Westerfiel

"The best my
for many reas~~_, _.~. _.~. .~.~~_ .~ which is the way
Jack Clark celebrates and rings a few changes on the
familiar private eye script . . . There's a memorable
moment [on] virtually every page."

--Dick Adler, Chicago Tribune

"A likeable protagonist and spirited, uncluttered
prose: a promising debut by a Chicago cabbie who
may drive a hack but doesn't write like one."

--Kirkus Reviews

Nobody's Angel

"My favorite fiction novel this year was written by a
taxi driver who used to [sell it] to his passengers.
It's a terrific story and character study of a cabbie in
Chicago during a time when a serial killer is
robbing and murdering cabbies. Kudos to Hard
Case Crime for publishing Mr. Clark's book."

--Quentin Tarantino

Nobody's Angel "is just about perfect. I won't urge
would-be novelists to forsake their writing classes
and become hackers, but they would do well to read
Clark's story, which doesn't contain a wasted word
or a false note. . . Its real beauty lies in Eddie's
bittersweet existence and the special romance and
danger of the cabdriver's life -- lives we often
glimpse but rarely give a second thought."

--Patrick Anderson, Washington Post

"From the driver's seat of his cab, Eddie negotiates a city splintered by race and class and rapidly losing its economic underpinnings. Nobody's Angel has the wry humor and engaging characters typical of the best of the hard-boiled genre, but Clark's portrait of Chicago in the 1990s, with its vanishing factories and jobs, its lethal public housing projects, its teenage hookers climbing into vans on North Avenue, is what gives it legs. Sure there are a couple murderers on the loose, but the larger violence is coming from systemic forces wreaking havoc in a place that, maybe, used to be better."

--Deanna Isaacs, Chicago Reader

"Nobody's Angel is a powerhouse of a book, a genuine work of noir and one of the best books of the year... Clark does something truly remarkable in a mystery novel, [he] chronicles the collapse of America's industrial base and its impact upon both our cities and the intractable problem of race in America through the story of an ordinary man... This is an incredible book that you will not soon forget."   --Tom Callahan, Book Reporter

"There's a world of intriguing and memorable detail expertly packed into two hundred pages and just the right amount of heartache. The book's close features one of the best final lines of any book I've ever read. Please don't pick it up and read that last page first, it's so worth getting there naturally."

-- Jedidiah Ayres, Barnes & Noble Ransom Notes

Nickel Dime Town

BOOKS BY JACK CLARK

nick acropolis novels
WESTERFIELD'S CHAIN
HIGHWAY SIDE
DANCING ON GRAVES
NICKEL DIME TOWN

eddie miles novels
NOBODY'S ANGEL
BACK DOOR TO L.A.

with mary jo clark
ON THE HOME FRONT
PRIVATE PATH

journalism
HACK WRITING & OTHER STORIES

one of these days
HONEST LABOR
THE B SIDE OF MISTY
PARIS IN A BOTTLE
MURDER REPORTER
THE MORNING SHE LEFT
THE COP NEXT-DOOR & OTHER STORIES

NICKEL DIME TOWN

Jack Clark

NICKEL DIME TOWN

Published by JACK CLARK INK
November 2024

jackclark.ink@gmail.com

For
Robin Rauch

You came back
just in time.

It was the middle of February, a cold and gray winter morning. The woman in the elevator with me wore a long down jacket and well-worn insulated boots. On the way up, she slipped off gloves and a stocking hat and used slender fingers to bring a few curls back to her dark brown hair. The scent of perfume or morning shampoo filled the small space. That was all it took to get me dreaming of spring.

We both got off at the fourth floor, the very top, and I followed her down the hall past doors for a travel agent, a dentist, two court reporters, a chiropractor, and an insurance broker. She stopped in front of the next door, the one with my name on it, and turned with a confused look on her face.

"What happened to Dr. Stern?" This was another dentist. The building had several.

I pointed straight down. "Third floor," I said.

Her eyeglasses were steamy from the clashing temperatures. But the brightness of her eyes shone through the fog. "I'm so stupid," she said. There was a glint of amusement in her eyes. "I've only been coming for ten years." She turned back towards the elevators.

—

I had a sudden urge to take another look at those eyes. "Stairway's right here," I said. When she turned, I pointed to the door across from my office. "Save you a few steps."

"Thanks." As she came back my way, her eyes shifted from me to my door. "That's you, I guess."

I nodded. "That's me." I had newspapers under my arm, coffee in one hand and keys in the other. Behind me the lettering on the frosted glass door read: *Nick Acropolis, Licensed Private Investigator.*

"You sort of look like what's-his-name," she said. "You know, from that movie." She gave me a two-finger wave, a wink, opened the door, and was gone.

I unlocked my door, dropped the newspapers and go-cup on the desk, and hung my jacket on a hook. I found myself humming 'A Foggy Day,' as I raised the blinds and opened the lone window a crack. Unlike the girl in foggy London town, my mystery woman had not managed to get the sun shining. "I'll never forget good old what's-his-name," I said to the clouds.

I started my usual looking-for-work routine, calling lawyers and fellow private eyes while paging through the morning papers.

"Hey, it's Nick Acropolis," I said to a string of voice mail systems, "just calling to say hello." This was a code they would all understand. *Poor Nick needs some work.*

I did manage to talk to one secretary. "Hey Patty, tell your boss it's winter up here on the North Side."

"Nick, you have the worst luck," she said. "The sun's shining so bright in the Loop I can't even see out the windows."

"Tough luck, kid. Don't forget to mention my name."

"Nick, it's February. He's in Florida."

"What was I thinking," I said, and went back to the

10

newspaper.

My horoscope said this was a good day for romance--which got me right back to my bright-eyed mystery girl--but advised me to be extra careful with financial matters. The Bears were looking forward to the draft, unfortunately they'd traded away all their high picks.

For years, I'd skipped the murders while reading the newspapers. But it didn't matter anymore. All my old partners in the homicide unit were either dead or retired. Nowadays it was usually the same murder over-and-over again, poor kids killing one another on all the wrong sides of town. I'd just glance at the headlines. "Sixteen-year-old slain on South Side." "Two Found Dead in Austin." "Twins Shot Outside School." There were plenty of murders but few arrests. Had the murderers gotten smarter or had the cops given up? The newspapers weren't saying.

I checked the obituaries and death notices but didn't find any familiar names. The Peanuts reruns were still better than all the other comics combined.

I was on my way to stretch out on the sofa when the phone rang. It was a lawyer calling but not one of my regulars. "Nick, Mitch Tourney here. How's tricks?"

"Long time," I said. Mitch had a neighborhood practice on the Northwest Side. He did real estate, personal injury, traffic, and criminal defense. Whatever walked in the door.

"Need a little help with a client," he said. "Nice lady. Single mom. She works overnight in a factory out in Elk Grove while her mother watches the kids. She takes the train to work, 'cause traffic's too bad in the morning and she doesn't want to be late getting the kids to school. A couple of weeks back she starts getting redlight tickets in the mail. Three one day, four the next, they just keep

---

11

coming."

"All from overnight," I guessed.

"Exactly," he said. "Suspect number one is her old boyfriend who she dumped two months back."

"He has a key to her car?"

"She never gave him one," Mitch said. "But he could have copied hers. But it's not necessarily the boyfriend. Client also had a beef with a neighbor about a shoveled-out parking space. So, I need somebody who knows what they're doing to look through these videos and try to get some clear shots of the driver. I hear you got a guy."

"I do," I said.

"He's good?"

"Like an eagle," I said, and my hand swooped down to grab the coffee. "If it's there, he'll find it."

"Name? Number?"

"Sorry, Mitch. But I'll be happy to show him whatever you've got."

"Single mom, Nick. I'm trying not to kill her with expenses."

"An hour for my time and whatever he charges. And he's dirt-cheap. That's why I can't give out his name."

"That doesn't make any sense."

"Word gets around, everybody'll be using him."

"I still don't get it, Nick. But open your inbox. Those are my videos you see coming in."

The videos showed up a few minutes later. There were eighteen clips. They all showed the same car running various redlights around town, always with the same driver behind the wheel. Each video came with a $100 fine. That was some payback for getting dumped or losing a parking space.

The redlight-running had all taken place in the dead

of night. The driver had long blonde hair, but you couldn't see much else. Oversized mirrored sunglasses obscured most of the face.

On the second time through, I spotted the driver giving the finger to one of the cameras. In another video, a squad car came around the corner with lights flashing and went after the car.

Someone knocked. I closed my computer and opened the door.

It was the bright-eyed woman who'd gotten off on the wrong floor. Her teeth were noticeably whiter. She looked relaxed now, and not confused at all.

"I decided it was a sign running into you," she said, and draped her jacket over one of the side chairs and sat down in the other.

I walked around the desk, dropped into my swivel chair, and flicked on the desk lamp.

She was in her mid-thirties, I guessed, and she'd been turning heads for most of that time. Her eyes were a brownish green. She was slender, a bit above average height. Her short, curly hair framed a fine-boned face. A slight smile crinkled the corners of her mouth. "Aren't you going to ask me about what's his name?" she said.

I shook my head. "I think I'd rather not know."

She took her time looking around my no-frills office, and then leaned forward with her hands on her knees. "Dr. Stern says I've been grinding my teeth." She brushed a stray curl away from her eyes. "He wants me to wear a night guard. But that's sort of evading the issue, don't you think?" She waited until I nodded and then went on. "I thought instead of a night guard, I could hire you to find out."

"Why you're grinding your teeth?"

"If my husband was having an affair. I thought he

13

was but now I'm not so sure."

I opened a desk drawer and pulled out a dog-eared magazine. Twenty-Five Ways to Tell if Your Spouse is Cheating, the headline on the cover read. Number one was the saddest on the list: Does your spouse seem a lot happier lately? I laid the magazine face down on the desk. "What changed your mind?" I asked.

She lifted a hand, spread her fingers wide, and gave me a shrug and a half-hearted smile. "Maybe if I knew for sure what he was doing out there I could, oh, I don't know, sleep through the night again. Or am I asking too much?"

"Tell me about your husband," I said, and grabbed a pen.

"He's dead," she said, and she ran a finger across her front teeth.

"Since when?" I dropped the magazine back in the drawer.

"Right before Thanksgiving. The year before last."

"How?"

"He had a heart attack in a motel in Iowa. And I used to be so mad at her, this woman I thought he was with. That she just left him for the maid to find. But now I think maybe he really was alone, which just makes it worse."

"How old was he?"

"Thirty-seven."

I scribbled the numbers on my pad. "Pretty young for a heart attack." I watched her eyes but all I got was another shrug.

"It runs in the family," she said. "His father. His uncles. None of them made it to 50. And Billy stopped taking care of himself. He was pretty good for years but then he went right back to being the life of the party, doing all the things they tell you not to do."

"What changed your mind about this affair?"

"I was at a party the other week, the Super Bowl." She raised one hand. "Don't ask me why I went. It was almost all cops, and this one drunk gets me in a corner and whispers how I've got Tommy by the short hairs and where did I stash the tape or something like that. That's what started me thinking."

"Who's Tommy?"

"Billy's old partner."

"Cops?" I asked, hoping she'd say lawyers, bridge players, or even gay lovers.

She nodded. "And now I live with Tommy."

"Okay," I said, and she must have heard my sudden lack of enthusiasm.

She sat up straighter. "Something wrong?" she said.

"I usually try to stay away from police-involved cases," I said. For years, this was how I made my living. But I was now reformed. "They're not big fans of the private sector. But keep going. Where were we?"

"I was telling you I was now living with Tommy. He was Billy's partner," she said, and raised a single eyebrow. "Comforting the widow. That's how it started."

"Okay," I said. This was my favorite new word.

"You used to be one, right?"

"One what?"

"A cop," she said.

"Long time ago."

"You've got the look," she said. "You know I could find somebody else. I don't want to get you involved in something that's against your religion. Is that it?"

"Very funny," I said. "No. This sounds okay." I didn't want her to go away. "Tell me about this tape you stashed. Video? Audio?"

She shook her head. "No idea."

"And what was your husband doing in Iowa?"

"He told me he was going to see his brother in Denver. I didn't believe him for a minute. I just assumed he had something going on."

"Why did it have to be another woman?"

"He kept disappearing and he never had an explanation. He wasn't getting drunk as usual so what else could it be?" She leaned forward and placed a hand on my desk. "And if he was going to see his brother, why didn't he call and let him know he was coming? Why make it a big surprise?"

"Iowa is on the way to Colorado," I said. "Did he say why he wanted to see his brother?"

She smiled. "I was on a need-to-know basis by then."

"What's his brother do out there?" I pointed west.

"Lawyer," she said. "His wife too. They drive me crazy. All they do is snipe at each other."

"Is it possible Billy was looking for legal advice?"

She waved a hand. "Maybe this. Maybe that. I've got a long list. He rented a car with 4-wheel drive. He was worried about snow in Colorado. But then it snowed in Iowa. Tommy thought he must have stopped because of the snow. And then the maid found him the next day."

"How about this drunk at the Super Bowl party. Who was he?" I pictured one of those square-shouldered cops with a stiff military haircut, and not a speck of humor.

She shook her head. "No idea."

"And now you've got Tommy by the short hairs?"

"Uh huh." She smiled. "And I know the crude way of saying that, too."

I smiled back. "He say anything else, besides the video?"

16

"He said something about drinking for free. But the entire party was on the house so everybody else was too."

"Did you find anything in Billy's suitcase or in the car?"

"I never saw the car. I guess the rental company took it back. I don't know what happened to his suitcase. Tommy might know. He went out to Iowa."

"What's Tommy's last name?"

"Burroughs," she said, and then gave me a very direct look. "But don't talk to him, okay?"

"Why not?" Was he jealous of a dead man?

"Oh, I don't know. He's maybe a bit on the paranoid side." She stopped dead for 30 seconds or so, while I wondered what percentage of cops would fit that category. In Chicago it had to be at least 50%, and the way things were going, that number would keep right on rising.

"I thought it was kind of natural, me and Tommy," she said. "He was Billy's best friend, but I always knew he had a thing for me. And after the funeral, I just let it happen. I mean, where's the harm, really? Of course, I was still pissed at Billy, so what better way to get back at him then taking up with his best friend? Isn't that every guy's worst fear?"

"You think he might know something about this tape. Is that it?"

She looked up for a moment, towards a big spider web in the corner above the door. "Sometimes I think he's not with me because he always liked me. He's with me to keep me from finding out what Billy was up to before he died."

"Did you tell him what the drunk at the party said?"

She nodded. "And he went all quiet on me. That's

usually a bad sign, and he never brought it up again. And that's another bad sign."

"Are you afraid of him?"

She gave me another of those direct looks. "Oh, I can talk myself into that but, no, not really." She looked away for a moment. "I don't think he'd ever hurt me. I heard all their stories for years. Billy would come home after a shift completely wound up and I'd sit and listen to him talk it out. Tommy was always doing crazy things on the job. Billy was always getting him out of trouble."

I drew a line through Tommy's name on my pad. "So, who's keeping Tommy out of trouble now?"

"He doesn't talk about the job. Never. He comes home and he sits in the kitchen sometimes, just looking out the back window. That's how I know it's been a bad shift."

"You could leave," I said.

She shook her head. "My house. I'd have to throw him out. But we're a long way from that. I don't want to overdramatize this. I just want to find out what Billy was up to."

"Okay, about your husband, what was his last name?"

"Daniels, the same as mine."

"You got a badge number, by any chance."

She shook her head. "I could probably get it."

"Don't bother," I said. That would be the easiest part of the job. "And your name?"

"Catherine. But I usually go by Kate."

I scribbled a few more details on my pad: The name of the motel and the car rental agency; Billy's brother's name and phone number; A few non-cop friends and the name of the saloon where they hung out. I filled out a standard form, stating that she was hiring me for help in a confidential matter, and had her sign by the X.

"What kind of work do you do, Kate?"

"I'm a photographer. But why would that make any difference here?"

"I have to figure out how much to charge you."

Her eyes widened. "That's how you come up with your rates?"

I nodded. "The more you make, the more I charge."

"Wow," she said, and showed me her bright, white teeth in a beautiful smile. "Believe it or not, I just got laid off."

"I'm sorry to hear that."

"I didn't realize there was an upside," she said. "I used to shoot for the Sun-Times. But they don't need real photographers anymore. Nobody does. So now I'm a freelancer. You know what that means."

"Two hundred a day," I decided, one freelancer to another. That was about as low as I went. "And let's say a four hundred retainer. You look like you can handle that."

"How about a hundred a day?" Her smile turned hopeful. "And I'll take your picture and make you a print, suitable for framing."

I pretended to think it over. "One-fifty," I said after a while. "Three hundred retainer. And don't worry about the picture."

"Do you take credit cards?" She reached for her purse.

"Sure." I got my phone out and hooked my credit card gizmo to it. I was as modern as could be. "If you're worried about Tommy seeing the charge, I'll put it under specialty products."

She shook her head, held a credit card up but didn't hand it over. "And for three hundred you'll be able to find the truth?"

I shook my head. "No guarantee and it might take more than two days. I've got to fit you in around some other cases. But one thing I can promise, you'll end up knowing more about Billy than you do now."

She handed me the credit card. I swiped it, handed it back, and promised to be in touch. She put on her coat and slipped a compact Nikon from a jacket pocket. "Now where do I want you?" she said.

"Let's skip the picture." I always ended up looking awful.

"Oh, no. Don't be shy. I'll make you look like that guy from the movies." She gave me a wave with a single finger. "Maybe out in the hallway."

I followed her out the door to the wide, florescent-lit hall. As she moved me an inch this way and an inch that way, I peered into her eyes but never found a connection. I was an object in the light, nothing more.

"You've got great eyes," I said. They were brown one minute, green the next, and always full of life. But they didn't react to sweet talk.

She finally got me positioned. She dropped an eye to the camera and backed across the hallway with the Nikon wrapped in both hands. "Great hands, too." I tried again. "I guess those are two things a photographer needs most."

She took several more shots then slipped the camera back into her jacket. "You're forgetting the most important element," she said.

"What's that?"

"Heart," she said, and this time she looked straight back.

"How could I forget that?" I was the first to look away.

—

20

I walked her down the hall to the elevator. She covered her curls with her stocking hat and climbed aboard. "I'll bet you've got some stories," she said, and gave me the warmest smile of the day.

"A few." I was expecting a wink, but it never came.

She waved with a gloved hand, held my eyes as the door closed, and then took her beautiful hands, eyes, and heart, down to that cold, unforgiving, world.

TWO

I went back to my cave and spent a few minutes gazing at the wall, letting Kate's image linger for a bit, then I picked up the phone and dialed Shelly Michalowski. This was a number I still knew by heart but rarely called. She was another lawyer. It was turning out to be that kind of day. Years back, I'd been her number one investigator. We'd first met when she was my defense attorney. That was her entire practice, cops in trouble.

"I'm calling for a favor," I said to her voicemail. "Would you mind checking your sources and see if there's anything funny on the record of Billy Daniels. He was in the 14th District, but he's been dead over a year. That's what I'm most interested in, right before he died, October, November, two years back. Anything you can find. I'd owe you big time. His partner was a guy named Tommy Burroughs. Maybe check him, too."

I put on my coat, took the elevator down, and walked up Lincoln Avenue, fighting a harsh wind all the way. Week-old snow was crusted with soot. The sidewalks were trails of slush, hiding patches of slick ice. The wind whistled through the trees and rattled bare branches. February might be the shortest month everywhere else. In Chicago, it felt like it's very own season.

Ten minutes later, I stopped at Rent-a-Dent, had a cup of lukewarm coffee with Caitlin, the manager, and picked up a battered Chevy. It was mid-afternoon but just about every car was running with headlights burning. The clouds were low and gray, and looked ready to unload.

On the way north, idling snowplows waited in front of convenience stores and donut shops with their beds full of blue salt. Most of the drivers sat behind the wheel, sipping coffee, paging through newspapers, or munching donuts. At the first flurry they'd spring into action and god help that poor little snowflake and all his cousins.

Sim's Video was the only store left in a strip mall on Clark Street in Rogers Park, about four miles north of my office. George Simmons had walked away from the place years ago, after a big Blockbuster Video opened down the block. He left everything, the stock, the name, the overdue bills and the back rent, to Phil, a chubby 16-year-old who worked there after school.

Phil switched the store over to video games and anything else that interested kids his own age. He'd help them film a YouTube video or put together a web or Facebook page. He was also a whiz at slowing down and enhancing videos to find details that no one else seemed to notice.

I'd found the place by accident one day and I'd been keeping Phil's identity a well-guarded secret ever since. Shelly used an expert witness with a PhD from UCLA to testify. He charged $400 an hour plus expenses. What he never told the court was that many of the details he pointed to had first been discovered by a high school dropout who charged less than a hundred bucks. Sometimes I also bought lunch.

"Oh, oh," Phil said when I walked in. "Sam Spade time again." He was still a big, cheerful kid, now with a wife and kids of his own. He also had an actual apartment. For years, he'd lived in the back of the store.

The place was comfortably cluttered. Computers sat one on top of the other. The sound of invaders being blasted to smithereens came from the back room. But something was missing. "What happened to your sign?" He'd had a big one in the window: WE OUTLASTED

BLOCKBUSTER!

"Turns out most of my current customers never even heard of Blockbuster." He shrugged. "What've you got this time?"

"Redlight videos." I handed him a thumb drive. "I need close-ups of the driver. The more the merrier. Also see if you can get some numbers off the squad car. You hungry?"

"Coffee wouldn't hurt," he said.

"Right back," I said, and 15 minutes later I was back with coffee and donuts.

"It's definitely a guy driving that Toyota," Phil said. He was on a stool in front of a monitor that was about the size of my kitchen table.

"How do you figure that?" On my laptop, I hadn't even figured out it was a Toyota.

He zoomed in on the driver. "Adam's apple. Hairy fingers. Bad wig."

"How about the face?"

"The problem is those mirrored sunglasses. The flash bounces back and obscures the entire area. I've got this profile here, where he was making a turn." He zoomed in again. But the only thing that was clear was the driver's cheek, a bit of jaw, the corner of his lips, and his actual hair, which was dark and turning gray.

"Any tattoos? Jewelry?"

"There's a ring on this one." He switched to another video. The driver's arm was resting on the window ledge. The hand was turned and a glittery ring with a black stone was facing the camera.

"Oh, that's good," I said. "Get me a still of that." If that was the boyfriend's hand, the client would certainly recognize the ring. "How about the squad car?"

A few seconds later, the squad came around the

—

corner and went after the Toyota. "Guy driving. Woman riding shotgun," Phil said. "She's trying to get her seatbelt on."

"I can't tell if you're kidding or not. How about numbers?"

"The last three numbers of the license plate, if that helps," he said, and they appeared on the screen. "That truck blocks the side numbers, and the light pole blocks the ones on the hood."

"How about on top," I said. "Between the gumballs."

"Gumballs?"

"The emergency lights. There should be a set of numbers right between them."

He moved from one video to the next. "This?" he said, and the screen moved close to a shadowy image, white smudges on a dark background. Before long the white smudges took up the entire monitor. "Hold on. I ought to be able to . . ."

It took a bit of fiddling. "How's this?" Phil said a few minutes later, and four dim numbers appeared. They were fuzzy but readable, and told me all I needed to know, the district and the beat number.

I scribbled the numbers in my notebook. "You know if you'd go back to school and get a PhD you could make a ton of money."

"Sure," he said, and he flashed one of his oddball smiles. "Soon as I get my GED."

THREE

Back at my office, I sent the close-ups from the red-light files to Mitch Tourney, along with an invoice for an hour of my time, plus $50 for Phil and eight dollars for the coffee and donuts.

I should have stopped right there. Maybe it was too much coffee and too many donuts. I made several needless phone calls.

The Chicago PD is big, more than 12,000 strong. I'd been gone for more than a decade, but I still had a few contacts. Billy Daniels and Tommy Burroughs were just another couple of patrol officers. But almost everybody I called had heard the story--how Tommy was sleeping with the widow before his partner was cold in the ground. Some thought it hideous behavior; others gave Tommy credit for pulling it off. "From what I hear, she's a knockout," a detective in Area 3 said.

Both Daniels and Burroughs had been in trouble here and there. Nobody had much in the way of details, but the consensus was that Burroughs liked to knock heads. He'd also been involved in several shootings, none of them fatal. My old Police Academy pal Lenny, who had somehow worked his way up to near the very top of department hierarchy, knew a bit about Burroughs, none of it good. He said he would do a thorough check on both names and give me a call. I told him I'd buy him dinner some night.

I was scribbling notes on a legal pad when Mitch Tourney called. "Hey Nick, good work," he said. "You were sure right about your guy."

"Yeah, he's good."

"And fifty bucks? Some of these guys charge that for a minute."

26

"And he only ate one donut," I said.

"I was wondering if you could track those cops for me?"

I got up and opened the window. "As long as I don't have to talk to 'em," I said. Outside, gray clouds were converging.

"That would be the whole point."

"We don't even know they were after your car. They could have been on a call."

"If they were, they were. What's the big deal?"

"Cops," I said, and I turned away from the window. "They're nothing but trouble." And they weren't very fond of private detectives, especially this one.

"I guess I could call..."

"No. Don't worry. I'll see what I can do." I dropped back in my chair. I hated to leave a job half done.

We said goodbye but I never put down the phone. Sergeant Jim Sheehan and I had grown up a block apart on the not-so-mean streets of the far West Side. Now he was running the desk at the 23rd District, which meant he'd know who was running all the desks in town.

He put me on hold for several minutes while he called around. "Rita Cunningham and William Flashing," he said when he came back. These were the cops in the redlight video. "Bill, I know. He's still in 18 and he's working today. You want me to see if he can meet?"

"Sure," I said. "Anywhere at his convenience." I was back on hold.

"How about two o'clock in the back of the station parking lot," Sheehan said a few minutes later,

"Works for me. How about Cunningham?"

"Her, I don't know. But she's in 15 now."

The 15th was a very active district on the far West Side in Austin. If you liked to work, this might be the

---

27

place you'd want to go. But if you didn't like all the action and were a troublemaker to boot, they might send you out there just for fun. They'd assign you to the worst beat in the entire district in the hope all the pain and misery of police work in a poor black neighborhood would eventually make you think about finding a more sedate occupation.

"Did she want to go?" I asked.

"She's working first watch tonight. You want to go out and ask her?"

"Sure." I was on hold again.

"She'll meet you by the desk after roll call. My guy says she's a ball of fire."

"I owe you, Jimmy," I said.

"Nick, if it wasn't for you, who knows where I'd be today."

"Ah, the good old days," I said. He couldn't have been more than 14 back then. I was a couple of years older. I found him crouched behind some bushes around the corner from where I lived and got him into a friend's basement. He'd crashed a stolen car into a light pole a block away with the police right behind him.

"How'd you ever get out of that car?" I asked. It had ended up upside down with the light pole on top, still burning bright.

"As fast as I could, Nick, and the fucking cops, they were everywhere."

That got us both laughing. "Let's get together for a drink some night," I said.

"Just make the call."

We'd each been saying those exact words for years-- and neither of us had yet to make the call.

———

FOUR

The snow started as I headed south, nickel and dime size flakes twirled in the wind, muffling the city sounds and hiding the grime. It gave the old town a pleasant winter-wonderland look.

The 18th District used to run from the Gold Coast to the slum. But the slum--better known as the Cabrini-Green housing project--had been replaced with something a bit closer to its glittery neighbor. At one time 15,000 residents, most of them black and poor had called the ninety buildings home. The old buildings had gone to the wrecking ball. Now there was a Target store, a new police station, and middle-class whites living in fancy condos.

If you looked east, you saw the Lake Shore Drive high rises. Southeast were the towers of the Loop. A bit south was the former headquarters of Montgomery Ward, now offices and high-end condos. The ancient weathervane was still in place atop the oldest building. Some said this was the original Angel from Montgomery.

If there were any real angels in the neighborhood their names were probably the ones inscribed on the honorary street sign in front of the station house. Sgt. James Severin and Patrolman Anthony N. Rizzato had been walking across a Cabrini-Green baseball field on a walk and talk beat when snipers opened fire. That had been decades back when the area was pretty much a war zone, before all the poor people had miraculously disappeared.

The snow had slowed by the time I pulled into the parking lot behind the station house. I drove to the very back and pulled next to a cop who was leaning against a squad car. His uniform was dotted with snowflakes. I rolled down my window. "Flashing?"

He nodded and I opened the door and got out. The cop in the passenger seat never looked up. He was absorbed in the glowing light of his phone.

William Flashing was my height, six foot or so, with steady blue eyes, a neatly trimmed mustache, and no chin worth mentioning. He had a bit of a gut, which is an occupational hazard in both our lines of work. He barely looked at me as we shook hands. He was too busy inspecting all the dents in my battered Chevy.

"It's a rental, believe it or not," I said, and then I gave him my well-rehearsed spiel about the advantages of Rent-a-Dent "They'll even bring a different car out sometimes when I'm on a stakeout. And, if I need a nice one, they've got those too. You've gotta pay extra, of course."

"I'm a car guy," he said. "And I gotta tell you, I'd be embarrassed to get behind that wheel." He put his hands up and backed away. "I'm afraid to even touch it. But you'd never get a ticket from me. You could run redlights and do handstands in the middle of the street and bump every car on the block and I'd just think, the poor bastard's got enough trouble already."

"Speaking of traffic stops," I said. "I want to ask you about one you made on December 16th."

"Go right ahead," he said.

"About three in the morning, a Toyota blew through the light at Halsted and Division. You went after it."

"Doesn't sound familiar. Where'd you get that?"

"From the red-light video," I said.

"Oh, yeah, yeah." He smiled. "They got it on video, of course I remember. We pulled her over by the shrimp shack."

"What can you tell me about the driver?"

"A very good-looking woman, blond, well dressed."

"Did you write a ticket?"

"No."

"Why not?"

Another smile. "You think I came on the job to write beautiful women traffic citations? And, as I explained to the lady, she'd also been caught by the redlight camera, and that ticket would arrive in the mail."

"Did you get her name by any chance?"

"Well, I know I looked at her license." He waved at a passing snowflake.

"And what was the name on the license?"

"I don't recall.

"Illinois driver's license?"

"Must have been. I would have remembered anything else."

"Did you run the license?"

"No."

"The plates."

"Same answer." He brushed a bit of snow from his hair.

"You're sure it was a woman?"

"I believe I can still tell the difference," he said. "But I gotta admit, it gets harder and harder all the time."

"Who was your partner that night?"

He looked up at the sky and then back at me. "Funny. For some reason, I don't remember."

"Would you be willing to sign a statement detailing what you've just told me?"

He shook his head. "Pal, I don't sign nothing, and I don't testify to things I don't remember." He pointed a steady finger at me. "You're a friend of a friend but that's as far as this goes."

I gestured towards his current partner who still had

his face down to his phone. "What's he doing in there, anyway?"

"Oh, who cares?" he said. "It's like babysitting. That's why I'm standing out in the snow like a fool. What's your excuse?"

FIVE

The snow had stopped by the time I took the eight-mile ride out to the 15th District. The snowplows were still pushing the slush around and dropping salt. But the winter wonderland was gone. We were back to a gray winter city.

The station was on a stretch of Madison Street a few blocks shy of the Oak Park line. Half the buildings had disappeared since I'd lived out this way. Back then Oak Park had been a dry town, and this stretch of Madison Street was loaded with bars and restaurants. Now it was mainly the home of empty lots and crumbling buildings. Not a single flash of neon or amber light. The station house, a recent arrival, was a modern, boring, cinder block building without a speck of history or romance.

Cops were changing shifts and trading places behind the front desk.

Cunningham made me the minute she walked out of the back room. Her uniform was sharply pressed, her shoes gleamed, her cap was tucked firmly under her arm.

"So, I'm supposed to talk to you because you used to be on the job. Is that how it works?" Her dark eyes flashed.

"Can we talk in the hallway? It won't take long." She shrugged but followed along. "Do you remember a traffic stop on December 16th, about 3:30 in the morning?"

"So that's what this is about."

"Why don't you tell me what you remember?"

She didn't say anything. She looked at me for a long while with her dark eyes and then shook her head.

"Look, I'm not wearing a wire. I'm not going to ask

33

you to sign anything. This doesn't involve the police department. It's a private matter."

She shook her head some more. But she didn't leave.

"If I told you it was his girlfriend's car, would that help?"

Another minute passed and then she pointed a stern finger my way. "If that's bullshit . . . "

"It's not," I said. "Scouts honor." I put up two fingers.

That brought a smile. "You don't even know how to do it," she said.

A minute or so passed and then she started talking. "Okay, so my partner and I, we observed a vehicle run the redlight at Halsted and Division. We activated our lights and went in pursuit, but the vehicle did not pull over or slow down. When we got close, I hit the car with my spotlight. The driver stuck his arm out the window and flashed a badge."

"But you pulled it over anyway."

"One of the few times my partner and I agreed on anything."

"Did you write a ticket?"

She held up a hand. "Let me tell it, okay?"

"Sure." I shrugged.

"The guy's wearing a blond wig and these huge sunglasses. He thought the whole thing was hysterical. He pulls the wig and glasses off and that's when it turns out that he's one of my partner's old friends from his days in some other district."

"Oh, well," I said. "I was hoping it was a fake badge." My day had been filled with cops and here was another one. I was about to run out of fingers.

"So don't try to make me testify."

"It's not going that far," I said. "His girlfriend dumped him, so he stole her car and drove around

34

running redlights, so she'd get the tickets."

"What a shit. I knew we should have taken him in."

"Come on," I said. We both knew that was never going to happen. Cops didn't arrest fellow cops for traffic violations, and if they were too drunk to drive, they gave them rides home.

"So where does it go from here?" Cunningham asked.

"I talk to her lawyer. Look don't worry. If the clown in the car isn't a total idiot, the department will never hear of it. And just so you know, your partner swears it was a woman."

"Yeah, that figures," she said.

I gave her my business card and we said goodbye.

SIX

Shelly Michalowski Esquire had me on the phone bright and early the next morning while I was still lolling in bed. "So, what's going on?" she said. "I thought you didn't do police work?" She'd been trying to talk me into working for her again.

"This one came in kind of sideways." I sat up and dropped my feet to the floor.

"Well, those two names you gave me, one of 'em's got quite a list. Burroughs. Let's see. Excessive Force. Excessive Force. Abusive Language. Excessive Force. You want me to keep reading?"

"No. I get the idea. How about Daniels?"

"He must have been the polite one. He got in on a few of the Excessive Forces, not many, but not on a single Abusive Language."

"How about those dates I was asking about?"

"Right where I was heading. They got a shoplifting call at a corner store on Kedzie Avenue. When they get there, instead of arresting the shoplifter, they ended up shooting the clerk. He pulled a gun on them and they had no choice. That's their story and for once there's no video."

"Lucky break, huh?"

"I don't know that luck had anything to do with it. The store had a surveillance system. The clerk says the cops erased it after they shot him."

"That's interesting," I said. "You got an address for the store?"

I scribbled the address on a bedside pad. "But if you're figuring on talking to the clerk," Shelly said, "you're too late. Aggravated battery of a police officer; he'll be out in four years. Pretty good deal, don't you think?"

"He must have got himself a real lawyer," I said. "Thanks, Shel. I owe you."

"I know you do. So why don't you help me out occasionally?"

"Cops, Shelly, I just can't do it anymore."

"Well, how about giving me your video guy, and then we'll call it even."

"No can do," I said. "How about lunch next week?"

"You're a selfish son of a bitch," she said and hung up without saying goodbye.

"I'm a stupid son of a bitch," I said. If I couldn't do cops anymore, what the hell was I doing with this case?

My last case for Shelly had been several years back. George McIntyre was 26 years old, an Area Six Homicide Detective, a rising star in the unit. One day he was working alone, reviewing a case file. There was something he didn't understand about the layout of a recent crime scene. His partner had taken their car to court to testify. He asked the desk sergeant if he could borrow a car.

According to McIntyre's Police Board testimony, the sergeant said, "Here. Take this one. It just came in." And he tossed McIntyre a set of keys.

"Is that ours?" a tactical officer at the other end of the desk asked.

"You're not going back out, are you?" the sergeant asked the officer.

"No. We're done," the tactical officer said, and then he turned to McIntyre. "We left a present in the trunk," he said.

After hearing that, McIntyre should have checked the trunk before he got in the car. He should have taken his own car. Yes. Gas was nearly $5 a gallon at the time. But he was only going a couple of miles. How much was he really saving?

He was at the crime scene drawing a diagram when he heard knocking. He opened the trunk and found Henry Adams, a 24-year-old black youth, curled up in a ball. He'd made the mistake of spitting on one of the tactical officers. The cops could have arrested him but decided on some street justice instead.

"What the hell are you doing here?" McIntyre shouted at Adams.

It was 25 degrees at the time. Adams was shivering so bad he couldn't even talk.

McIntyre should have called for an ambulance, and then called the Watch Commander and put it all in his lap.

But there was a hospital a few blocks away. So that's where he took Adams. He helped him out of the trunk outside the emergency room. He had to hold him up for a minute or so, until Adams could stand on his own, and then he led him to the automatic doors. When they opened, he pushed Adams forward and then turned and walked away, the very picture of a man who did not want to get involved.

He should have known the hospital would have surveillance cameras. The video was a highlight on many news shows.

When Shelly first told me about the case, I assumed we'd be defending McIntyre. "Shouldn't be too hard to get him off," I said. "I mean, he took him to the hospital."

Shelly smiled and shook her head. The tactical cops were her clients. My job was to help them keep their jobs. The only way to do that, was to make McIntyre the fall guy.

"I can't do it," I told Shelly.

Maybe my reluctance had something to do with McIntyre being a homicide detective. I couldn't help but identify with him.

But my lack of participation didn't hurt the tactical officers. They both lied at the Police Board hearing and they both got off.

McIntyre told the truth and was fired. The last I heard he was working as a dispatcher at a trucking company. The two tactical officers were still on the force, serving and protecting.

SEVEN

Chicago Avenue looked better than it had in years. The proof that in some neighborhoods less was truly more. Plenty had disappeared since my last trip out this way. Back then the street was home to a 24-hour open-air drug market. The police had finally installed surveillance cameras and the dealers had moved a couple of blocks north where they could hide in the shade of the trees.

Fences surrounded a few of the empty lots, making them look a bit like parks instead of signs of disaster. "Keep it up. Keep going. Keep trying," was written in large letters on one of the fences. It was a gray day, a few degrees above freezing. That didn't stop people from hanging on the corners--the unemployment rate was probably higher than the temperature — and watching traffic pass was more entertaining than anything on basic cable.

A few miles to the east, I could see the elegant towers of the lakefront shrouded by a misty gray curtain. Dead ahead, a few miles west, sat the tree-lined suburbs of Oak Park and River Forest. In this in-between land, the big money hadn't stopped by in decades. Those who could afford to get out did, leaving even more vacant land.

I turned on Kedzie Avenue. The store where Billy Daniels and Tommy Burroughs had shot the clerk was a deserted, desolate-looking place, a perfect fit for the neighborhood. So many buildings had disappeared, and many others were wrecks like this, which left nobody to shovel the snow. Pedestrians walked in the street instead. The exceptions were the kids. They'd walk anywhere. Kids of all ages with absolutely nothing to do and, on the wrong day, they might do anything at all.

One small group of boys hung on the corner in front

of the store, dancing and prancing in the grimy slush. None of the kid's jackets looked very warm. They were all in running shoes. Not a single pair of winter boots. Nobody had ever heard of galoshes.

The building, a single story with a flat roof, had been boarded up and enclosed by a cyclone fence. A faded sign read SWEET'S FOOD & LIQUOR MINI MART. Another said, WE ACCEPT ILLINOIS LINK. That was the food stamp card. A dim rainbow curved towards the ground. BE A MILLIONARE was written above the colors, an advertisement for the Illinois Lottery. The newest sign was pasted on the front door, courtesy of the City of Chicago. REVOKED. That was for the liquor license.

The building sat a bit cockeyed, and there were holes here and there. A gutter had fallen or been pulled down, exposing the rotting wood behind it. A fire or a bulldozer would finish the job in the not-too-distant future. A dump truck would cart the remains away, and there'd be one more empty lot for weeds to grow and garbage to blow, and not even a glimmer of a pot of gold.

I pulled alongside the kids and lowered my window. "What happened to the store?" I asked, and they moved closer.

"Lit it up," somebody shouted. Across the street, a curtain fell back on a second-story window.

"Shot that Indian motherfucker dead," the biggest of the bunch said. He was 15 or so.

"He was an A-rab," another kid said.

"Who shot him? Why?" I said.

"We don't talk to no five-o," the big kid said with a smile. And that was a big part of the city's crime problem in neighborhoods like this. Nobody would talk

41

to the police.

"I'm six-o," I said, and way too old to be asking pointless questions. I took my foot off the brake.

"You should bring us another store, Mister," the youngest of the bunch said.

"That's right." Even the big kid agreed. They knew it was easy to get killed buying cupcakes too far from home.

"Wish I could," I said, and I started away, just another white man passing through.

I thought of driving to Iowa, to the motel where Billy Daniels had died. It was only two hundred miles. But what would I find more than a year after the fact?

EIGHT

When I got off the elevator, a tall guy with slick, wavy hair was loitering outside my office. He wore a leather jacket, which looked much too light for the weather and barely concealed the gun on his hip.

"You Acropolis?" he asked before I was halfway down the hall.

"Who're you?"

"Oh, that's pretty funny," he said, and he moved his weight from one foot to the other. "You've been asking all over town about me and you ain't got one fucking idea who I am, huh?"

"Burroughs," I said.

"Good going, Nick." He snapped fingers on both hands and then pointed straight at me. "They told me you were smart. I knew we'd get along."

He had broad shoulders and long arms. But there was no thickness to him. You could stick him on a billboard, and he would look right at home trying to sell you something you didn't know you needed. But I had a hard time seeing Kate Daniels on the same billboard, or even down below in a passing car.

I unlocked my door, dropped my go-cup of coffee on the desk, flicked on the overhead lights, and hung my coat on a hook.

Burroughs followed me in, but not too far. He leaned back against the door, keeping it open.

"So, what can I do for you, Mr. Burroughs?" I said, standing behind my desk with one hand behind my back, holding my imaginary gun. The real ones were locked up in my file cabinet, much too far away.

"Just tell me what's going on." He shrugged like he didn't have a care in the world, but his eyes betrayed

43

him. He couldn't keep them still. "I mean, we're all on the same side, right?"

"I can't really talk to you. Not now, anyway."

"You know I couldn't figure it at first." He did a little dance, an inch my way and then danced right back to where he'd started. The door barely moved. "Why would some private eye be asking around about me? Even when I saw your address that didn't do anything, but when I pulled out front, the light bulb finally popped. You got a deal with the dentist? Get your teeth cleaned and get a free consultation with a washed-up dick. Something like that?"

"You must have better things to do."

"You know, I hate to say it, but you could use a little teeth-cleaning yourself." He danced my way again but, once again, danced back to the safety of the door. "You'll wonder where the yellow went. Remember that one?"

"Thanks for stopping by. We're done now."

"And you're done with Catherine. Or did she call herself Kate. Yeah, I'll bet she did. You should feel honored."

"I really don't know what you're talking about and, even if I did, I couldn't tell you anything, anyway."

"Don't worry about that. She'll be calling you in a while to cancel whatever it is."

He turned to leave. "Whoever she is," I said to his back.

The door had almost closed when he turned and pushed it open again. "You miss the job?" he asked, and now he sounded like he was talking to an old friend.

I shook my head. It had taken years, but I'd finally gotten over it. That's what I told myself.

He opened his jacket and showed me the big automatic holstered on his hip. "This is what I'm gonna miss," he said. He grabbed his crotch. "I got my little guy here." Then his hand moved to the gun. "And then I got my big one up here. One way or the other, you're gonna get fucked. Just tell me how you want it."

He kept his hand on the gun as we stood looking at each other. I was trying to pretend I was relaxing on a street corner somewhere, watching passing traffic while waiting for a bus. Burroughs was waiting too, but he was twitchy as hell. He wanted something to happen, and he wanted it to happen right now. He didn't care what anybody thought or said. He knew he'd get tossed off the force eventually. It was just a matter of time. That's why he was already thinking about all the things he was going to miss someday.

My phone rang. I took it out very slowly and looked at the screen. Mitchell Tourney. "You get anywhere with those cops?" he asked after I pushed the button.

"Hold on a second," I said, and then I looked back at Burroughs. "Are you still here?"

"You should be asking yourself that same question." He backed into the hallway and the door closed softly behind him.

"What's up?" I said into the phone and dropped to the safety of my chair.

"Did you get anywhere?" Tourney asked.

"Let me ask you a question. Your client's ex-boyfriend, he a cop by any chance?"

"How'd you get to that?"

"You could have warned me," I said. "It shouldn't come as a surprise that neither of the cops are signing statements. Did she ID the ring?"

"She can't say for sure," he said.

"Too bad."

"Well, look, send me their names and whatever else

you've got along with your invoice."

"One cop," I said. "William Flashing."

"How about the other one?"

"Let's leave the partner out of it. She's an innocent bystander."

"Maybe you should let me be the judge of that."

"You don't need her. Ask Flashing if he ever worked with your client's ex-boyfriend. That should do the trick."

"I guess I've got to trust you, Nick. Is she hot?"

"Who?"

"The partner. Come on, why else would you be doing this?"

"You're right, Mitch. That must be it."

I pushed the button to end the call and then sat there with the phone in my hand. But I wasn't thinking about Rita Cunningham.

I was trying to picture Kate Daniels and Tommy Burroughs together. Too many pieces were missing. This was one puzzle I'd never make work. I'd spent too much time staring into Kate's eyes. That was part of the problem. Maybe I didn't want the pieces to fit. I'd seen plenty of other cops like Tommy Burroughs, guys with a badge and a gun, with eyes that were long dead and well beyond caring what anybody else thought. Guys just waiting for the right moment to say, "Fuck it," and throw it all away.

The Kate's and Tommy's of the world had been getting together forever. There were probably entire branches of psychiatry devoted to figuring out why some women chased squad cars and fire trucks, with or without a camera.

I'd asked Kate if she was afraid of Tommy. *"Oh, I can talk myself into that. But, no, not really,"* she'd said. *"I don't think he'd ever hurt me."*

"I hope you're right, Kate," I said, without much confidence, and then punched in her phone number. I was relieved to get her recorded message. I waited for the beep. "Just a heads up, Kate," I said. "Tommy just walked out of my office. He knows you were here. And it's my fault so I owe you an apology and lunch one of these days. If you need any help, please don't be afraid to call. I mean it."

She'd asked me not to talk to Tommy and I hadn't. Not directly. Instead, I'd talked to a half-dozen cops from districts all over town. Cops love to talk. Maybe it's those long hours spent together in a car, where every thought that comes into your head eventually comes out. And before long the entire department knows your every kink. *What had I been thinking?* I hadn't been thinking at all, obviously. If I had, I'd have simply waited for Shelly to call. She'd given me all the information I needed.

NINE

Later that night, I drove by Kate Daniels' small house on a quiet side street in Cragin. It was a neat brick bungalow with no sign of life. The blinds were closed. No lights except for the one on the front porch. I tried her number again. It rang eight time before her message kicked in. I wondered if she'd heard my last message and hung up without leaving another.

I turned on Laramie, went south to the Eisenhower Expressway and headed west out of the city. On Interstate 88, I paid a couple of tolls and picked up coffee at a service area. I hit a bit of snow near Dixon but none of it stuck. A sign said this was the birthplace of Ronald Reagan. After that the road was clear.

It was two in the morning when I merged onto Interstate 80 and crossed the Mississippi River into Iowa. Less than an hour later, I was ringing the night bell at the Crosswinds Motel, a small one-story place with about twenty rooms. Six cars were parked in the lot. All but one had Iowa plates.

After a while, the lights in the office came on. A guy in a striped robe came to the door with sleep in his eyes and gave me a long look. I pointed to the neon VACANCY sign that was burning in the window off to the right. He opened the door. "Fifty-five dollars, and you've got to be out by ten."

"That won't be a problem," I said. He stepped out of the way. I signed in and handed my money over.

I pulled down to number eight and parked in front. The room was clean enough and had a pleasant smell to it. The bedspread, the carpet, and the wallpaper were fading into their retirement years. The bed felt somewhat firm. I pulled the sheet back, didn't see anything moving, and went in search of a pop machine.

TEN

I heard the maid's cart go by at 8:30 in the morning. I went down a few doors, stuck my head in, and said hello. "I'm in number eight."

A young woman in a blue smock was pulling the linens off the bed. "You have to be out by ten," she said without looking my way. A hairnet covered her dark hair.

"No problem," I said. "I was wondering if you have a few minutes."

Now she looked up. "What I have is three kids waiting at home." She was not as young as I'd thought.

I folded a twenty and held it out. "I just want to ask a few questions about my friend Billy who died here."

She took the bill and tucked it away in her apron. "The cop," she said.

"That's the one."

She smiled. "You got the wrong girl, mister. That was Mary. I wasn't here yet." She went back to making the bed. My twenty was already in her piggy bank.

"Where would I find her?"

"The cities," she said. "Minneapolis."

"Do you have a phone number?"

She turned my way and pursed her lips. I held out another twenty.

I dialed the number as she gave it to me and then listened to a recorded message.

"No answer," I said, and pulled out one more twenty. "Would you mind trying her on your phone?"

She reached for the bill. I pulled it back. "If she answers," I said.

A minute later, I traded the twenty for the phone. "Hi Mary." I walked outside and then back to my room.

—

"Hi," she said. "There's not much to say. I took one look and went and got the boss."

"How'd you know he was dead?" I pushed bunched up covers out of the way and sat on the bed.

"The smell for one. He went in the bed. I guess that's what happens. And he knocked over his pizza and beer when he fell."

I walked back out to the fresh air. "He was on the floor?"

"No. He must have been sitting up in bed, you know watching TV, and he just fell over sort of sideways and knocked the pizza and the lamp off the nightstand. There was something hanging out of his mouth. I think it was a piece of pizza, but I didn't look too close. I thought he'd choked but then I heard it was a heart attack, huh?"

"It runs in his family." I let her know.

"He was young, I heard."

"I assume the door was locked." I turned and examined the lock on my door.

"The Sheriff asked me about the door. It was locked. "

"No sign of a struggle or anything like that?" I asked. "No sign that there might have been somebody else in the room with him?"

"The door was locked from the inside. You can tell. "

"Can you think of anything else?"

"It looked so lonely. The TV was on, but it wasn't on a channel. He must have been watching a movie."

"What time did you find him?" I walked over and took a close look at the TV.

"The place was full because of a snowstorm, a lot of truckers. He was my last room. His car was parked right in front, so I left him 'til the end. I knocked and then... It must have been almost noon."

"You didn't happen to find a DVD in the machine

50

when you cleaned the room?"

"Mister, I never touched that room until it was all cleaned and had a brand-new bed and everything. But they didn't have DVD players back then. They were still using those big old tapes."

"What was the room number, anyway?" I asked.

"Nine," she said. I was right next door.

"Thanks for your help, Mary," I said. "You've got a great memory."

"Yeah," she said, "and sometimes I wish I didn't."

I walked back to the room the maid was cleaning and handed her the phone. "You should send Mary half that money," I said.

She gave me an odd little smile. It was the only one I got out of her. Maybe she was saving them up for her kids.

A bell rang when I opened the door at the motel office. A woman wearing a Cubs hat came out of the back. She had a sweater over a paint-splattered T-shirt. Her jeans were spotted with various colors. She smiled and said, "Good morning."

"Hello," I said. "I'm in number eight. I'm here on behalf of Catherine Daniels. Her husband William died here about a year and a half back." I handed her one of my business cards.

"Poor Mr. Daniels," she said. "And he was so young."

"I was hoping you could tell me a bit about that day."

She shook her head. "I don't really know much. My husband Vernon checked him in. I never actually saw him. The maid came in and told me he was dead. I called Vernon and he had to leave work to get back here and handle everything with the police. I'm Janet, by the way."

51

"Nick," I said.

She looked down at my card. "Vernon told me you weren't the usual guest."

"Maybe I should talk to him."

"He won't be back from work until after six. That's assuming we don't get more snow."

"Could I call him at work?"

She shook her head. "It's not that kind of job. Only for emergencies."

"What happened to Daniels' belongings?

"The Sheriff took everything," she said, and her eyes narrowed. "His wife should have them back by now."

"Where do I find the Sheriff?"

"You go west on the interstate to the next exit and then you'll see the building right off the service road."

"What I was wondering, could there have been a tape left in the VCR or the DVD machine that day? Something that was found later."

"Once again, that would be Vernon's department. But we do have a Lost & Found box and you're welcome to look through it. That's where a lot of miscellaneous items end up. "

She led me back through a bright kitchen into a laundry room. She flicked on the overhead lights and pointed to a large cardboard box with a cutout opening in front. "You can just stack everything on top of the machines, if you want."

Most of what I found was clothing, many sweaters and light jackets, items easy to overlook when you check in at night and out in the light of day. As I got towards the bottom heavier items began to appear, shaving kits and makeup bags, books, CDs and cassettes.

At the very bottom of the box, I found two VCR boxes. The first held a tape from Disney and the other was empty.

A few minutes later I dropped my room key on the desk and said goodbye.

#

The Sheriff's office looked a bit like an interstate highway rest stop. It was a low brick building conveniently located within a few feet of the westbound lanes.

I stopped at the front desk. A guy in a deputy's uniform sent me around the corner to waste ten minutes talking to a Sergeant who didn't seem to understand a word I said.

"Do you think I could talk to the Sheriff?" I finally asked.

"You can try," he said, and that's how I found myself in a bright and sunny corner office with the sheriff himself.

He looked much too young for the part, but it was an elected office. He had rich dark hair, a firm handshake and a ready smile. "Vote for Jim," a framed poster said. "Keep Viaud County a country place."

I showed Jim my P.I. license and backed that up with my driver's license and the authorization signed by Catherine Daniels.

He looked it all over and then said, "It seems pretty late in the game for any serious doubts."

"It's not about doubts," I said. "Mrs. Daniels is curious about her husband's last days. I was down the road at the Crosswinds Motel. I thought I should stop here too. You have to admit, 37 is fairly young for a heart attack."

"Well, who you should really be talking to is Doc Decker. But he's in the hospital himself right now. I can

53

tell you what he told the officers from Chicago who came out a few days after the death."

"Thanks. I'd appreciate it."

"Okay. Let me see if I can remember. He said the heart stopped and that was the cause of death. But that wasn't enough to rule it a heart attack. And here's the part I'm confused about. If Mr. Daniels had lived a few hours longer, it would have been easier to diagnose the cause. There would have been evidence in the heart or the vessels, something like that. But because he died immediately, there was no such evidence. The only way to make the diagnosis was to rule out all the other possible causes and that's what Doc Decker did. He ruled out everything else and that's how he arrived at his conclusion." He looked up. "Did that make sense?"

"Good enough for me," I said. "How about his belongings. I take it those were sent back to Chicago."

"We gave the Chicago Police everything we had. I know they called back looking for something. But I don't remember what it was. It might have been a cell phone, something like that."

"A video tape by any chance?"

He thought it over for a moment and then nodded. "Maybe that was it. Maybe."

"Well, thanks for your help," I said.

We shook hands again. "You know this is a good country kind of place. If you're ever looking to get away from the big city. We've got all sorts of recreational opportunities. It's also a great place to retire, if you don't mind a little snow now and then."

#

In daylight the road back was bright from fields of snow.

I debated calling Kate Daniels. What could I tell her?

The maid's description seemed too depressing to share. *It looked so lonely.* On the other hand, it should be enough to convince Kate that Billy was not having an affair. Instead, he spent his last hours alone with pizza and beer, watching television in a dreary motel room.

I stopped at a service area near DeKalb and picked up coffee and gas. While there, I tried Kate's number; I got the same cheerful recording. I didn't leave a message.

The sun broke through for a few minutes outside of Aurora and I found some decent jazz on the FM dial.

Otherwise, the trip was a bust.

ELEVEN

The knocks came at five in the morning, patient, solid, knocks that were never going to stop. I could either answer or go out the window to the roof next door.

They were at the front door of the apartment, which meant they'd gotten through the flimsy lock on the downstairs door; *they, because cops never came alone.*

I grabbed a pair of pants. "Yeah?" I said, standing off to the side of the door.

"Police."

"Yeah?" The floor was ice cold. I debated going back for socks.

"We'd like to speak to you."

"I'm listening." *What the hell were they doing here?*

"Come on, Nick. You know how this is done. Open the fucking door."

"Who's the First Deputy?" I asked, and then realized I wasn't sure of the answer.

"It's on the tip of my tongue," he said after a while. "Big black guy used to play football for CVS. Close enough?"

I opened the door. They were both in suits and ties, which meant they were detectives. The one on my left held up a badge. He had a bit of hair left, all white, and an even whiter face. His eyes were a bit bloodshot. His gray suit had been tailored for a much thinner man. His tie and the top button of his shirt were loose. "Detective Swanson," he said. "Like the frozen dinners." He hooked a thumb to his right. "This is Detective Craig, as in Jenny."

Craig was a good twenty years younger than his partner. He had a very square jaw, dark hair and hooded eyes. He was a bit taller than me, maybe 6'2". He hadn't liked the Jenny Craig comparison. He looked like a man who didn't laugh often. "Get dressed and we'll take a ride," he said.

"Is that really necessary?"

"Come on, Nick," Swanson said. "You of all people should know how it's done."

Yeah. I knew how it was done, alright. *But why were they doing it?*

A few minutes later I was in the back seat of their roomy Ford and, just like old times, nobody said a word. The only difference, I was in the wrong seat. Now I was supposed to be scrambling to get my story straight while the dicks took turns watching me in the rear-view mirror.

After a bit, I realized we were no longer going south, towards the new Police Headquarters. We were heading west. This made the old Area Five, now called Area North, an easy guess. Was the Austin District where Rita Cunningham worked part of the area? I knew they'd changed borders recently, but I hadn't paid much attention. Could this have something to do with her?

All the way out to Grand and Central, into the parking lot, out of the car and up the stairs, I kept telling myself to relax. It would soon make sense. And then we turned right at the top of the stairs and Swanson dropped his briefcase on one of the desks reserved for Violent Crimes, the old homicide unit. And suddenly it made too much sense. "Who's dead?"

"Let's just keep playing by the book," Swanson said, and he pointed towards two dark windows at the back of the room. Two-way glass. On the other side were the interview rooms, where the same glass looked like a mirror.

Craig switched on the inside light and held the door

open. "Give us a minute or two," Swanson said. This was straight out of the playbook. They'd let you sweat for as long as they thought necessary. But that was okay. I needed time to think.

The room was eight by ten, with a bench bolted to the wall and a table to the floor. I took a look in the all-seeing mirror. I looked a bit worried. Who was dead?

No. That wasn't all of it. Why do they think I might be involved?

I couldn't come up with a single name. I didn't keep an enemies list. I hadn't had any real beefs lately. Tommy Burroughs was as close as I could get. But wasn't he threatening to kill me? Had someone done the world a favor and taken him out? That would be a cause for celebration.

And then I had a sickening thought. Burroughs had told me Kate Daniels was going to call and cancel our agreement. She never had. I'd called several times and she'd never answered or called back.

"Fuck," I said softly, and I sat down on the bench and dropped my head into my hands.

They'd been watching through the two-way glass, of course. So now the door opened, and they both came in dragging chairs behind them. This made for three rather large human beings in a room no bigger than the standard bathroom.

Before the door closed behind Craig, I spotted a woman standing several feet back. She was a bit off to the side, just far enough to give her a good view of the phony mirror. I knew I'd seen her before, but I couldn't remember where.

Swanson had an oversized envelope in hand. "Want to show you a couple of pictures," he said. Craig leaned back against a wall and kept his eyes on me.

"Tell me what happened," I said.

Swanson laid a photograph on the table between us and slid it my way. There I was, standing outside my office. Photographers usually have a hard time catching me with a smile. But Kate Daniels was a pro and she'd managed to find a small one.

"What can you tell us about this?"

"I'm not saying another word until you tell me what's going on. I've played it your way up 'til now. That's over. Tell me what happened, or I want my lawyer. You decide."

"That picture," Craig said. "That's your I-want-to-fuck-you smile, isn't it?"

I folded my arms, closed my eyes, dropped my head, and took a deep breath. I wasn't very good at sleeping in a sitting position, but that didn't mean I couldn't pretend.

"You know how long we can keep you here?" Craig said.

In my days on the other side of the table, we'd considered sleeping in the interview room almost a sure sign of guilt. You could relax at last. You didn't have to wait for the knock on the door. It had already come. The worst had happened. You were locked up. You could finally close your eyes without fear and get a little sleep.

I was keeping myself from thinking about Kate Daniels by trying to decide which lawyer I would call when I finally got my phone call. This was really an exercise and nothing more. I'd call Shelly. We'd both been losers at my Police Board hearing. Now she'd have a chance to even the score.

I heard one of the cops leave the room, but I kept my head down. The door opened again. Something landed on the table. "There's your answer," Swanson said.

—

"Page seven."

I opened my eyes to the morning Sun-Times, Kate Daniels' old paper. On the bottom of the front page, a large headline read: RAMPAGE IN CRAGIN. On page seven, I found Kate Daniels staring back at me under the headline, "Former Sun-Times Photographer Two Others Dead." I closed my eyes again and saw that small wave as the elevator door was closing. That was all I got. I couldn't bring her smile back. I'd never be able to do that.

The story was short on details, a double murder followed by a suicide. Daniels was found shot to death in her darkroom. Tommy Burroughs name wasn't mentioned at all. But he had to be the shooter. There was a short bio of Kate Daniels. She'd been born in North Dakota, of all places, and had come to Chicago to attend Columbia College. She'd won a Stick-o-Type Award from the Chicago Newspaper Guild for a series of photographs she'd taken at a fire, a mother dropping an infant towards the waiting arms of a police officer. They'd reprinted one of the photos. The baby was in mid-air. The cop's outstretched arms were still far away. The mother was leaning far out the window. Behind her the building was engulfed in flames. According to the story, the mother and the baby had both survived.

I read the story twice and then looked up. "Burroughs," I said.

Swanson nodded.

"And then he killed himself," I said.

He nodded again.

"Who's number three?" I asked.

He shrugged. "A neighbor he had a beef with."

I spread both hands wide. "So why am I here?"

He dropped the same photograph on top of the

newspaper. "What can you tell us about this?"

"That's me outside my office."

"Who took it?" Swanson probed.

"Catherine Daniels."

"What was the occasion?"

I was looking into her eyes hoping she'd look back. Instead, I said: "She asked if she could take my picture. I said, okay."

"And you had no other connection with her?"

"No," I said. "Not really." Unless you count dreams.

"And that's your story?"

I nodded. That was my story, as ridiculous as it sounded.

"And you're sticking with it?"

"Right." I nodded.

"So how do you explain this?" He took another photograph out of his envelope. It might have been the same shot, but it was hard to be sure. Someone had used the photo as a dartboard or maybe they'd taken an ice pick to it. My eyes were gone. The smile had disappeared. My name was no longer legible on the door. My occupation had been scratched out as well.

"Burroughs?" I asked, and there was a sick taste in my mouth.

He shook his head. "Doesn't look like it. You know who that leaves?"

Yeah, I knew. She'd asked me not to talk to Burroughs, but I'd tipped him off anyway with all my stupid phone calls. And Kate apparently knew it. I could almost hear her screams as she punished me the only way she could while Tommy Burroughs was busy kicking the door down. "She got off at the wrong floor," I said. "She was getting her teeth cleaned at the dentist downstairs."

61

"And then?"

Craig had been inching closer, as Swanson asked the questions. He slid his chair into mine. They met with a bang. He put a foot on the seat of the chair.

"She came back and hired me," I said.

"She hired you to do what?" Swanson raised an arm.

"I don't think I have to tell you that."

"Nick, it's a homicide investigation," he said softly. "Remember?"

"And it's already cleared. Psycho cop goes berserk. No. I'm sorry." I pushed the photo aside and turned back to page one. "Psycho cop goes on rampage. What more do you need?"

"How's this?" Craig jumped in. "She had a tape she wanted you to . . ."

Swanson shouted over Craig's voice. "She thought her husband had been murdered. Isn't that what happened?" He was pissed, but not at me. He was pissed at Craig for letting the tape out of the bag.

So now I could relax. They were worried about some tape that was nothing but a vague rumor. I decided to try the truth. "She hired me to find out if her husband had been having an affair."

"Two years after he died?" Craig said. Now he was shouting too. "You really expect us to believe that?"

I looked at myself in the mirror. See how well the truth works, Nick?

"My hearing's fine," I said. "And it's not even a year and a half since he died. But she'd been worrying about it. She told me that's sort of how she'd ended up with Burroughs. She was punishing Billy for screwing around. So after he died she took up with his best friend. And now she was having second thoughts and feeling bad about it. "

62

"Second thoughts about being with Burroughs?" Swanson asked.

"That too, I think," I said. "But mostly she was wondering if she'd misjudged her husband."

"And what did your investigation find?"

"I barely got started," I said. "I have other cases. I didn't have much time to give it."

"Did you talk to Thomas Burroughs?"

I nodded. "For a couple of minutes."

"What about?"

I shrugged. "He'd heard I was asking around about him. He wanted to know why."

"I'd like to know why myself," Swanson said. "If you were interested in Daniels, why were you asking about Burroughs?"

"I was asking about both. They were partners and best friends according to Kate."

"Kate?" Craig said.

"Catherine. That's what she went by. And she told me Billy had been acting funny before he died. That's why she thought he was having an affair."

"Funny how?" Swanson asked.

"He quit drinking for one, but he was still staying out late. She figured if he wasn't at the bars, he must be with another woman."

"Just like a woman," Craig said, and he pulled his chair back a bit. "You quit drinking and your wife thinks you're fucking around." He sounded like he might be talking from experience.

"You know how you can tell your wife is having an affair," Swanson asked. He pointed Craig's way.

Craig ignored him. "So, cause of death for Catherine Daniels," he said. "Instead of homicide how about we write in: inept private eye? You have a problem with

63

that?"

"It sounds pretty accurate," I said. Maybe I'd put that on my business cards, so people would know what they were getting themselves into.

"Look," Swanson said. He was trying to be a nice guy. "If word got around about this . . . "

"And it will," I said. "Believe me."

"Yeah," Swanson said. "But if we pushed it around, gave it to the press, made sure every lawyer in town knew."

I nodded. I saw where he was going.

"We'd like to ask a favor," Swanson said. "I don't have to spell it out, do I?"

I shook my head. "Got it," I said. Case closed. This is why they'd pulled me out of bed in the middle of the night. But what was the big deal? I didn't have a client anymore. Who would I send my report to?

"We know you had a little trouble a few years back," Swanson said. "But that doesn't mean you're not part of the family. Once a cop always a cop, but try to remember, you're on our side. Deal?"

"Sure," I said. "Deal." But where was that big blue family when I'd needed it?

"This isn't just from us," Swanson said. "Come on." He opened the door wide. "We'll give you a ride back."

"Thanks," I said, and I followed them out the door and down the stairs. I stopped by the front desk. "You know, I think I'll walk for a while. I need some fresh air."

"You sure?" Craig asked.

"Sure."

"Well, thanks for coming in, Nick," Swanson said. "I've heard your name for years. It's nice to finally meet you."

"Likewise," Craig said. And we all shook hands, like

any other happy family.

The woman I'd seen upstairs was on the telephone on the customer side at the far end of the desk. She was dressed in civilian clothes, but I had no doubt she was cop. She was forty or so, tall, with reddish-brown hair. She had eyeglasses in hand, but apparently didn't need them. She held my eyes with a steady gaze. *Where did I know her from?*

TWELVE

I walked north up Central Avenue. Alongside Hanson Stadium the sidewalks were covered with dirty snow. I tried following the packed down footprints. I hadn't worn boots and kept slipping this way and that. I switched over to the street, which was wet from salt and melted snow. Cars splashed slush my way and tooted their horns, while the salt tried to destroy my shoes.

I took a break at Fullerton and looked for a taxi. I was three miles north of where I'd grown up. We used to ride our bikes up this way, to the stadium to see high school football games, or to the hamburger stand that had been across the street, Henry's, or something like that. It was a forerunner of McDonalds or maybe an early copycat. Now the neighborhood was mostly Mexican. There wasn't a cab in sight. But there were plenty of taquerias, which meant the food was better than ever.

I crossed Fullerton and continued north, now on the sidewalks, which had all been shoveled. I tried to think of every stupid thing I'd ever done. Some nights I couldn't sleep because they ran through my head like an endless train, one dark car after another. Now I had a new one to add to the collection. Kate Daniels had gotten off on the wrong floor and had compounded that mistake by asking for my help. Her real mistake was trusting me. I'd set her up for Tommy Burroughs and then in my great attempt to save her, I'd made a few phone calls and had taken one pass by her house. Isn't it funny how this wasn't enough? Cause of death: inept private eye.

Fair enough.

The neighborhood went from predominantly Mexican to predominantly Polish. These were the hardest working ethnic groups in town. They'd cut your grass, fix your roof, tuck-point your bricks, hang your drywall, install a new toilet, and rod out your sewer. They'd do the job right, usually at a fair price, and then they'd take some of that money and send it south of the border or across the sea.

I'd walked over a mile when I came to a pancake house. I went in, sat down and ordered breakfast. I was staring into the blackness of my coffee, telling myself it wasn't my fault that Kate Daniels was dead. Yes. It had been stupid of me to make all those phone calls and alert Burroughs that Kate was up to something. But Tommy Burroughs was the one who had pulled the trigger. And Kate was the one who had put herself in the line of fire, another good girl who couldn't resist taking up with a very bad boy.

I dumped a bit of coffee whitener into my cup and mixed it with my finger. *That's right, Nick. Go ahead. Blame the victim.*

Someone slid into the booth across from me. I looked up to find the familiar looking woman I'd seen at the police station. "Tommy Burroughs was always a psycho," she said. "It was just a matter of time."

"Hello again," I said.

She slipped off a pair of dark blue gloves. "Do you mind if I join you?"

I gave her a welcome wave. "I know we've met."

"My father's wake," she said. "John Whalen." She placed her gloves on the edge of the table.

"My first boss." He'd been the district commander when I was a rookie patrol officer. "He was a good man," I said. "And you're?"

"Barbara." She reached out a hand and we shook.

"Nice to see you again," I said. "That's gotta be like

twenty years."

"Sixteen," she said.

"You weren't on the job back then?" She was probably still in high school.

She shook her head. "Dad wanted me to keep my hands clean and become a lawyer," she said. "I hope they didn't give you too hard a time, Swanson and Craig."

I shrugged. "I don't know why they bothered."

"Rumors all over the place," she said. "You probably heard."

I shook my head. "About what?" *You mean that mysterious tape?*

That got me a smile and a business card. "If you hear anything interesting, something you might not want to share with the boys in the area, I'd appreciate it if you'd call me instead." A blue police star on a white card. *Sgt. Barbara Yates, 15th District Tactical Squad.*

"Sure," I said. Here was another member of my big happy family who hadn't been around when I'd needed her.

"Everybody's against us now" she said. "Have you noticed that?"

"Weren't they always?"

"The important thing is not to add fuel to the fire." She held my eyes.

I looked straight back. "You don't have to worry about me," I said.

"I'm not," she said. "Dad was proud of you, you know. 'One of my boys,' he'd say whenever your name came up."

"Your dad told me, 'Take the dick's test. You're never gonna last as a street cop.' I didn't even know what a detective was back then."

A minute later, the waitress came with my breakfast.

"I'll let you eat in peace," Barbara said. She slid out of the booth. "Don't beat yourself up over Catherine Daniels. Tommy and I came up together. Every woman he ever went with ended up in the emergency room. She should have known better."

"Maybe nobody told her," I said.

She shook her head. "She knew." She turned and walked away.

So now everybody agreed. It was Kate Daniels' own damn fault.

I moved the food around my plate and even ate a bit. After a while, my phone buzzed. I looked at the screen, Lenny, my old friend down at Police Headquarters. I'd asked him to check out Burroughs and Daniels for me.

"Nick, sorry to call you so early," he said. "Look, those guys you asked about, I got a bunch of stuff, but I don't think most of it matters anymore."

"Just give me the highlights," I said.

"Thomas Burroughs killed himself last night. And I've got to cover my ass a bit because I was just asking about him."

"Just give 'em my name," I said. They wouldn't pick me up again, would they?

"Christ, are you nuts? That's what I'm trying to avoid. Look don't worry. You're not the first person I had to wake up."

"Tell me more about Burroughs," I said.

"He's got a file takes up an entire cabinet. We've been trying to get rid of him for years. He took a neighbor and his girlfriend with him. He'd been having an ongoing beef with the neighbor. I guess the guy liked to cut the grass at the crack of noon. Burroughs kicked the door in and pulled him right out of bed."

"Why couldn't they toss him?"

That got me a snort. "People like your old pal Shelly," he said, and his voice dropped. "And he had somebody down here, too." Meaning police headquarters.

"Tell me about his girlfriend."

"They didn't find her until later," he said. "Looks like she tried to lock herself in a darkroom down in their basement. She used to work for the Sun-Times. A rumor says you knew her."

"Just a little," I said, and I could see those beautiful hands trying to hold back a flimsy basement door. "Hardly at all."

THIRTEEN

When the waitress came by, I asked her to call a cab.

By the time the cab came, it was snowing again. I gave the driver my address but then about ten minutes later, as we cruised down Irving Park Road, I changed my mind. "Could you take me to Belmont and Lincoln instead?" This was my office.

He grunted which I took to mean yes.

We were waiting for the light at Sacramento when it hit me. "Should have known better," I said.

"What's that?" the driver said.

"Just talking to myself." I pulled out my phone and dialed.

"Crosswinds Motel," Janet answered.

I said hello and told her who I was. "Your lost and found box," I asked, "how long do you keep that stuff?"

"Oh, we go through it every couple of months and pick out whatever's been there a while. Oh, I see what you're getting at. That thing you were looking for, it wouldn't be there now, would it?"

"What do you do with the old stuff?"

"Most of it goes to the Salvation Army store in Mayfair." She gave me directions to the town, three miles north. "Go halfway around the square and make a right and then you'll see the store on the left."

I thanked her and said goodbye.

"Sorry," I said to the cabdriver. "I changed my mind again." I gave him the address for Rent-a-Dent.

"And then you are out," the driver said.

"Sure."

"One, two, three strikes," he said. "Just like the ballgame."

Buddy, you've led a charmed life, I thought. Those were barely strikes at all.

FOURTEEN

The snow was coming down pretty good now, billions of tiny flakes, whipping around and sailing on the wind. Rent-A-Dent didn't have any cars with 4-wheel drive. However, an old Jeep Cherokee with all-wheel drive was available.

"How many wheels does it have?" I asked Caitlin, the girl behind the counter.

"Very funny, Nick," she said. "I'll ask Jose to take one off for you."

The snow stopped before I got to the service area at DeKalb. I picked up coffee and chocolate chip cookies. The road was clear the rest of the way.

Mayfair, Iowa looked pretty good at first. On the same block there was a restaurant, a grocer, a hardware store and a bar. Unfortunately, the town square was one empty storefront after another. FOR RENT signs papered many of the windows. The movie theater looked as if it had been closed for decades. A series of construction jacks supported the marquee which read, "THE END," in crooked letters.

In the center of the square a Union soldier stood at attention on top of a tall pedestal. There was a plate at the base of the statue; probably a list of names, those who had or hadn't come back to what had surely been a prosperous town.

The Salvation Army store was on a corner just off the square. The smell of dust and mildew, old clothes and bug spray, greeted me as I opened the door. Otherwise, it was a cheerful room. Sunlight streamed through big front windows. Much of the furniture looked better than what I had at home. The wood parts had been polished. The pillows puffed.

A woman sat behind a high desk towards the back with a pen in hand. She looked up and waved. "If you need help finding anything," she said, "just call." Her head went back down.

I took my time browsing--more useless stuff to clutter up my apartment--and eventually made my way to a back corner where books and tapes were shelved. There must have been several hundred VCR tapes. And if Mary the maid was right, that's probably what Billy was watching on his last night, his last moment, perhaps.

But what were the odds of it ending up here, I wondered as I started going through the shelves. And what were the odds that it was still here, or that it was the tape from the corner store? Billy might have been watching anything for his last picture show.

With the two trips, I'd already driven over six hundred miles with nothing to show for it. So, I took my time and opened every box. Most of what I found were Hollywood movies. I set aside the tapes without movie covers. Some of these were hand-marked with Hollywood movie names. Others were either unmarked or seemed personal. "Irene's Wedding," one said.

I carried one of the unmarked ones up to the clerk. "How much are these?"

"Fifty cents each or five for two dollars."

I found a hand basket and began stacking tapes inside. My plan was to spend the day at Sim's Video. But a bit of reflected sunlight found its way into the back of the store. A single word in very light pencil on one of the unboxed tapes caught my eye. "Sweet's," it read. This was the name of the corner store.

I went back to the woman at the desk, held up the tape and handed her a buck. "Do you happen to have a VCR where I could take a quick look at this?"

The woman turned towards the back room. "Robert," she called.

Robert was a small, thin man who moved with the lightness of a dancer.

"This gentleman was wondering if we had a VCR in working order," the woman said.

Robert gave me a one-finger wave and I followed him into the back room, to a small alcove that had been partially walled off with bookcases. Two easy chairs and a sofa all faced an old 26-inch TV.

Robert pulled the chain on an overhead light, took the tape from my hand and slipped it into a VCR machine. "Unfortunately, there's no remote," he said. "This button starts it. This is fast forward, and this is reverse." He pulled a chair close to the machine. "If you need help, I'm right around the corner."

It took me a while to get the hang of it but, before too long, I was looking at customers coming and going in a small corner store. I recognized some of the kids from the other day, but I couldn't hear a word. The tape had no audio.

None of the stock was out in the open. Everything was behind a counter, all of it protected by a yellowish sort of Plexiglas which went clear to the ceiling. It would be a tough place for even the best shoplifter.

There were two clerks at first. One was forty or so, the other still in his twenties. They both appeared to be Indian or Pakistani. The clerks would get the items the customer asked for and bring them back to the cash register. The customers had to put their money in a miniature revolving door. The clerk moved the door to his side, took the money and rang up the sale, and sent the change and the items purchased back. At least half the sales were liquor or tobacco. Most of the rest was candy, chips, soda, and other junk food.

I fast-forwarded through the tape looking for cops. When they showed up, I reversed for a while and then waited for the shoplifter to appear. But none ever did.

The older clerk put a jacket on, went out a security door to the main part of the store, and then out the front door. The younger clerk looked out the front window. I thought he was probably watching the older clerk all the way to his car.

A few minutes later a young black guy entered the store. He was in his late teens, tall, wearing a leather jacket over a sport's jersey. His running shoes sparkled. So did one of his teeth. Several others were missing.

He put his money in the revolving door, but the clerk sent it straight back. They went back and forth for a while but without audio it was hard to figure out what was going on. At one point, the youth pushed the revolving door to the clerk's side and held the door in place with both hands. The clerk got off his stool and began rearranging stock. He never touched the money.

And that's where things stood when the cops entered. Tommy Burroughs went straight for the black kid. He spun him around, slammed him against a wall, and did a pat-down search. Burroughs pulled a half-pint liquor bottle from the kid's back pocket. He held it up for the clerk to see.

The clerk waved his hands around. I couldn't hear a word, but I knew exactly what he was saying: *He didn't get that here!*

The cops split up. Burroughs stayed with the youth, riffling through his other pockets, looking though his wallet, whispering in his ear. Billy Daniels talked to the clerk.

After a bit, Burroughs waved the clerk over to the

---

customer side of the store. The clerk unlocked the security door, ducked down, and stepped into the customer area.

Burroughs held up the half pint and then some kind of ID. He pushed the ID right into the clerk's face, and pointed at the money, still on the far side of the revolving door. The clerk got very excited, jumping up and down. He turned and pointed straight at the camera. Both cops turned to look that way.

Daniels opened the front door and the black kid started out. Burroughs handed the half pint to Daniels who handed it on to the kid, who carried the evidence out the door.

Burroughs and the clerk got into a shouting match. This went on for a while with Billy Daniels running interference between them. The clerk made an end run, got up on tiptoes and he and Burroughs were suddenly face-to-face. Burroughs knocked the clerk back with one hand, pulled out his gun with the other, took very deliberate aim, and fired. The clerk fell to the floor and grabbed his knee. Burroughs kicked him in the side and took aim again.

Billy Daniels jumped between them. He pushed the gun to the side and pulled Burroughs away from the clerk. Burroughs still had his gun in hand. He spun around, looked right at the camera, and then walked behind the counter and disappeared into the back room.

Billy Daniels spread his arms wide, leaned over the clerk and said something. A few seconds later, the tape stopped.

"That looked like one of those videos you see on TV," the woman said behind me. I hadn't heard her come in.

"An old police show," I said.

"I forgot to give you your change," she said, and

reached out with fifty cents.

"You better keep it," I said, the last of the big-time spenders.

FIFTEEN

I played the If game most of the way back to Chicago.

If I'd found the tape on the first trip; If I hadn't made all those useless phone calls; If I'd kept my big mouth shut. That was the biggest if of all.

If Kate Daniels were still alive, I'd probably be whistling a tune about now. I'd drive one-handed while patting myself on the back. *See Kate, I told you I'd find out what was going on. You want to know why your husband had a heart attack. Take a look at this.*

I would have made a few copies of the tape before I showed it to her. I'd want one for my safety deposit box, one for the store clerk or his attorney, and maybe one for a reporter friend at the Tribune. I'd ask Kate for permission, of course. But if she refused, I'd probably make sure the tape got out just the same. How else was I going to get Tommy Burroughs out of my way?

But what was the point of distributing the tape now? Tommy Burroughs was out of everyone's way forever. He'd given himself the ultimate punishment, although it didn't feel anything like justice.

What I really wanted, I decided after I'd crossed the Mississippi, was to talk to that kid with the half pint. What had he and Burroughs been whispering about? Did that really matter now, I wondered. And then I answered my own question. It did.

Because someone had to pay for Kate Daniels' death and, if I let myself off the hook, that kid was the only one still standing. Had Daniels and Burroughs sent him in with that whiskey? That was a mystery worth investigating.

I drove back into the snow right about where I'd left it. From the looks of things, it had been coming down continually.

SIXTEEN

Sim's Video was still open when I bulled my way into the unplowed parking lot. Most of the lights were off but a couple of kids were playing video games in the back room.

"Oh, no," Phil said when he saw me. "Twice in a week. Things are getting wacky around here."

I held up the tape. "Can you copy this?"

"Tomorrow," he said. "Sure."

"Tonight."

He shook his head. "The problem is, it's analog, so if it's an hour and a half long, that's how long it takes to transfer it. I have a dinner date with my lovely wife. It's her birthday so I can't be late. And it's snowing so traffic's a mess, right?"

"How about just ten minutes of it. Can you do that much now?"

"Well, why didn't you say so?" He started digging around under the counter.

"And then tomorrow you can make copies of the entire tape."

"Sure. Once it's on a DVD I can make you as many copies as you want." He dropped a clunky machine on the counter, brushed off a layer of dust, and hooked it up to a much slimmer machine.

I handed him the tape, told him where I had stopped it, and he started rewinding, stopping here and there.

"Back more," I said once, twice and then, "Right about here." And several seconds in, the youth in the leather jacket walked into the store. "Stop."

The tape stopped and gave us a beautiful closeup, which included a shiny gold star on one tooth. "Can you get me a still of this?" I asked. "Make sure you get that tooth."

"Tomorrow," Phil said. "Let's get the copy out of the way first."

"Do me a favor," I said, as the tape moved along. "Don't watch it, okay?"

"Why not?"

"It's a bit gross," I said. "It's your wife's birthday and I know it's going to upset you." He'd been bothered before by some of the violent videos I'd brought in.

"Whatever you say," Phil said, and he clicked the monitor off.

The kids finished their game in back. Phil went back to turn off the lights. I used the toilet.

When I came out, my DVD was ready. The original tape stayed with Phil.

It snowed all the way home.

SEVENTEEN

I spent a couple of days hiding out in my apartment or in one of the nearby saloons. If it wasn't snowing it was cold and if it wasn't cold, it was snowing. Sometimes you couldn't tell if it was fresh snow or if the wind was blowing the old snow around.

But I had good winter boots and a down parka. Most of the sidewalks had been shoveled, and the saloons were warm enough and not too far apart. A couple of them even had working fireplaces, where people stood around, warmed their hands and pretended they were in Bavaria not Lincoln Square. I pretended I'd never seen the tape.

In the old days, you might visit a friend in the State's Attorney's office. Then the two of you would go have a quiet talk with the prosecutor in charge of the case and then you might all gather in the judge's chamber to watch the video. Once it was determined both cops were dead, the rest would be easy. They'd call the defense attorney in and give him some plausible story, and then they'd either toss the conviction or reduce the sentence to time served. Everybody would go home happy, including the poor sap in prison. The video would never be made public.

But that was before videos of police shootings became the rage. Now nobody could risk hiding the video and then having it surface later, after they'd made a deal obviously based on it.

I knew the right thing to do was to distribute copies to all the interested parties. The State's Attorney's office, the store clerk's defense attorney, the newspapers and TV stations, and not worry about what it did to the police department's image.

81

The problem was that blue blood still pulsed through my veins, more than a dozen years after I'd been tossed off the police force. And Barbara Yates was right. The tape would add more fuel to a very large fire.

It wasn't just Chicago. You couldn't turn on a TV without seeing one cop or another shooting someone in the back. From Natchez to Mobile, Minneapolis, Memphis and old St. Joe. Didn't these cops watch TV? Didn't they realize in the seconds before they fired that they were just fanning the flames of the anti-cop brigade? Didn't they realize there were cameras everywhere?

Shelly woke me late one morning. "Officer Thomas Burroughs," she said. "Anything you'd care to tell me about him?"

"He's dead."

"I know he's dead, Nick. But don't you think you should have told me?"

"Sorry." I sat up in bed.

"I was just calling around about him. And that got other people calling around and now those people are getting questions and I'm getting questions from them and the man with the answers is still in bed. So, could you please tell me what's going on?"

"His girlfriend was my client."

"The same one he killed?"

"That's the one."

"And that's it? You're not involved in this mess in any other way?"

"Right."

#

I was at my office an hour later armed with a cup of coffee and my adding machine.

—

And for three hundred dollars, you'll be able to find the truth?

No, Kate. Sorry. Not quite.

I'd spent your advance and a bit more. I knew some of the truth but not all. Tommy Burroughs was definitely a psycho. You learned that the hard way. He wasn't as harmless as you'd thought. But what was the game at the corner store?

Was it just a simple shakedown? Were Burroughs and Billy Daniels just looking for a Thanksgiving bonus?

Why was Daniels heading to Colorado? That was one of the questions Kate wanted answered. He had the tape along, so maybe he planned to show it to his lawyer-brother. If I turn this tape over, he might have wanted to ask, will I go down with my best friend Tommy?

Not for the shooting. He'd probably saved the clerk's life. But what about the shakedown attempt? Could the CPD overlook his role in that?

It didn't really matter. I was off the case, and all your money's gone anyway, Kate. I spent every dime.

But could I really charge her for that second trip to Iowa? It had been stupid on my part to assume the tape might still be in the lost and found almost a year and a half after the fact. If I'd asked one question, I would have found it on my first trip.

If I deducted charges for the second rent-a-dent, for tolls and gas, I ended up with $60 yet to spend.

So, I was back on the case, but only a bit. There was no reason to get any higher on the CPD's shit list. I would forget I'd ever found the tape. But I'd try to find the kid the cops had used inside the store. Maybe he could answer some of the questions I still had.

And then I could find Kate Daniels grave, spend whatever I had left on flowers, and whisper my report straight into the ground.

I made a quick stop at Sim's Video on the way home.

"Boy, am I glad to see you," Phil said as I walked in. This was the exact opposite of his usual greeting. "I was afraid something happened."

"Just holed up for a while," I said. "I meant to call."

He went to the back room and returned with two slim envelopes. "Ten dvd's of that tape," he said, and slid one envelope towards me. "And ten stills." He slid one out of the second envelope, a 6 by 8 of the kid from that ghetto food store, grainy but good enough for identification. The star on his tooth gleamed like a real star next to a black hole. The black hole was the gap where his front teeth had once been.

I paid the bill and added a tip. "Where's the original?"

"Bad news," Phil said. "It got shredded in the machine. If you give me a couple of days, I can probably get it back together."

"Sure," I said. "No hurry. I'll stop by next week."

EIGHTEEN

I started out at Sweet's Mini Mart, which now had a huge West Side skylight where the weight of the snow had caved in most of the roof. It wouldn't be long before the wrecking ball arrived.

The kids were gone. Could they actually be in school?

I found the big kid, the one who'd told me he didn't talk to no five-o, walking in the tire ruts a block away. Even with all that snow, he was still wearing running shoes.

I tooted my horn, pulled around, and rolled down the window. "Hop in," I said. "I'll give you a ride." His jacket didn't look warm at all.

"Ain't going nowhere," he said. He'd probably never been downtown. He took a quick look at my car. "Nice truck." I'd paid extra for a fancy SUV with barely a dent.

I held up one of my pictures. "Don't talk to no police," he said, before I could ask a single question.

"I'm private," I said, and held out a business card. He backed away and the card fell to the slush. "Call that number. There's a reward, anyone knows where to find him."

"Big reward?" The kid smiled.

"Big." I nodded.

"A whole bottle of wine, for real?" His smile got bigger. He was having a good time.

"A pair of winter boots. How's that sound?"

"Don't need no boots." He was back in the hood.

And that's how it went as I drove around the West Side. Nobody wanted to talk and only a few took me up on the offer of a ride.

"What kind of pervert are you?" my very first rider

asked.

"Information," I said, and tried to show him a picture. "I'm buying."

"Not from me you're not." And he opened the door while the car was still moving. I stopped. He walked away without looking back. I slipped the photo back into its envelope and my business card back into my shirt pocket, and then reached over and closed the passenger door.

You could see for blocks through the ruins. Was that why nobody would talk? The odds were someone, somewhere, was watching. If only those ruins could talk. That would be one heartbreaking tale. But who would listen?

"Yeah, he was around a few years back," a guy who looked to be about fifty told me. "But you can bet he's either dead or in jail by now. These kids, that's all they know."

"Has he got a name?"

"If I make one up, do I still get the reward?"

"A street name?"

"That's cop talk. A name is a name is a name. It's all the same."

I gave him my card and a ten. "If you hear of anything, use the number on the back."

"Go around the corner and drop me by the alley," he said. Nobody wanted to be seen with me.

Late afternoon, I took the long drive up to Rogers Park to find Sim's Video closed.

NINETEEN

The next morning, I went downtown to the library to look at a crisscross directory. This was a phone book that listed phone numbers by address.

Back in my days as a real detective, this had been a great tool. You didn't have to ring the bell at the house across the street from the shooting while the entire neighborhood looked on. You could make a discreet phone call right from your desk. You'd be surprised how forthcoming someone might be if no one was watching or listening in.

But that had all been in the days of old, the days before cell phones took over the world.

I only found two active landlines in buildings with views of Sweet's Mini Mart, and only one of those answered when I called.

"Why no, I'm sorry, I can't eat sweets anymore," a very old-sounding woman said. "It's my diabetes."

Before I could explain, a much younger voice took over the phone. "What do you want?"

"I want to ask..."

"We don't need your damn windows," she said. "How many times do I have to tell you?" And that was the end of that call.

I went back to the West Side. I walked into several corner stores, but they were hard to find, and saloons were non-existent. That was one of the minor tragedies of life on the poor side of town. It was harder and harder to get a drink. A tavern could be around for years and then one night someone would pull a knife or a gun, the police and an ambulance would come, and the city would decide the business was a nuisance and revoke the liquor license. Try making a living selling potato

---

87

chips and soda pop.

After a few decades of this, the inviting blush of neon was as rare as an actual supermarket. This was one of the neighborhoods they called a food desert, meaning it was a mile or more to a grocer that was anything more than a junk food emporium. It was a saloon desert, too.

The clerks at the corner stores were Indians or Pakistanis, or from some African country. For them the store was probably one small step on the road to the American dream. I only found a few black clerks and most of them spoke with foreign accents. Nobody knew anything about the man in my photograph. Nobody knew anything about Sweet's Mini Mart. I slipped my card under bulletproof glass.

A small travel trailer sat on blocks in the middle of an empty lot on Chicago Avenue. It looked like a Christmas tree lot waiting for next season to arrive. But then a young girl walked out of the place, and down the few steps to the ground. She had a plastic bag in one hand and a half-gallon of milk in the other. On the trailer door, a hand-lettered sign said: PEOPLE'S FOOD STORE. A smaller sign said: BUY LOCAL.

I parked at the curb, walked across a layer of fresh gravel, and up the steps. Musical notes sounded as the door opened. A woman stood behind a low counter with a feather duster in hand. There wasn't a bulletproof shield or a miniature revolving door in sight.

To her right, a cooler was stocked with milk, eggs, butter and yogurt. To the left open shelves held breakfast cereal, rice, flour, and cooking oil. Unlike the typical store on this side of town, you could pick the items yourself. But there was plenty of empty shelf space.

"Welcome," the woman said. "Are you looking for anything special?"

"Lifesavers," I said.

"I do not sell junk food," she said, and I knew she'd said it a thousand times before. "I do not sell tobacco or alcohol. I do not sell lottery tickets."

"Must be tough."

She shook her head. "Not particularly," she said. "And you're certainly not here for mints."

"No. You're right." I showed her the picture of my mystery man.

She barely looked. "Oh, yes, I've heard about you, you and your picture," she said. "You don't really think anyone is going to talk to you, do you?

"Why not?"

"You've lost the trust of the people," she said. "The entire police department..."

"I'm not the police," I said, and I handed her a business card.

She looked at the card and then up at me. "You stink of the police."

There wasn't anything to say to that. I turned and headed for the door.

"Wait," she said behind me. "Would you like to help our cause?"

When I turned back, she pointed to a sign off to the side. "Help us build a real store," it read. "Good food. Good prices. Good jobs." An arrow pointed to a donation can on the shelf beneath it.

"You're kidding, right?"

"That's going to be our new home."

Next to the sign was an artist's rendering of this same corner occupied by a shiny two-story building. "People's Food Store & Neighborhood Center," a sign above the front door read. The trailer I was standing in was perched on the roof, surrounded by grass, picnic tables,

89

and a small playground.

"The bible says those who plant the seeds will be rewarded one hundred-fold," she said as I turned her way. "That's better odds than just another scratch-off ticket, don't you agree?"

"Lady, you're one hell of a salesman." I checked my roll. The smallest bill I had was a twenty. That would just about finish off Kate Daniels' retainer. "This is a lucky bill," I said, as I stuffed it into the can.

"Bless you," she said. "One hundred-fold."

I went out the door, got back in the car and turned east. There was an extra-large convenience store a few blocks down, "24-7," a big sign read, "Fast Food & Groceries." A uniformed cop stood outside but there wasn't a squad car in sight. He was more than likely working on his day off to provide a bit of security, and to keep the gangbangers from cluttering up the parking lot. Offering a place for gang members to congregate could get your license revoked, too.

In the old days, I would have pulled in and showed the cop the photograph. In the old days, I would have driven right to the station house. The old days, as in last week.

I spent the better part of two days driving around, visiting stores and giving out rides.

"Oh, hell, he's been dead for years," one of my riders said.

"Down Pontiac way," another said. This was a prison town downstate.

"Probably in Menard." This was another prison, way, way, downstate.

"That the rapper, right? Fuck the po-lice. Fuck the po-lice. That one?"

A few people thought the man in the photo looked

familiar. That was as close as I got. No names. No addresses. No such luck.

"Can you take me out to the Sears at North and Harlem?" one guy asked.

"Sure. What's out there?"

"Underwear."

#

I was on my way back, after an Italian beef in Elmwood Park, when I looked in my rear-view mirror and spotted Rita Cunningham in a private car right behind me. She was the Austin District cop who'd been involved in the redlight case.

I pulled to the side at the next light and waved when she came alongside. We both pulled to the side at the next corner.

"Just so you know, nobody's got your name," I said. We stood talking between the two cars.

"Yeah. I figured. Flashing called. He got a subpoena. He was wondering if I got one, too."

"It's not going to go too far," I said. "The boyfriend's just gonna have to make some kind of deal with his ex."

"That's sweet," she said, and did a little dance without moving her feet.

"Pretty rich, isn't it?"

"You know I asked around about you." She tried to hold my eyes.

I looked away. "Don't believe half of what you hear."

"You should still be on," she said.

"I'm over it," I said. "Hey, let me show you a picture." I reached into my car and found the picture of the kid with the gold tooth.

She gave it a glance. "So?"

"Oh, well," I said, and slid it back in the envelope.

___

"Wait a minute," she said, and I slid the photo back out and handed it over.

She took her time looking. "Can I keep this?"

"Why?"

"Those teeth," she said. "They're pretty close to a description I heard a while back."

"In reference to what?"

She shook her head. "I'm not sure. Let me show it to someone. If she says it's him then... "

"You'll call and we'll compare notes." I handed her another business card. "I'll bet you threw the other one away," I said. That got me a smile.

TWENTY

I probably gave out a couple dozen business cards and I got a few calls. None sounded very promising.

"I hear you wanna talk to me," a squeaky voice said. It sounded like he hadn't yet reached puberty.

"What about?" I asked, and I pulled into a bus stop.

He managed to get the voice a bit lower. "That's my uncle in your picture. That's what Ellis say."

"Where do I find your uncle?" I found my note pad and pulled out a pen.

"I don't know."

"How about Ellis?"

"He's sleeping." His voice was back in the high range.

"What's your uncle's name?"

"Don't know."

"You don't know your uncle's name?" I tossed the pad onto the dashboard.

"Ellis didn't tell me which uncle."

"What's your name?" A last-ditch effort.

He had to think it over. "Don't know," he said finally.

"Call me back when you know something."

"And then I get the reward?"

"Sure." A bus tooted its horn behind me. I pulled across to the far corner.

I checked the phone after he'd hung up. He might have been a kid, but he'd known enough to block his number.

The light on my office phone was blinking when I stopped by.

"You want to know about Sweet's store call me," a man with a heavily accented voice said. He left a suburban number.

And then another message, and a muffled voice that

sounded more white than black: "Whatever you think you're doing, stop. We had a deal, remember?" Detective Swanson? I played it back several times, but the voice didn't become any clearer. Detective Craig?

I dialed the suburban number and the same accented voice answered. "You called me about Sweet's Mini Mart," I said.

"You are the detective?"

"Right."

"And what is your interest in the store?"

"I'm looking for a man who was seen there."

"A young man with a star on his right incisor?"

"That sounds about right," I said. "What's your interest?"

"Fifty percent," he said. "I put up the money to open the store and my brother and his sons operated it. We were to split the profits. A very bad investment for me, fifty percent of nothing is very, very small."

"Was that your brother who got shot?" I doodled on a legal pad.

"His son. And now he's in jail for something he did not do."

"You sound pretty sure of yourself," I said.

"If you knew my nephew you would also be sure."

"So, how'd he end up getting shot?"

"He is young, so he believed in technology. We had a camera that watched the store. The man you are looking for came in with his tooth and tried to buy whiskey. My nephew said no. The man was too young. Then the police come in and find whiskey in the young man's pocket. My nephew says he did not sell to him. He thought the camera would save him. But what he did not know was the police would shoot him and steal everything, including the film from the camera. New technology, old technology, it makes no difference if the police are thieves."

"What did they steal?" I asked.

"All the cigarettes. All the whiskey."

"That's a little hard to believe," I said, and wrote *cigs and whiskey* on my pad.

"As soon as the ambulance leaves and all the police leave, a truck pulls in back and they take everything but old potato chips that no one buys."

"A police-truck?"

"A U-Haul."

"That could be anybody," I said.

"No. We have many friends in the neighborhood. They look out their windows and see all the stealing. And one unmarked police car waits around the corner. As soon as the truck leaves, they leave too. And all the while my nephew is chained to his hospital bed and arrested for nothing."

"Aggravated Battery of a police officer is what they call it."

"I swear he did not do it."

"What's your name?"

"I am Ankur Sharma," he said and spelled it out for me. "And you are Nick Acropolis a private investigator. Can you help us?"

"If I ever find that kid with the gold-tooth he might be able to help."

"We have looked. The lawyer hired an investigator and he looked and looked and could not find."

"Another investigator," I said. "I'm sorry to hear that. What's the name of this lawyer?"

"He is a Patel," he said. "Pushkar Patel with offices on Devon Avenue."

"I might call him," I said. He recited the number. I

wrote it on my pad and boxed it off so it wouldn't get swallowed by doodles.

"My nephew, he came for the dream, make enough money to go back to India and marry his fiancée. Now he has no money. No knee. Probably no more fiancée. We take up a collection to get him a new knee, but the prison will not allow."

"If I hear anything, I'll give you a call."

"I hope you will find it in your heart to help us."

I pushed a couple of buttons on my phone. "I'm sorry, I've got to take this call," I said and made my escape.

A Chicago Police Department envelope came with the junk mail later that same day. Inside I found a ten-page press release from City Hall, listing suspended and revoked city licenses. Sweet's Mini Mart was on page three. Somebody had used a yellow highlighter to make sure I wouldn't miss it. "Sweet's Mini Mart LICENSE REVOKED. Licenses held: Tobacco, Retail, Package Goods. License revocation effective December 23."

That was it. No note. No explanation. No other highlights. And it didn't tell me anything I didn't already know.

I flipped through the pages. It was one revoked license after another. Almost all the addresses were on the wrong sides of town. One dream after another, right down the toilet.

TWENTY-ONE

One day a stuttering salesman called. He was so incoherent I couldn't figure out what he was trying to sell.

"Sorry." I cut him off. "I can't buy anything right now. I'm out of work."

"I'm sorry to hear that, sir," he said as clear as a bell and I recognized the voice.

"What's the gag?" I closed my newspaper and dropped my feet to the floor.

"No names," Lenny said.

"Got it. Why the hush?"

"Rumors," he said. "They're all over this place."

The place would be police headquarters. "Nothing new about that," I said. "Hey, was that you, sent me that list?"

"I haven't sent anything. But a certain name keeps coming up. Someone you're familiar with and someone everyone down here knows I'm familiar with, and I don't want to get squeezed like some monkey in the middle. I'd appreciate a heads up, as much as you can give me."

"When I can," I said. "I know I owe you."

"And I'm calling it in," he said. "I'm sorry but now's the time."

I listened to the fizzes and pops on the line while I tried to figure out what I could give him. Outside a truck blasted its horn. I could hear a siren somewhere in the distance.

On the worst days of my life, Lenny had come through for me. He'd also probably saved my life once with a bit of information. He didn't know the difference it had made. But I did.

"Where do we meet?" I asked.

"No meets. Just tell me what's going on."

"It'd be easier to show you. Can I mail it?"

"Mail what?"

"A video," I said. "I'm afraid you're not gonna think it's much of a payback."

"Jesus Christ," he whispered. "Another one? How bad?"

"It's not pretty," I said. "And I think it's coming out."

I knew it was coming out because I knew I'd never be able to silence that voice: *I hope you will find it in your heart to help us.*

"They all get out eventually," Lenny said. "Where'd you get it?"

"The Salvation Army."

"Okay, I won't ask any more stupid questions. Send it to the old address."

The old address was the house where he'd taken me in.

We said goodbye and then I put a DVD in an envelope, along with a sheet of paper with the name and address of Sweet's Mini Mart and the date of the shooting. I took the elevator down, walked around the corner and down a few blocks to the post office.

It was a beautiful day if you didn't look down. The snow was melting and all the dog shit, cigarette butts, and other garbage hidden under that cool blanket was being revealed. "Dog Shit Day," my old partner Andy used to call it. And now I was going to drop a bit of that shit on my old pal Lenny.

TWENTY-TWO

The phone stopped ringing. No West Side voices. No lawyers. No Swanson or Craig. Nobody. It was the kind of peace I could never find when I wanted it.

But instead of peace, the uncle's words kept ringing in my ears: *I hope you will find it in your heart to help us.*

I was waiting instead; waiting for Lenny to call and tell me everything was under control, the nephew was being released from prison; waiting for Lenny to slip the video to a friendly reporter, someone who would show it to the world and get me off the hook; waiting for someone to make up my mind for me.

I was whiling away an afternoon with my feet up on the desk and a newspaper spread wide when a call finally came.

"Nick Acropolis?" a woman asked. She didn't sound West Side at all.

"That's me."

"This is Virginia Laubett. Phil's wife."

The name didn't sound familiar. "Phil Laubett." I said, and waited for her to fill me in.

"From Sim's Video."

"Oh, Phil, of course. How was your birthday?"

"So, you haven't heard from him?" she said.

I closed the newspaper and grabbed a pen. Phil, who had copied the Sweet's video for me. "He's missing?"

"And nobody's heard from him," she said. "Nobody. I keep thinking I'll wake up but when I do, he's still not here."

"I stopped by the store the other afternoon, but it was already closed," I said. "I was thinking he went home early."

"That's something he rarely does," she said. "Well, thank you. If you think of anything . . ."

—

"Wait. Wait," I said. "Where are you? Can we talk in person?"

"I'm at work. Downtown. I can't talk here. But I'll be home by seven."

She gave me her address and I scribbled it on my legal pad.

#

I took the bus out Irving Park Road. This is a wide commercial street that runs from the lake to the edge of the airport and beyond. But I wasn't going far and got off a block after Kedzie Avenue. This was the same Kedzie that ran by Sweet's Mini Mart. But four miles north, the neighborhood was white, Mexican, and middle class.

The Laubetts lived in a yellow brick two-flat, on a tree-lined side street without a single empty lot. Virginia had asked me to call from downstairs and when I did a buzzer sounded. I opened the door and heard children coming down the stairs.

The door to the first-floor apartment opened and an older woman peered out. She was 50 or so 60, with brown hair and suspicious eyes. "Ginny's on the way down," she said.

The kids came running down the stairs, a girl of five or six, with her little sister, who was probably three, trailing after her. "Hi, Michele," the older girl called as she came down the last flight and headed for the open apartment door.

"Better catch your sister," Michele said. The older girl turned just in time and caught her little sister as she was about to go airborne.

"Give me that little gal," Michele said. She took the girl in her arms and now she didn't look wary at all.

The woman who followed the kids was 30 or so, and she looked exhausted. "Thanks, Michele," she said, and waved. "They promised to be good."

"We'll see about that," Michele said, and closed the door.

"Virginia." She stuck out a slender hand and we shook.

"Nick," I said, and followed her up the stairs and into a large living room overflowing with stuff, lots of dolls, toys, and art projects, also plenty of books, newspapers, and magazines. An orange and white cat hid under the sofa.

Virginia Laubett had wavy red hair, and a freckled roundish face that reminded me a bit of her husband's. "Sit anywhere," she said.

I picked a not-too-overstuffed armchair and pulled out my notebook. "Let's start at the beginning," I said. "When did Phil go missing?"

She shrugged. "He didn't come home Monday night." That was four days ago.

"And?"

"And I haven't seen or heard from him since." She rubbed her hands together. Four days could feel like years, especially with two kids to worry about.

"What did you do that night besides wait?"

"I called the store, of course. No answer. I called his cell over and over. No answer. Then I went back to waiting and calling again and again, and then there came a point when I knew that something had definitely happened. I guess that was about ten. So, then I started calling some of his friends. I called the kid who works at the store. And nobody knew anything. They were all as surprised as I was. That's when I called the police."

"And he's never disappeared before?"

"No," she said and shook her head. "But he used to threaten to all the time. 'One of these days I'm going to go down to the corner for a pack of cigarettes and never come back.' He claimed it was something his father used to tell his mother."

"Mine always said he'd be going out for matches. And he didn't even smoke."

"Neither does Phil," she said, and she gave me a very direct look. "Nick, I know Phil likes you. But I have two concerns. I don't see how I can afford a private detective. And what can you do that the police cannot?"

"Don't worry about money. I'll take it out in trade at the store after he's back," I said. "So, what did the police tell you?"

"I met them at the store the next morning. But there was nothing unusual to see. The store was locked as usual. The alarm was set. Phil's car was gone. Vince, a high school kid who works for Phil, came in after school. He said they both left about five o'clock. That was about two hours earlier than usual. Other than that, he didn't notice anything out of the ordinary."

"Any idea why he left early?"

"He told Vince he had something to do. But he didn't tell him what that was."

"So, what did the cops say?"

"They thought Phil had left on his own. But then they had all these theories. Maybe Phil was on a drunk. Maybe he was with another woman. Maybe he won big on the lottery, which he doesn't play, and took his winnings out to a casino. They said they'd look for his car and file a missing person's report and the best thing to do was to just relax and wait for him to come home. They told me to relax. Can you believe that?"

"Was there anything special going on at the store

recently?"

She shook her head. "Not that I know of. Most of what he did was for kids. I think that's why he liked when you came by. My very own Sam Spade was in today, he'd tell me. Most of the time he wouldn't tell me what he was doing for you. The other week he told me, 'It's so secret even I don't know what it is.'"

"Do you know if he had any enemies?" I asked. "Fights with neighbors, anything like that?"

She shook her head.

"Is the store making money?"

She nodded. "It does better every year. And I do the taxes."

"Anything else about work?"

She shrugged. "For years, Phil talked about building a real recording studio. Then he decided he hated most of the music the kids made. He said it would just encourage them to make more."

"He was happy with the store?"

"He kind of outgrew it," she said. "He got older and his customers stayed the same age. He talked about putting it up for sale--this is a few years back--and I think he would have but the only degree he has is from grade school. He couldn't figure out what to do besides the store."

"So maybe he decided to walk away."

She gave me another long, direct look, and then shook her head. "From his family, no. I'll never believe that. Never."

"Did he ever tell you what he did for me?"

She shook her head. "Not much."

"How about this last time? Did he say anything besides it being a secret?"

"He said I'd probably see it on that someday." She

pointed to a flat screen TV.

So, Phil had watched the video. Of course, he had. He was a video guy. My asking him not to watch it had probably made it even more inviting. But why had he held on to the original? Maybe his story about the shredded tape was true. Maybe. And if it wasn't?

"What else has Phil been up to recently besides family and work?" I asked.

"He was out with the guys the other weekend, the ones he grew up with. They get together several times a year. Supposedly it's just poker and drinking in someone's basement rec room."

"Why supposedly?"

"This is where I've been going slightly crazy," she said. "They've been getting together for as long as I've known Phil. But what I didn't know until last year was that sometimes some of the girls from the old neighborhood stop by to say hello. I don't know, maybe Phil's old flame dropped in . . . "

"And then he waited until the banks opened to grab a bunch of cash for their big adventure?"

The cat came by and rubbed against her leg. She petted it for a moment, but I wasn't sure she really knew it was there. "Except he never went to the bank" she said. "He hasn't used our credit cards."

"So, these guys, you talked to them?"

She nodded. "They didn't know anything."

"Could you give me names and phone numbers?"

She left the room. The cat gave me a look, then slipped back under the sofa. Virginia came back with an address book. "He didn't take anything with him," she said. "Nothing. Maybe the old flame is rich."

"Do you know her name?"

She gave me a faint smile and shook her head. "I

never even thought she existed until this. Phil and I never had that conversation, you know, where you talk about all your exes. I always thought I was his first real girlfriend. But now I'm not so sure."

She began paging through the address book reading off names and phone numbers. I scribbled them in my notebook. "What's he do?" I asked, and she started giving me occupations too.

"Truck Driver."

"Lawyer."

"Fireman."

"Something in finance."

"A chain of sandwich shops."

"A police officer."

"Terry Lopher," I repeated the name. "Chicago cop?"

"Right. I called him and he was as shocked as everyone else," she said. "I gave him the name of the detective and he said he would call and put a bug in his ear."

I added the detective's name to my notebook.

"Anything else?"

"Terry said he would call me back," she said, and then she took a deep breath. "I'm still waiting."

I underlined Terry's name.

"There's a tape of mine inside the store. Can I get in there sometime and take a look for it?"

She gave me one more name, Vince, a kid who worked at the store. "He'll be in tomorrow after school. I'll call and let him know you're coming."

"How'd you and Phil meet?" I asked after I put my coat on.

"I was spending another Saturday night alone and I went to Blockbuster to rent a movie and they'd gone out of business. So, I walked down the street and I saw Sim's

---

105

Video was open. I went in and they didn't have a single recent movie. Not one. I said, 'How can you call yourself a video store?' And Phil was such a gentleman. He apologized and then he opened a newspaper and started reading off the titles of the current movies. 'No Country for Old Men,' what do you think?' 'Too violent,' I said. 'There Will Be Blood. No.' he said. 'That's not going to work. How about "The Queen?' 'I saw it,' I said. 'Juno? Eight o'clock at the Davis. So, we've got to hurry.' And that was our first date."

TWENTY-THREE

The next morning, the first of Phil's friends to answer my call was Dave Peterson, the fireman. He told me he was working his side job, remodeling a house in Albany Park. This was the neighborhood just north of where Phil lived.

I took the Ravenswood train out. The Western Avenue station was across the street from my apartment. I got a westbound train and took it four stations to the end of the line, and then walked a few blocks further west.

The house was probably 60 or 70 years old but, if you didn't look too closely, you might think it was new construction. The tipoff was a block of cement steps that led up to the front door. They'd obviously been there for decades.

The front door was brand new and opened a few inches. The hardwood floors had a nice shine to them. I followed the sound of a nail gun and found a man on a ladder installing crown molding. He was wearing blue jeans and a Chicago Fire Department T-shirt.

"Dave?" I said when the gun took a break.

He turned my way, came down the ladder, and pulled out a pair of earplugs.

"Dave?"

"In the bathroom." He pointed to an interior stairway. "He told me to send you up."

Dave was on his knees fitting ceramic tile in a shower stall. He stood up when I said hello. He was a healthy-looking guy in his thirties. He had curly brown hair, a bushy mustache, and an easy smile.

"Let's get some fresh air," he said, and he pointed towards the back of the house. "These chemicals are worse than smoke."

I followed him down a hallway that ended in a room that ran the width of the house. "Master bedroom," he said. "Every house we do, there's gotta be a deck off the master. It's a big selling point." He picked a sweatshirt off the floor, put it on, and zipped it all the way up.

The deck was almost as big as the bedroom. A folding table, looking something like a well-used painter's pallet, was surrounded by a group of folding chairs. Several six-pack coolers were scattered about. A five-gallon paint bucket was now full of tools. A large maple tree would offer plenty of shade when the leaves came back.

"So how long have you known Phil?" I asked as Dave lit a cigarette.

"We pretty much grew up together. I moved into the neighborhood about fourth grade. Phil was already there."

"Near the store, right?"

He nodded and sat on one of the chairs. "Not far. You're working for Ginny, right?"

"If that's Virginia, yes."

"Okay," he said. "Just wanted to make sure."

I sat down across from him. "Any reason Phil would just take off?"

He shook his head. "It doesn't make sense."

"How about the last time you saw him?"

"It was a regular night down in Bobby's basement, the guys from the hood. We played a little poker, drank beer, and watched some Cubs highlight films."

"Did you talk to Phil?"

"Oh, sure. But nothing special, the old days mostly."

"If Phil had troubles, who would he talk to?"

"Tony probably." He bent over and began undoing the laces on his boots.

"Tony Cantore?"

He nodded. "Anywhere you saw Phil, Tony was usually somewhere nearby. They lived in the same building on Pratt when we were kids."

"Did you see them talking that night?"

"I'm sure I did but I don't really remember. We always overdo it."

A car passed on the street a few doors north of us. The radio was loud. "I lost my chance for happiness," a woman sang.

"How about the girls? Did any of them show up this time?"

He shook his head and smiled. "You've been busy."

"So, Phil's old flame wasn't around?"

That got me a snort. "Phil's old flame? Is that what Ginny thinks? Oh, the poor kid."

"What's her name, anyway?"

"The closest Phil ever got to a girlfriend before Ginny was a girl named Karen. But that was over back in sixth grade when her family moved to the suburbs. It broke Phil's heart. It broke all our hearts. She was great. I've always wondered what happened to her."

"How about Terry?" This was the cop.

"What about him?"

"Did you happen to see him and Phil talking?"

"Like I said I was pretty wasted by the end of the night." He looked away, then back. "How much is this gonna cost Ginny?"

"What?"

"You don't work for free, do you?"

"When Phil comes back, I'll take it out in trade. He's been doing work for me for years. We're friends, too."

"You're..." and I could see Sam Spade on his lips. But he stopped himself. "...a friend, too. That's cool. What kind of work does he do for you?"

"Anything to do with video," I said. "Now getting back to Terry. He's a cop. So, isn't that where Phil would go if he was having problems with someone, if someone threatened him?"

"Yeah, maybe." He started searching through the tool bucket and finally came out with a slender chisel. "But I don't see Phil getting into those kinds of situations."

"You're sure you didn't see him and Terry talking during the party?"

He shrugged. "I really don't remember. Why don't you call Terry?"

That had been the first call I'd made. "I'm waiting for him to call back," I said.

"It's like he fell off the end of the earth," Dave said. He took off a boot and started using the chisel to dig white caulk from the crevices on the bottom. "We retraced his route, me and Bobby. Clark to Peterson, Peterson to Western, Western to Irving, that was the way he usually went. Unless there was a Cubs game and then he took Bryn Mawr to Kedzie."

"And?"

"And nothing. To get home, he had to go over the river. On Irving Park, the only way to get a car into the river is to fly. We looked for his car, here and there, gas stations, side streets, alongside the river. Nothing. And we tried a few other routes, too."

"What got Phil depressed?"

"The Cubs."

"But they finally won." Who could forget that night?

"That just depressed him more, I think. He thought it was going to be the greatest joy in his life and then, when it finally happened, it was kind of a letdown. That's what he told us when we got back from Cleveland. Five of us drove over there for the last two games. Even with the hotel room, it was cheaper than going to Wrigley. Phil couldn't close the shop that long. We brought him back a counterfeit Cleveland shirt that said 2016 World Series Champs. It was a riot. They were practically giving them away after the game."

"You can't think of a single thing that might have made him walk away."

"Nothing." He cleaned the caulk off the chisel with his fingers and put the boot back on.

"How about enemies?"

"Nobody I know. Phil is just a regular guy. He's honest. He's fair. Always been straight as an arrow. This is something I can't say about some of the other guys. I could usually read Phil like an open book. At least, I thought I could, until this." He took off the other boot and started in with the chisel.

"He might be dead," I said.

He nodded. "I've been thinking the same thing."

#

I spent the better part of the day tracking down and talking to Phil's old friends. Nobody remembered anything special about their last party. Tony Cantore, who'd lived in the same building as Phil when they were kids, was now a lawyer. He thought Phil seemed a little less lively than usual. Bobby Shelly, who hosted the last get together, told me it was Phil who had asked him to call the party. They usually waited until after opening day. That was all the unusual behavior I could find.

Terry Lopher, the cop, was the only one in the group who didn't return my calls. Maybe he'd asked around about me and found I was now *persona non grata.* But maybe he had other reasons not to talk.

———

TWENTY-FOUR

I got up to Sim's Video about three in the afternoon and the place was closed tight. I spent a bit of time tapping on the glass door with a quarter but that didn't bring anyone out of the back room.

Around back, a ten-year old Ford was parked crossways behind the back door. A note was taped to a side window. "Phil, sorry, I broke down. I'll have it out this afternoon for sure. John."

I punched in the phone number scribbled under the words.

"Yo," a guy answered.

"This John?"

"Yo. You?"

"I'm over by Sim's Video."

"Shit, about the car. I'll have it out tomorrow, first thing. I couldn't get in the shop today."

"Phil's missing," I said, and leaned back against the car.

"Who're you again?"

"Nick," I said. "I'm a friend of Phil's. I'm also a detective. I'm trying to find him."

"You mean, it's something serious. Like he's really, really, missing?"

"Looks that way," I said. "How well do you know him?"

"I live across the alley," he said.

I turned my head. "The six-flat?" It was a three-story brown brick building, two apartments to a floor, with a big wooden porch on the back.

"Yeah. And Phil lets us park in his lot overnight, or in the back there. We've got to be out in the morning, but if you call him and ask or leave a note, he's usually cool about it."

"When's the last time you saw him?"

"Oh, I don't even know. I haven't been in the store in months. Sometimes I'd see him taking the trash out. I'm on the first floor, so if I'm in the kitchen... But that's been a while too."

"Did he have friends in the neighborhood?"

"The kids in his store, I guess."

"Nobody else?"

"Everybody in my building, pretty much. We all use him for computer problems, stuff like that. He's a whiz. My girlfriend calls him my geek."

"You home?"

"Fuck no. Work."

"Is there anybody else I could talk to in your building?"

"Go knock on the back doors. Just about everybody else works nights. It's a good crew."

I said, "Thanks," and then followed his advice. I didn't learn anything new. Everyone mentioned the free overnight parking and said that Phil was a good guy. But nobody had seen anything unusual in the last week or so.

I walked back to the store--still empty--and then out to Clark Street, where I started walking in and out of storefront businesses.

Phil had fixed the scanner at the convenience store, occasionally had lunch at the Mexican restaurant, bought small gifts at the gift shop, beer at the liquor store, and fixed just about everyone's computer at least once. Everybody seemed to know him, although a few didn't know his name. Some thought he was Sim himself. "He's my biggest competitor," the guy at the computer repair shop said. "But he's a great guy. I hope you find him."

When I walked into the immigration law office, half the waiting room looked ready to flee. "Never mind," I said, and backed out the door.

Kenny at the auto repair shop said Phil had a thing for a waitress at the Holiday Grill down the street.

"What's her name?"

"Jenny." He put down his wrench and I followed him back to fresh air outside the big overhead door. "But she's missing, too."

"When?"

"Oh, a couple years back. She was so beautiful." He shook his head. "Every guy in the neighborhood went there for lunch. I'm not kidding." He was smiling just thinking about her. "Nobody could take their eyes off her. Some girls get off on that but not Jenny. It really bothered her. She stopped wearing makeup and that made her even more beautiful. She started wearing baggy clothes and cut off all her hair. And she was beautiful that way, too. She finally gave up and moved back south, somewhere in Tennessee. That's where she was from. You should have heard that twang."

"Any chance Phil might have kept in touch and then followed her down."

"Last I heard she was married with kids. That's some lucky devil, I'll tell you that." He went back to work.

I was on my way to ask around at the Holiday Grill when I spotted a light on inside Sim's.

A skinny kid who looked about fifteen answered my knock by holding up a hand-lettered CLOSED UNTIL FURTHER NOTICE sign. I flashed my P.I. license and he put down the sign and unlocked the door.

"You're the detective," he said.

"Yeah, Nick Acropolis," I said. "And you are … "

"Vince," he said, and then he decided that wasn't

enough. "Vincent Robertson."

He stepped to the side and then followed me back to Phil's workspace, which was piled high with papers and assorted equipment. I added his full name to my notebook.

"How long have you worked here, Vince?" I looked around. I'd never seen the store without Phil.

"Almost a year. After school and on Saturday."

"Were you here Monday?"

He nodded. "But only for an hour because Phil closed early."

"Why?" The place was too quiet. That's what I was missing, I realized, the whirl of computers, the sound of video games from the back room. Phil's easy laughter.

He shrugged. "He sent me home."

"Why did he close early?"

"He had to go somewhere."

"Where?"

"I don't know." He looked a bit annoyed by my questions. "That's all he said." He added a phone number to the CLOSED sign.

"Can you remember Phil's exact words?" I asked.

"He was in a real good mood, kind of funny, He said something like, 'Places to go. People to see. Things that need doing.'"

"Things that need doing?"

"Something like that." He held up the sign. "I'm going to put this up before I forget."

"Whose phone number is that?"

"Mine," he said. "Just in case anybody needs to get in."

I pulled my notebook out and scribbled the number after Vince's name.

"Anything else unusual?" I asked as he taped the sign

115

on the front door.

He shook his head.

"Did he take anything with him, do you know?"

He shook his head again.

"He wasn't carrying anything?"

"His backpack. He always carried that."

"I left a VCR tape with Phil," I said.

"I was looking for it," he said, and he started sorting through the clutter on Phil's workspace. "Mrs. Laubett told me you were going to come by. Phil was working on it right around here. But I can't find it."

"What was he doing with it?"

He shook his head. "I don't know. Every time I'd come by, he'd quick turn the monitor off."

"What could you see?"

"Cops." He scrunched-up his face, as if that word all by itself was distasteful. "But not faces. Just like an arm or neck or something and then sometimes the uniforms and the badges. That's how I knew they were cops."

"Do you remember seeing name tags?"

He shook his head, and then turned towards Phil's oversized monitor and held out both hands, the size of a basketball. "But the badges were really big."

"Phil didn't tell you what he was doing?"

He put his hand in front of his mouth. "He said it was top secret."

"Was he working on it Monday night?"

He nodded.

I spent some time looking through Phil's desk and found a copy of "Juno." This was the movie that Phil had taken Virginia to on their first date.

A notepad sat on the desktop. There were all sorts of scribbles and circles on it, figures and single words, some of them boxed off, others were circled. The letters

"OPS" were underlined. That might stand for the Office of Professional Standards, which had once investigated excessive force complaints against Chicago cops. But they'd been replaced a couple of years back by another set of initials IPRA, the Independent Police Review Authority, which was now being replaced by COPA, the Civilian Office of Police Accountability.

"*The more letters the better,*" Shelly had once said. But I doubt she was happy with the idea of a civilian office. For decades, cops had investigated other cops. That had usually worked out pretty good for Shelly and her clients, present company excluded.

I said goodbye to Vince, then stood out front and waylaid pedestrians. This got me nowhere. Nobody had seen anything special. Many of them wouldn't answer a single question.

It was so much easier with a badge.

The Rogers Park police station was a few blocks down the street. But I couldn't go in and see if they were making any progress on Phil's case without worrying about it getting back to Detectives Swanson and Craig. I'd promised them I was off the case.

But that was another case, wasn't it?

No. Not if the badges were as big as basketballs on Phil's monitor. That could mean only one thing. Phil wanted to know the identity of those cops. So now it was all one case.

In my head Terry Lopher was the link. I tried his number again and left another message. "Hey, Terry, I'm over by Phil's store. I thought we might be able to meet."

I tried my luck with a few more pedestrians. Lopher didn't call back.

I took the long way back to Rent-a-Dent and cruised by Wrigley Field and then the 23rd District Station. I could go in and see if Sgt. Sheehan was working. This was my old friend who had helped me track down the cops in that redlight video. He'd probably be willing to help. But I couldn't drag him into this.

Phil had probably wanted to help too, to see justice done. Where had that gotten him? I didn't have a single worthwhile lead.

Wasn't I a real detective? Did I really need help from the police department to make progress on a simple missing persons case?

Apparently, I did. So maybe I wasn't a real detective at all, and exactly what part of Phil's disappearance did I think was simple?

I dropped the car at Rent-a-Dent, walked across to the Third Base Inn, and barhopped all the way home.

TWENTY-FIVE

"How's the boy?" Frank Stringfellow asked on the phone the next morning. He was a private detective with offices out in the far reaches of suburbia. Every so often, he threw some city-work my way.

"Don't ask." I'd showered, shaved, and had breakfast. Now what was I supposed to do?

"Got just what you need, Nick, a quick trip to Paris. What do you say?"

"When do I leave?"

"Tonight, if your passport's up to date. United's got a direct flight at 6:30. Means you should be at O'Hare in about five hours. Can you make it?"

"You're pulling my chain, right?"

"Straight as an arrow," he said. "Flight gets in at nine tomorrow morning. I gotta get somebody over there and I know you've been before. Also, I know you won't kill me on expenses. It shouldn't take more than a couple days."

I found my passport just where I'd left it. Inside were 70 Euros, and also stamps from a single trip, Chicago to Paris and return. I'd taken a lovely woman along. We were celebrating after getting her brother out of jail.

"Passport's good for another two years." I sat on the edge of the bed and slipped on a pair of socks.

"You want to leave tonight or tomorrow?"

"Slow down, Frank," I said. "Gimme a minute to think." Could I really leave town with Phil missing? Not only was he missing--he was missing with my lost video. Well, then again, maybe it was time to use my copies of that same video to help find him. If I sprinkled those around, Paris might be a good hideout, and who knows, they might even have an early spring.

119

"What's the job?" I walked into the kitchen and poured myself a cup of coffee.

"You gotta find a guy."

"I hope you don't mean finger someone."

"No. No. It's an old client of mine. His son wants to find him. He walked away from an assisted living place and absconded to Par-ree."

"Well, good for him," I said. "That's the best story I've heard in months."

"Yeah. My whole office is on the old man's side. And the son's a mope. But he needs his father's signature on a couple of documents so he can keep the family business going. And he's willing to pay top dollar. So that's the job. Get him to come home or get him to sign the docs."

"What's the business?"

"Raven Moving and Storage, biggest mover in town. I've been doing work for Al Raven for damn near 20 years."

"Big blue trucks, right?"

"That's part of the battle, believe it or not. The kid started selling advertising space on the side of the trucks and Al went ballistic."

"How do I find him? Paris isn't exactly a small town."

"It should have been easy. He was using the company credit card and that gave us the hotel. But the son fucked that up by calling him direct. Al hung up and checked out. We're assuming he checked in somewhere else. But, if he did, he's either paying cash or he's got cards we don't know about."

"Lot of hotels in Paris," I said.

"He's been going for years. He usually stays in the same neighborhood. A couple other hotels he's used before. So, you've got that. Also, he was taking cash advances with the corporate card. He was getting the maximum five hundred almost every day until the son got wise and canceled the card. He's living large."

"That's nothing for Paris," I said.

"He's probably got another card or two but, if he's staying in that same neighborhood, he might still be using those same ATMs. So, start with those and the hotels. It's a lot of pounding the pavement but that's the only way you're gonna find him unless we dig up a new card."

"And if he says no?"

"Try talking some sense into him. And if he still won't sign, try to convince him to come home. That'll give the mope a chance to use his charms. You can tell Al that I personally guarantee his son won't try any funny stuff."

"Funny stuff like sticking him in a nursing home?"

"Assisted living, Nick. There's a difference," he said. "You in or out?"

"Of course, I'm in." I was just hoping I didn't suddenly wake up.

"You wanna leave today or tomorrow?"

"What the hell." I couldn't think of any reason to wait another day. There wasn't anybody to call. I had enough clean laundry. I'd leave a note for the neighbor asking her to take care of my mail. "Let's go."

"How about I meet you at O'Hare at 3:30. That'll give us time to go through the file."

"I might be a little late," I said. "There's something I gotta do first."

"You wanna go tomorrow instead?"

"No," I decided. "I think I've got enough time. About money?"

"Your standard day rate," he said. "You're okay with that, right?"

"Perfect," I said. Frank usually asked for some kind of

discount.

"We'll get you a room at the Best Western he checked out of. He either went right or left. That'll put you right in the middle."

"Don't forget walking around money," I said.

"I'll bring a thousand to the airport."

"Paris, Frank. You better make it two."

TWENTY-SIX

I packed and then went downstairs and found a cab around the corner on Western Avenue. "How about taking the long way to O'Hare?" I asked as the driver stowed my suitcase.

"If you've got the money, I've got the time," he said.

"I've got to stop at Belmont and Lincoln, then on Devon Avenue, and then a couple of stops downtown. How's that sound?"

"Sure. Let's make a day of it."

"I gotta be at O'Hare by three."

The cab made a tire-screeching U-turn. "Those stops better be quick," he said, as we turned left and sped down Lincoln Avenue.

At my office I packed DVDs in four separate envelopes and hurried back to the cab for another U-turn. We were heading back north.

Pushkar Patel's office was above an Indian Restaurant on a stretch of Devon loaded with Indians and Pakistanis. This was the lawyer for the corner-store clerk who took the bullet in his knee.

I went up the stairs and down a narrow hallway. I found a locked door and knocked.

A very skinny, dark-skinned guy in a suit and tie opened the door. "Yes?"

"Mr. Patel?"

"I am Push Patel," he said, and he gave me a tiny bow.

"Watch this." I handed him an envelope.

"What is it?" he said to my back.

"You'll know when you see it." I was almost back at the stairs.

I could hear him hurrying down the hallway. "Who

are you?"

I went down the stairs and out the door to the taxi. "The Tribune on lower Michigan," I said to the cabbie.

"Got it," he said.

I was looking at the waves on the way down Lake Shore Drive when Shelly, my favorite lawyer, called and said, "Thomas Burroughs." She was the one who'd dug up his dirty past for me.

"He still dead?" I asked.

"That's how you're going to play this?"

"What am I supposed to do?" I looked to my left. A guy was running down the lakefront path wearing only shoes and shorts.

"Look at this nut," the cabdriver said.

"You're not involved in any way?" Shelly said. "That's what you told me, right?"

"Uh huh."

"And this rumor about a photograph mutilated almost beyond recognition that was found at the murder scene?"

"Where'd you get that?"

"Three sources so far and the calls keep coming."

"Oh, well." Evidently Detectives Swanson and Casper had decided to call our deal off. So now it was mutual.

"I'm gonna need more than that, Nick. Why don't you come down and buy me that lunch you're always promising. And you can tell me all about it."

"I'm on my way out of town," I said. "Something for Frank. Look, I'll call you the minute I get back. Promise."

The phone beeped. She was gone.

After the Tribune, my next stop was Tony Cantore's office. This was the guy who'd grown up in the same building as Phil. He was now a lawyer on LaSalle Street, a few blocks north of the river. "The wrong side of the river," he'd called it when we'd talked on the phone.

I killed a few minutes paging through a real estate magazine. It was page after page of people living in glass houses without curtains, across from scores of other glass houses. Half the houses came with telescopes. Before I could get too carried away imagining what they might observe, Cantore opened the door to his office, winked at the receptionist, and waved me inside.

He had wavy black hair and a long, olive-tinted face. His shirtsleeves were rolled. "New developments?" He closed the door behind us.

"Do you have a DVD player, by any chance?"

He pointed to a computer alongside his desk.

I pulled the DVD out. "Would you mind playing this?"

"What's this about?"

"Ten minutes," I said. "It's what Phil was working on for me."

He picked up his phone. "I'm out of the office for ten minutes." He took the DVD from my hand, swiveled around in his chair, and slipped the disc into the computer.

I dropped into a side chair as the youth with the bottle stashed in his pocket entered.

"Where are we?" Cantore asked without taking his eyes from the screen.

"West Side corner store."

When the cops walked in Cantore leaned forward. "What's going on," he asked a minute later. "Jesus fucking Christ," he whispered after Burroughs shot the clerk. "What the fuck?"

Burroughs headed into the back room and a few seconds later the video stopped.

"You say Phil was working on this?" He closed the

computer and turned my way.

"He was supposed to make copies for me. The original was a VCR tape. I wanted to have some backup copies. When I picked them up, Phil told me the original had gotten shredded. He was going to try to get it back together for me. That's the last time I talked to him. But the kid who works for him says Phil was working on this video the day he disappeared."

"When was this shot?"

"About a year and a half ago."

"That doesn't make any sense." He swiveled away from the desk. "Why haven't I seen it before?"

"Nobody's seen it. I just found it."

He gave me a big smile. "You were just walking down the street, minding your own business, and there it was sitting on the sidewalk?"

I nodded. "Something like that," I said. "Look, I asked Phil not to watch it."

"Why?" He spread his hands wide.

"I wasn't sure what I was going to do with it. I was afraid it would upset him. It was his wife's birthday."

"You think this has something to do with his disappearance?"

I nodded. "What Phil usually did for me was to enhance videos. I didn't need anything like that here. I just wanted copies. But it sounds like he enhanced it for himself and got the names and badge numbers of those cops?"

"Why would he do that?"

I got up and looked out the window. I could just make out the statue on top of the Board of Trade, the goddess of grain, something like that. "At your party, he gives Terry the names and badge numbers and ask him to check them out." When I turned back around, Cantore

126

was standing behind his desk.

"Same question. Why?" he said.

"He might wonder if they got punished."

"Did they?"

I shook my head. "No, but they're both dead."

"What happened?"

"One had a heart attack, the other committed suicide."

"I'm sorry. You're going to have to spell this out for me." He came around, moved some papers out of the way, and sat on the edge of the desk. "How does all this connect with Phil disappearing?"

"Well, let's assume he asked Terry about the two cops and Terry asked some of his police friends."

"So, Terry tells him they're dead and that's that," Cantore said.

"But what if one of those cops asks Terry what it's about. And Terry says he's just doing a favor for his friend Phil who owns a video store. "

"What's wrong with that?"

"I'd already been warned off the case. People in the department knew the video was out there somewhere. I was told not to look for it. They don't want it seen."

"Can't blame 'em for that. What happened to the guy who got shot? Is he okay?"

"He's in prison for aggravated battery of a police officer. Four years."

He pushed himself off the desk. "Are you kidding me?" He looked at me, but he was playing for the jury. "The victim went to jail?"

I nodded. Welcome to Chicago, Tony.

"What are you asking me to do?"

"You could get all the guys together and show them the tape, and then decide what to do with it."

He spun around and pointed a finger my way. "You want us to do your dirty work for you, is that it?"

"Look, this isn't my first stop. It's coming out one-way or the other. But if you can tie the video to Phil, you're going to get some action on his disappearance. The police won't be able to pretend it's just another missing person's case. And if someone's holding Phil to stop this from coming out, that motive goes right out the window."

"And what do you get out of it?" He gave me a phony smile.

"Same as you," I said. "Maybe we find Phil."

He let that sink in, then came my way and stuck out his hand. He had a nice firm grip, and he kept his eyes steady on mine as we shook. "Okay, I'll see what I can do. And if we do decide to call a press conference or something like that, where do I say I got it?"

"I'd appreciate it if you'd keep my name out of it," I said. "Maybe you just found it in your mail slot one day."

TWENTY-SEVEN

A cold rain fell on Paris. "This is nothing," I said to my cab driver on the way in from Charles de Gaulle. "In Chicago they'd be dancing in the streets if it got this warm."

"Shee-cawgo," he said. "Obama! Obama!"

"Those were the days." I looked out the window as a huge truck splashed past. *Warszawa Polska* was written on its side.

"Shee-cawgo, Uber?"

"Oh, yeah. That too."

"Fuck Uber," he said.

"You told me you didn't speak English," I said.

The Best Western was in the middle of Rue Odessa, a narrow, one-block street of restaurants, shops, and movie theaters. There must have been a big sale on dark jackets. Everybody had one. People crowded the sidewalks and used the street for a passing lane. They weren't dancing but they were certainly moving about, with or without umbrellas.

There was a huge, open square at one end of the block, bigger than a couple of small towns sitting side by side. Odessa was one way and my taxi had to go around the block and come in from the other end, through a much smaller square with a parkway in the middle. Stairways led down to a metro station. Cafés sat on four of the six corners. It was lunchtime and they all looked packed.

My room was small but comfortable. I stretched out on the bed for a short nap and then took a shower.

The best picture of Al Raven had been taken at the 40th Anniversary party of Raven Moving & Storage. Raven started out with a single truck and two helpers.

That was the entire company, three men and a truck. Now there were over 100 trucks, three warehouses, hundreds of movers, and an office staff of 25.

Raven was front and center in the picture, surrounded by as many of his workers as could get in the frame. He looked a bit like a truck himself. His shoulders were wide. His feet were pointed off to the sides and firmly planted. He had a cane, but it was held crossways in both hands, as if it were for decorative purposes. He had a full head of white hair, streaked with grey. He looked tough as hell, and pretty pleased with himself, but he looked like fun too.

Just about everyone seemed to be leaning towards Raven and he took the weight easily. He didn't look like a man who'd had two hip replacements or like nursing home or assisted-living material. Not two years ago when the photo was taken. But who knew what else might have happened to his health. He'd be 75 in the fall.

The man who wanted him back in that nursing home was standing alongside. He was 25 years younger and had a big smile on his face. It looked like he could hold the smile for hours if necessary. He was standing as straight as a fence post, and he seemed as tall as his father was broad. He wasn't leaning towards his father. He wasn't leaning away either. But he looked like he wanted to be somewhere else. Anywhere. According to Stringfellow, he'd been working as an investment banker in New York when the old man talked him into joining the family business a few years back.

It had stopped raining by the time I walked down to a cafe at the quiet end of the block. It was too cold for sitting outside but several people were doing just that. I found a tiny table inside with a good view of the square, sat down and ordered a *café au lait*.

"*Café crème,*" the waiter said. I couldn't tell if he was correcting me or just making a suggestion.

"Half coffee, half milk," I said.

He repeated my words with barely any accent and then returned a few minutes later with a half cup of coffee and a small pitcher of hot milk. "*Grand crème, monsieur,*" he said. It looked exactly like a *café au lait* to me.

I unfolded the computer-generated map Stringfellow had given me. My hotel was marked, as were the two where Raven had previously stayed. One was on Boulevard Montparnasse, the other on Avenue du Maine. They were several blocks apart and the square where I sat was almost dead center. The ATMs he'd been using were on those same two streets.

If Raven was still in the neighborhood, and I sat here long enough, he was bound to pass. But he wouldn't stand out in the crowd. In the hour I sat sipping coffee plenty of old-timers went by. Many had white hair. Several were using canes. One zipped by in a motorized wheelchair. I didn't see many obvious tourists. This was quite a bit different from St. Germain where I'd stayed years back.

I stopped by both hotels and tried to leave a message for my uncle Al Raven. Both clerks said they had no one by that name. Neither seemed entirely sold on my story. I'd have to figure out a better approach.

I strolled by both ATMs. I wasn't expecting to spot Al Raven and I didn't. He picked up most of his cash in the morning.

The ATM on Boulevard Montparnasse would be easy to watch. There were cafes to sit in and plenty of excuses for window-shopping. But Avenue du Maine was another story. It was a wide street with express lanes in the middle, making it virtually impossible to cross. Stairs went down to a Metro station. But the only café with a view was across that wide, fast street, and I'd get even fatter if I kept walking in and out of the corner bakery.

I could sit on the ground next to the ATM and hold out a paper cup but the guy there now might take offense. I could buy a bunch of hats and walk in and out of the Metro station. The easiest thing would be to take another nap, in preparation for some Paris jazz.

But, back at the hotel, I had a hard time finding sleep. Images from that tape kept popping into my head. And I could see the same images appearing on televisions and in newspapers back in Chicago. What had I started? How would it end? And where the hell was Phil? Would he end up as another name on my list of regrets?

Was the entire sting a setup? That's what it had looked like to me. Burroughs and Daniels had sent an underage kid in to buy booze and then had come in behind him.

The clerk had either sniffed the cops out, or he was actually straight. But the cops had a contingency plan for that, a half pint that they'd planted in the kid's pocket.

The clerk made two clear mistakes. First, he'd come out from the safety of his bulletproof cage, then he'd shown the cops the camera that was busy recording them.

They could have grabbed the tape without shooting the clerk and maybe they would have if the clerk hadn't gotten in Tommy Burroughs face. It didn't take much to set him off apparently; shouting about an obvious setup; mowing your lawn too early in the day; hiring a detective.

What would have happened if I'd pushed back at my office? But maybe if I had, Kate Daniels would still be out in the world taking her pictures. Another thought that kept me from sleeping.

I wasted an hour fiddling with my laptop, trying to find some Chicago news. According to the Tribune and the Sun-Times nothing of interest was happening.

TWENTY-EIGHT

The next morning, I was up early with jazz melodies lingering and just a slight hangover. I had a *petit dejeuner* at my favorite corner café, and then spent several hours walking back and forth, staking out one ATM and then the other. I varied my route. The most direct way was down Rue de Gaieté, past peep shows and legit theaters, restaurants, bars, and a fancy-looking hotel, across the small square to Rue Montparnasse, a block of wall-to-wall creperies, and then up to the boulevard.

I had to give Paris credit. It was a great town for a detective. Nobody paid any attention, no matter how many times I passed, humming tunes from the night before.

About twelve-thirty I gave up and had lunch at one of the creperies on Rue Montparnasse. I then headed back to my hotel for a nap.

An hour later the phone rang. "We got a hit," Stringfellow said. "He rented a car at Hertz four hours ago on a French bank card."

"So, where's he going?"

"That's your job." He gave me the address. "Up and at 'em, buddy."

The woman behind the counter at Hertz gave me a big smile and said, "Of course," when I asked in my best pigeon-French if she spoke English.

"I was supposed to meet my uncle here this morning," I said.

"Please. More slowly," she said.

"*Mon* uncle," I said. "My mother's brother." And then I went into as many details as I could about my dear uncle Al Raven, and the surprise trip we were going to take. "Did he leave a message for me, for his nephew?"

"Uncle Al," she said, and I began to suspect that her English was better than she was letting on. "Like Al Capone from Shee-cawgo."

I pretended to be offended. "My uncle is the farthest thing from a gangster you could imagine," I said. "Did you meet him?"

"*Oui*," she said.

"And he reminded you of Al Capone?"

"I'm only repeating his joke. Is that how you say?"

"And a great sense of humor he's got, I might add."

She dumped a basket of keys on the counter. As we talked, she searched through a pile of paperwork, matching keys as she went, stapling them to the paper.

"How you say Shee-cawgo?" she asked.

"Chicago," I said. "Shhh."

"Same as Uncle."

"Did he leave a message or say where he was going?"

She shook her head. "But lunch in St. Lo."

"Really," I said. "Normandy?"

"*Oui.*"

"How was my uncle's French, by the way?"

"Much better than yours," she said, and now she didn't sound French at all.

The phone rang. She started out in French then switched to flawless English, while explaining how much it would cost to keep some car for an additional two days.

"How long did you spend in the states?" I asked when she hung up.

"Three years in Philadelphia. Does that count?"

"You know that old W.C. Fields joke?"

"Your uncle has already told me," she said. "So, you want to rent a big shiny car to chase?"

"Maybe I'll just wait until he comes back. Do you

have any idea when that might be?"

"I am forbidden to give out information about our customers," she said. "It is wrong to even ask."

"Sorry."

"But today we offer early the weekend special."

"It's only Thursday."

"And this is why it is so special," she said and winked. This was something she should have done the moment I walked in the door.

"Do you like jazz, by any chance?"

She shrugged. "A little," she said. "My husband he like it very much. You wait. He come on big motorcycle."

#

I tried calling Stringfellow from my cell phone but all I got was a recorded message in French. I went looking for a pay phone. There wasn't a single-one in the whole damn town. What would you do if you couldn't afford a cell phone or a hotel, and you had to call someone to borrow money?

Back in my hotel room, I used the room phone and told Stringfellow what I'd found. "He's probably heading for the D-day beaches," I said. "You want me to rent a car and track him down?"

"You got any idea how many beaches there are?"

"No. Not really." But I'd always wanted to see them.

"Christ, who knows how long he'll be gone."

"He'll be back in two days, that's what the girl at Hertz said."

"Why didn't you start with that?" he said. "Hey, you ever heard of a Chicago P.I. goes by Sam Spade?"

"What?" This was Phil's nickname for me. Did that mean the tape was out?

"Sam Spade," he said again, "like Bogart in that movie with the dingus."

"In Chicago?"

"It's all over the news, another one of these crazy cop videos." Oh, boy, and I was 4000 miles away and would miss all the action. But I had to admit, it was a relief not to worry about someone kicking in the door.

"So, what should I do about Raven?" I asked.

"Well, just hang tight, I guess. If you look, you might find his new hotel. Maybe he'll come back to it. I'll talk to the son; see how long he wants to keep you twiddling your thumbs."

TWENTY-NINE

Paris isn't the jazz town of legend but it's still a good one. That's how I spent my nights, bouncing from club to club, spending bits of my walking-around money. During the day, I searched for Uncle Al's hotel. I had a thick, important looking envelope with his name on it, and I went hotel to hotel. "I'd like to leave this for my uncle," I'd say. "I'm afraid I don't have his room number."

There were hotels everywhere, even on the smallest of streets. I decided to concentrate on the Best Westerns and the Holiday Inns. Al Raven had stayed in one of each. They'd always been interchangeable in my mind and maybe they were in Raven's too. They also both had directories listing all their locations and often they sat on a strip with several other hotels. I started just around the corner from my hotel on Boulevard Montparnasse and then hopped across the big square to Rue de Rennes.

"I'm sorry nobody here by that name."

"Not one of ours, chum."

A few desk clerks just took the offered envelope and said "*Merci*."

"Are you sure he's here?" I'd ask.

"Let me check," some said. But others knew the game and almost threw me out on my ear.

On Rue Raymond Losserand, the Holiday Inn clerk said, "I'm sorry. He checked out Thursday."

"That doesn't make any sense," I said. "He knew this was coming."

"Let's see," the clerk said, and he shuffled some papers and then looked at his computer screen. "It looks like we are holding a room for Sunday night. But it's not guaranteed. If we fill up, he'll be out of luck."

I took my envelope back. It was full of flyers from various jazz clubs, the pages the son wanted Raven to sign, and a small, sealed envelope with "Dad" handwritten on the front.

On my last trip to Paris, we'd spent our nights listening to jazz and our days going from one museum to another. I'd seen enough art on that trip to carry me through this one as well. But besides museums, jazz clubs, cafes, restaurants, and bakeries, Paris was loaded with movie theaters and surprise, surprise; most of the American movies were shown in English with French subtitles. So, when I needed a break from the hotels, I'd go to a movie. After a few days of this, I was certain there were more movie theaters within a block of my hotel than in all of Chicago. Maybe it was time to start calling my hometown a movie desert.

I spent most of Sunday watching the Holiday Inn. Uncle Al never appeared. When I got there Monday morning, the clerk said, "You just missed him."

"He checked out?"

"Oh, no." And then he said something about a promenade.

"Where's that?" I asked.

"Is outside."

There were cafes in either direction from the front door. I checked both without finding Al Raven and then ordered coffee at the second one. I was a football field away from the hotel, but I had a clear view of the front door, and I knew Al Raven was going to walk down the street before too long. I felt proud of myself for a while. Who said I wasn't a detective?

I was on my second *grande crème* when a truck came up the block and stopped mid-way between my cafe and the hotel, in front of a large apartment building.

Demenagements, the truck said on the side, *Longues Distances.* A crew of three got out and went right to work. One of them went into the building. The other two started fiddling with the piece of equipment they'd towed behind the truck. It turned out to be a portable elevator. It went right up the outside of the building.

I was on my way to the second café, where the truck wouldn't block my view, when the mover who'd gone inside stuck his head out a sixth-floor window. The guys on the ground loaded a platform with packing supplies and sent it up the elevator.

I didn't really need more coffee. I found a patch of sunlight midway between the Holiday Inn and the truck and leaned back against a building and watched the men at work. Stacks of furniture pads went up and wrapped furniture came down. It was hard work, but it was honest. It made me consider my own mission, talking an old man into checking himself back into a nursing home. Nobody would call that good, honest work.

After a bit, the old man came down the street, helped along by a familiar looking cane.

"*Bonjour,*" I said when he was a few feet away.

"*Bonjour,*" he said, and he came to a stop.

"*Ca va?*" I asked. It goes?

"*Ca va,*" he said. It goes. Then he said something else in French and, just like that, I was lost.

"*Pas parle,*" I said. "*Parlez vous English?*"

"I thought you sounded like one of us," he said in English. "Where're you from?"

"Chicago."

He got a smile on his face, and it pretty much broke my heart. I knew the smile would disappear as soon as he found out why I was there. "Well, well, well," he said. "Isn't that something? Me too."

140

"Funny," I said.

He pointed across the street as the elevator started down with another load of furniture. "That's quite a contraption, don't you think?"

"It's got to beat carrying all that stuff down the stairs," I said.

"You are so right about that, my friend. That's how you kill a good furniture mover; send him out on high stairs every day." He slipped the cane into the crook of his arm and leaned back against the building. "What brings you to Paris?"

"I was hoping you wouldn't ask," I said.

"None of my business. Forget I did."

"No. It is your business, Mr. Raven. I came to see you."

The smile changed as quickly as I thought it would. He pushed himself off the building. The cane sounded like a firecracker when it hit the pavement. "My son sent you."

I nodded.

"So, you're a lawyer?"

I shook my head.

"A cop?" he said, and he gave me a closer look. "No. That doesn't make any sense. Accountant?"

"Private investigator," I said.

The smile was back, and his back was back against the building. "A private eye. You must work for Frank Stringfellow. I'll bet you're the guy who was asking around at Hertz. How'd you find me?"

I held up my important looking envelope.

He didn't even look. "I hope you didn't fly business."

"Coach," I said. "But extra leg room."

"You're not that tall," he said. "You know who's paying your bill, don't you?" I shrugged and he pointed to his chest. "So, what's my son want?" He stabbed the sidewalk with the cane again.

"He'd like you to come home," I said.

"Yeah." He smiled. "And I'd like someone to give me real hips again."

"And if you won't come home, he'd like you to sign some papers."

"I'll bet he would." He waved his free hand at me, like I was some annoying housefly. "Well, you can run along and tell him no on both counts."

Neither one of us moved, we stood there watching a tall sofa as it made a wobbling trip to the ground.

"Oh, what the hell am I getting mad at you for?" Raven said after the sofa landed. "You're just the messenger, right?" I nodded. "And you've got me at an unfair advantage. You know my name, but I don't know yours."

I told him my name.

"Pleased to meet you, Nick," he said. "Call me Al." He stuck out his hand for an all-American shake. "Can I buy you a cup of coffee?"

We walked down to a bakery he said was the best on the street, and then walked to a café across the street and grabbed a table in the sunlight. We nibbled our pastries and sipped coffee, and talked about all the things that were wrong with the new days in Chicago. He didn't sound or look anything like nursing home material to me.

"So where are these papers he wants me to sign?" Raven asked after a while.

I opened my envelope and separated the papers from the jazz flyers.

Raven slipped on a pair of glasses and then spent a minute or two flipping through the seven or eight sheets.

"He must think I'm senile," he said. "I don't know where he gets his lack of judgment." He set the sheets aside and then I handed him the sealed envelope with "Dad" written on the front. He pulled out a single sheet of paper, unfolded it, and took his time reading.

"Oh, this is funny," he said after a while. "He lost his key to the safety deposit box. He'd like to borrow mine."

"Wouldn't the bank give him another one?" I asked.

He shook his head and smiled. "He needs my signature."

"So, what's your answer?"

He folded the note and slipped it back into the envelope, ripped it in two, and then handed it back to me. He picked up the other papers and tore them into quarters. "Is that clear enough?"

I nodded, picked up the pieces, and put them back in my envelope.

"So, what do you do now?"

"I'm supposed to talk you into coming home."

He smiled. "Start talking."

"It was looking-like snow when I left. Don't you miss that?"

"Well, you tried. What else have you got in that envelope?"

"Just filler," I said and pulled out the flyers from the jazz clubs. "You like jazz?"

"You kidding?" He started going through the flyers. "Let's see. I've been here, here, don't know this one, here. Hell, why would you want to go back to winter in Chicago? Why don't we go hear some music instead?"

"I'm game." Music always sounded better when friends were along.

He leaned back and stretched. "And it's on me. How's that sound? The whole night."

"Sure," I said, and then I couldn't resist adding. "One way or the other."

That brought a quick laugh. "Oh, that's right. I'm footing the bill even if you foot the bill. Oh, well, I'd rather spend it on you than leave it to him. Now ain't that a shame?"

THIRTY

The first night we went to the Universal Café on a quiet stretch of Rue St. Jacque. The entire club was about as big as my living room.

A piano trio fronted by a very sultry brunette was on stage when we walked in. Her long red dress shimmered in the lights. Half the songs were in English, many standards. But the ones I loved best were the ones in French. Some I knew. But with others I might only pick out a word or two, or none at all. The meaning was in the melody, and at first, they all seemed to be love songs.

I caught the singer's eyes late in the set, and for some reason it was Kate Daniels who looked back. *You're forgetting the most important part,* she'd said, and I had to look away.

On the break, half the room went outside to smoke, including the entire band. We ordered another round and stayed at the table.

"This place is great," Al said. "I can't believe I've never been."

"The only problem, they don't pay the musicians. It's nice that there's no cover. But the poor guys have to pass the hat."

"My son doesn't get jazz," he said. "You know what he gets. Money. That's what he understands."

I shrugged. "You could say that about half the world."

"So did you read his letter?" he asked.

I smiled.

"Of course, you did. You're a detective."

"Does it make a difference?" Most of the note was obvious bullshit about how much everyone missed grandpa. The interesting part was about the "fresh lettuce" which the son had nowhere to put because he'd misplaced his key to the produce box. I wondered why he didn't just find another box or stick the lettuce in the refrigerator or under the mattress.

"Because if you did read it, you might end up getting the wrong idea."

"All business fringes on the illegal," I said.

"What the hell does that mean?"

"Just something I heard a judge say once." I'd been trying to figure it out ever since.

"I played it straight my entire life," he said. "Declared everything. Paid all my taxes. Followed the rules. But my hotshot son, he went to business school. You know what he learned? How to cheat, lie, and skim. That's what they teach 'em. Cash jobs. Cash discounts. Paying under the table. Paying off the union. Stuffing as much as you can in a bank box and when that fills up getting an even bigger box, and then winking at the girl who works the vault, like she's in on it too.

"But I promised him free rein and that's what I gave him. We only really had one fight about the business. That was when he started selling advertising space on the side of my trucks. 'The trucks already have advertising,' I told him. 'It's for Raven Moving and Storage.' We've got two automatic truck washes. You have any idea what those cost? But it gives me the best-looking trucks in town. And now I'm gonna sell that space to some other schmuck? That just makes the trucks and the company look cheap. Two ex-cons and a clown behind the wheel, if you see what I mean."

The smoke break ended. The band began passing the hat around.

"You got a fifty?" Al asked and held up a 50-Euro note.

146

"For the band?" This was about $60 US.

"Sure, one from you, one from me. That'll make a pretty decent tip, right?"

But how would it look on my expense report? "How about twenty?"

"Hey, it's my money. Remember?"

That got us both laughing. I handed him a fifty and he dropped both bills in the hat.

The second set was worse than the first. I didn't even have to catch the singer's eyes to see Kate Daniels. *And for three hundred you'll be able to find the truth?* Before long, we were in the hallway outside my office, looking into each other's eyes. Then that final wave as the elevator door was closing.

Raven looked my way. "You okay?"

"I'm fine." I just couldn't sit still. "I'm gonna grab a smoke," I said when the song ended, and I got up and walked outside.

Raven came out right behind with both our coats and found me puffing my imaginary cigarette. "You don't like the band?"

"No. They're pretty good," I said. "I just can't get my mind off a job I'm working back home."

"You find people. Is that what you do?"

"Not most of the time." I couldn't bring myself to talk about Kate Daniels, so I told him a bit about the redlight case as we strolled down to Boulevard Port Royal.

"Cops," he said after we settled in a café. "I had two good friends who went on the force when we were young. And that was it. We were never really friends again and, when I did see them, they never looked very happy."

"It's a tough job," I said. "And there're plenty of guys who have no business doing it." I kept right on talking.

This was my new disease. If I found someone who'd listen, I'd talk myself silly like the worst barroom bore.

Al nodded his head as I kept going. He said, "Uh huh," here and there, and then called to the waiter, "*Le meme chose, s'il vous plait*," and another couple of drinks appeared on the table and I kept blabbing.

I ended up telling him what had happened at Sweet's Mini Mart but managed to avoid mentioning Kate Daniels or Phil. I'd failed to keep one of them from getting killed and had no idea what had happened to the other. But it wouldn't be good news. A guy like Phil doesn't suddenly walk away from his wife and kids.

"You gotta get that tape out," Raven said when I finished my story.

"It's out," I said. "I dropped off a bunch of copies just before I left town."

"That makes you a hero in my book."

"Not to the cops," I said. "Money back guarantee, they won't be happy." They already weren't happy, and they were busy telling the world about my failure to protect Kate Daniels.

"I was thinking more about that clerk," Al said, and he held up his glass for a toast I didn't deserve.

"Yeah," I said, and I could still hear that plea: *I hope you will find it in your heart to help us.* That was the real victim here, the guy with the bullet hole in his knee doing four years for the crime of yelling at a cop who was trying to set him up.

"I can't imagine anything worse than being in prison for something you didn't do," Al said.

"Yeah," I said again, and I tried to push the image of Kate Daniels holding back that darkroom door out of my mind.

"What you need is more music. Why don't you hang

around a couple more days? A lot more jazz in this town."

"What would I tell Frank?"

He thought it over and then smiled. "You could tell him you're bringing back the key."

"That'd buy me some time," I said. "Only problem is, I'd have to really do it."

He pulled out his wallet and found a small red envelope. He opened it and slipped out a long narrow key. "This is it," he said, and he handed it over.

"You're not pulling my leg?" He shook his head, and I held up the key. "Because this is what your son really wants."

He nodded. "Do you know what's in that box?"

"Lettuce," I said. "You're right. I read the letter."

He shook his head. "No. That's what used to be there. I wonder what happened to my son's key." And he pulled a second key out of the same small envelope. "Well, well, well," he said. "Where did this come from?"

THIRTY-ONE

On the plane back, I wrote two reports for Frank Stringfellow, one investigative, the other listing my various expenses. They were both more fiction than true crime.

While the plane taxied at O'Hare, a brigade of snowplows cleared the parallel runway as snow whipped overhead. The grassy areas were now the whitest part of the field and were covered with drifts as big as circus trains.

Frank Stringfellow stood behind a pack of limo drivers outside customs. He caught my eye and pointed to the exit doors. I rolled my suitcase that way, and then came the surprise. "Have a good time in old *Par-ee*, Nick?" Detective Swanson was walking right beside me. He put a hand on my arm.

On the other side, Detective Craig grabbed my shoulder with one hand and my suitcase with the other. "Let me help you with that," he said, and we pivoted away from the exit.

"My wife is so jealous," Swanson said. "She says to me, some loser gets Paris, and we get a blizzard. That's not fair. What do you think, Nick? You think that's fair?"

"Hey! Hey! Hey!" Stringfellow's voice boomed behind us, and then he cut us off with waving arms. "I get him first. Isn't that the agreement?"

"Where the hell were you hiding?" Craig asked, and we came to a stop with Stringfellow blocking the way.

"I don't think I was the one hiding," Stringfellow said. "Come on, Nick. Let's get out of here."

Craig hesitated, and then stepped away from my suitcase and gave me a little take-it wave. "We make a deal, we keep it," he said, and caught my eye.

"We'll see you later, Nick," Swanson said. "We're not done."

"Oh, no. We haven't even started," Craig said.

I took control of my suitcase and followed Stringfellow outside and then to his extra-large SUV in the parking lot. I climbed into the passenger seat. "How'd you pull that off?" I asked.

"We made a deal," he said, and pulled out into traffic. "But first I had to give you up."

"Keep going," I said.

"They came to my office. They knew you were working for me, and they wanted to find you. There were all the usual threats when I wouldn't tell them anything. But then I thought what the hell, you're 4000 miles away. So, I told them I'd tell them where you were if they'd guarantee I'd get a couple of hours with you after my job was over, a little debriefing session. Swanson was pretty-amused to hear you were in Paris. Craig not so much."

"Did I miss anything?" I asked after we passed the WELCOME TO CHICAGO sign.

"Another police video," he said. "These guys never learn."

"Are they following?"

"If they are they're keeping way back. So, you got the key?"

"Right here." I slipped the key out of the envelope with my report and handed it over.

"Good work, Nick," he said. "This gets you a free ride home. And I'm gonna try to get a bonus out of Raven for you. But he's tighter than two Swedes at a smorgasbord so don't get your hopes up."

"How'd they get to you?" I asked. "That doesn't make any sense."

"Who'd you tell you were working for me?"

"No one," I said, and then I remembered that my old pal and lawyer Shelly had called while I was in that cab distributing those tapes. I'd told her I was on my way out of town. Had I mentioned Frank's name?

"You're not pissed that I gave you up?" Stringfellow asked after we pulled in front of my apartment.

"No big deal," I said. "It's not like they don't know where I live."

THIRTY-TWO

They knew, alright. Somebody had torn my apartment apart. They hadn't been subtle about it. They'd looked for hiding places and they'd found most of them. But they'd gone overboard, dumping the sugar and salt on the floor, slicing open the sofa and my mattress. The only things missing were my few movies and every single CD. My entire jazz collection was gone. "Son of a bitch," I said.

I went right back out, grabbed a couple of newspapers at the corner store and took a cab down to my office.

A box on the bottom of the front page of the Sun-Times said, "Sweet's clerk expected to be released. Page 5." I turned the pages and found the headline: SHARMA HEARING SET FOR TODAY. This was the clerk with the bullet wound in his knee. It was late afternoon. The hearing would have ended hours ago.

At first, I thought they'd missed my office. But no, they'd been there, too. They'd just used a lighter touch. The remaining copies of the Sweet's Mini Mart tape were gone. So now they knew for sure.

I checked the Sun-Times online and there it was. "Sweet's clerk limps out of court a free man." The story said the judge and prosecutors had agreed to toss the conviction and set Sharma free. "The State's Attorney's office has not announced whether it plans to retry Sharma. Veteran court observers say a retrial is highly unlikely after the discovery of a video which shows Sharma being shot by police with no apparent provocation."

I went back to the paper paper and started flipping through the pages. MYSTERY MAN IN VIDEO SOUGHT, a headline read. "Police are looking to question the unidentified customer seen in the video of the police shooting at Sweet's Mini Mart. Area North Violent Crimes detectives say the man is a person of interest in a double murder that occurred on the West Side in early December."

The story went on to say witnesses to the December shooting had come forward after seeing the video on TV. Anyone with information about the man's name or whereabouts was asked to contact Detective Swanson or Detective Craig at Area North.

THE MYSTERY OF THE CHICAGO POLICE, a headline on the editorial page read. "The video that seems to show the true circumstances surrounding the shooting of Pankaj Sharma by a Chicago Police officer nearly two years ago has the city in an uproar. The identity of the purported leaker, who apparently uses the *nom-de plume* Sam Spade, isn't the biggest mystery here. The real question is how the Chicago Police Department can allow these embarrassing and criminal incidents to keep happening.

"The video in question was likely stolen by police at the scene of the shooting and then buried. Instead of the police officer involved in the shooting being punished for his actions, Sharma, who looks like another in a long list of wrongly convicted, was given a pair of crutches and sent off to prison.

"A few years back we chastised a weekly newspaper that called the Chicago Police Department the biggest street gang in town. Today we'd like to apologize for that editorial. The more of these videos we see, the more we are beginning to agree. If the police are going to act like criminals, they should be treated as such. We call for a federal investigation of the shooting and the entire police department and ask for federal oversight as well.

The CPD has had years to try to fix this problem. They've failed. It's time for the Feds to step in."

The Tribune covered the same ground with the same tone but also wrote about the money. "Since 2004 the city has paid out more than $600 million in police abuse verdicts. This figure does not include millions of dollars in outside legal fees. Only New York City has paid out more and both their population and police department are three times the size of Chicago's."

Another story profiled Tommy Burrough's two victims, Kate Daniels and Walter Hulgret. "Both would be alive today if the right man had been arrested after the shooting at Sweet's Mini Mart." I had to hold my hand over Kate's picture. But even then, I found it impossible to read the story.

In my search through both papers, I never found a single mention of Phil Laubett or of Sim's Video. I went online and checked the last week with the same result. Nothing.

This made no sense. Sam Spade was Phil's name for me. How could the name get out without the fact that Phil was missing?

I spent the rest of the day calling Phil's old friends and leaving messages. No one called back. I called Sim's Video and got no answer. I tried Phil's wife with the same result.

I took the elevator down and walked around the corner to the Walgreens and bought a throwaway phone. When I came out, Swanson and Craig were parked right in front of the store. They followed me back to my office, tooted the horn, and continued down Lincoln Avenue, a couple of homicide detectives wasting their time a long way from home. No wonder they couldn't solve any murders.

Upstairs, I used the new phone to call the Rogers Park Police station.

"Hey, I think I saw that guy from Sim's Video," I drawled when a Sergeant answered.

"Who?"

"That Phil guy, the one who's missing, works at Sim's Video right up the street."

"Hold on," he said, and then came back and asked for my name and number.

A minute later the phone rang. "Hello Mr. Jones," a man said. "This is Officer Lopher. I'm returning your call. You say you saw Phil Laubett."

"Sure did," I said.

"Where was this? And when?"

"Just a little while ago. He was pulling into the drive-thru at McDonald's. The one over there on Ashland north of Diversey."

"How long ago again?"

"A couple of minutes," I said. "Somewhere . . ."

He cut me off with a quick goodbye.

I went downstairs and around the corner and joined the crowd at the Ashland Avenue bus stop. I heard the siren far away but as the squad got closer the driver also started blasting the air horn. The emergency lights flashed, the horn and the siren bounced off the buildings but, even with all that, the squad still almost got clobbered by a CTA bus moseying east. The bus stopped with inches to spare. The squad never slowed down.

As it cleared the intersection the car went into silent mode. I waited until it pulled into the McDonalds several blocks down, and then went back up to my office. So now I knew that Phil Laubett was still missing, that the police were actively looking for him, and that his old pal Officer Terry Lopher was leading the charge.

———

THIRTY-THREE

I hired a cleaning crew to get my apartment back in order and then spent a couple of days leaving messages and waiting for return calls that never came. I spent the nights on the town---mostly in various saloons within a few blocks of home---telling everyone I was curing my jet lag.

Swanson and Craig followed me around from time to time, but they never hung around long. Sometimes they'd just wave or toot the horn and then be gone. Something funny was going on here. I'd assumed that Stringfellow had only bought me a couple of hours.

Late one night I took a cab down to the Third Base Inn. *Last Stop before Home,* the sign above the door said, and that's how it had turned out on many occasions. It was only a few blocks from my office and almost directly across the street from Rent-a-Dent.

I put a twenty on the bar. The bartender dropped an Old Grand-Dad, on the rocks, in front of me and left the twenty sitting. It was an old game. I'd once found a missing bus boy for Jay, the owner of the place. It had taken about five minutes of my time. I'm not sure I ever left my barstool. I couldn't very well charge Jay for making a single phone call, so he'd been paying me back with free drinks ever since. In appreciation, I over-tipped the bartenders. The bus boy was back at work. He and Jay had made amends, and everyone was happy.

I slid a couple of bucks into the jukebox. Frank, Sarah, Patsy, and Merle, one heartbreaker after another and, before long, I was lost in a fog of self-pity. It brought me back to an earlier time when I was wallowing in alcohol and that most bittersweet of emotions.

I'd been in the prime of my career as a homicide

detective, happily married to my high school sweetheart, when one of my partners decided to rob a bank while I was waiting in line to cash my paycheck. This was his idea of a practical joke.

I did the wrong thing. I didn't turn him in. It just isn't done. I lied at the Police Board hearing and in Federal Court. But my partner went to prison anyway, and I got thrown off the force.

What was it Detective Swanson said? *Just 'cause you lost the badge, that doesn't mean you're not part of the family.* That was a sucker's line. I was part of the family when they needed me. As soon as that was over, I'd be out in the cold again. Of course, I'd pushed them, so I was already out in the cold. And not a single lawyer had returned my latest round of calls. Had they all heard about the part I'd played in Kate Daniels' death?

Before I had finished my drink, the bartender put a fresh one in front of me.

"You think you're doing me a favor?"

I almost told my new friend on the next stool all my problems. No. I stopped in time. That's how I'd gotten Kate killed, by thinking everyone else was part of my very own ex-police force and talking out of turn.

And now even that small force was gone. They'd left me completely alone, a force of one.

I scribbled a few lines of this reasoning on a cocktail napkin so I wouldn't forget, folded it, slipped it in my shirt pocket, stood up, finished my drink, and went out the door.

My jet lag was lingering. I hadn't even made last call.

Swanson and Craig were waiting at the curb. "Alright, Mr. Acropolis, right this way, please," Swanson said. He turned me around and pushed me against the car. Craig slapped handcuffs on my wrists while

Swanson did a pat down search.

"We're done playing," Craig said, and he turned me back around.

And then we all stood there waiting for something.

"You really think the cuffs are necessary?" I asked.

No answer.

"So, what am I charged with anyway?"

No answer.

"If I told you I wanted to call my lawyer . . . "

Nothing.

"You find that kid with the star on his tooth yet?"

A paddy wagon came around the corner and stopped alongside the detective's car.

"Here's your stagecoach, Nick."

"Oh, come on, you're not really gonna put me in that thing," I said.

"That's just the beginning." And in I went.

"Enjoy your ride," Craig said.

The door slammed shut behind me.

The driver started away and then decided to check his brakes. I ended up bouncing along the slimy floor.

THIRTY-FOUR

I lost track of time. It was one paddy wagon after another, blood or vomit on the floor, to one lockup and then the next. Nobody questioned me and nobody answered my questions. They didn't hear me at all. I didn't exist. I was on the merry-go-round.

I was usually in the farthest corner of the lockup, away from the prying eyes of the watch commander, if he should happen to stop by; away from all the other prisoners, prisoners who I might persuade to make a phone call for me after they got out.

One night I spent hours freezing to death in the back of a parked wagon.

Another night, a group of drunken cops stopped by with a 12-pack to say hello and take turns pissing into the floor drain outside my cell. Sleep was the best way to while away the hours. Sleep and dreams. But if the cells were packed, I had to fight the constant noise.

I tried to imagine Paris with the right companion. Some French woman, tall and thin perhaps, with deep brown eyes, a sly smile and a sexy accent. And then Kate Daniels jumped into my daydream and that was the end of Paris. I was back to my grim surroundings.

One day I heard the key turn in the lock. The cell door opened. Somebody came in. The key turned again.

I sat up from my nap to see a uniformed police officer sitting on the bunk across from me. He had wavy black hair, hair he would have been ordered to cut back in days of old, and bushy eyebrows over steady gray eyes. We looked at each other, nobody saying a word, and then I broke the silence. "So, what'd you do?"

"Good one," he said. Time passed before he spoke again. "I want to ask you a few questions about a missing person's case."

I looked for his name, but the tag was gone. That didn't matter. I knew who he was. "Hello Terry," I said. Terry Lopher, Phil's childhood friend who would never return my calls. Here he was in person.

He blinked. "Who's that?" he said.

"I just saw Phil pulling into the drive-thru at McDonald's," I said with a drawl.

He hesitated for several seconds. I could see him thinking it over. Finally, he grinned. "So that was you."

I pointed. "And that's you. So why am I here?"

"Look." He lifted a hand, palm up. "I've got nothing to do with this. I heard you were here. I just want to ask you some questions about Phil."

"Ask away."

"You wanted him to do what on that video?"

"I just wanted copies."

"Why?"

"What does that have to do with finding your friend?"

He thought about that for a few seconds, and then nodded. "Okay. Fair enough."

I heard someone talking and got up to look. A guy was all by himself several cells down. He was wearing a suit without a tie and giving himself a pep talk. "You are so stupid," he said. "You're an A-one, stupid fucking idiot, you know that?"

I turned back to Phil's old friend Terry. He hadn't moved. "I told him not to watch it," I said. "I know that was stupid on my part. He enhanced it. He got the names and badge numbers of those clowns and then he talked to you."

"It could have happened that way," he said, and he looked towards the floor. "But anything after that I had nothing to do with." He looked up. "I swear."

161

"You said something to someone, and they said something to someone else and eventually it got to someone who did not want that video to appear. And they decided to do something about it. That's what happened."

His head went back down. "Even if that's true and I'm not saying it is, I still don't know who those people are."

"You sure you want to know?"

"Hey, fuck you," he said, and his head was up again and hard gray eyes tried to stare me down. "You're the one who got him into this shit."

"Well, if we're going to go that way, we could blame his wife's birthday." I held his eyes. "If it wasn't for that, he would have copied the video while I waited." I sat back down.

"You gotta believe me. I want to find him."

"Have you gotten anywhere?"

"I've got one lead. But I can't figure out what it means."

"What?"

He thought it over, took a deep breath and then exhaled. "One of our license-plate reading cars recorded Phil's plates about eight hours after he left the store."

"Where?"

"Archer Avenue. Heading west right at the city limit."

"That's it?" I'd been hoping for more.

"I found a gas station video from Willow Springs, about fifteen minutes later. It looks like Phil's car again. I can't say for sure. It's still going west on Archer."

"If we could let Phil take a look at that video, he'd tell you whether it's him or not."

"I'm pretty sure it is. Because the same pickup truck is

right behind him in both videos."

That sat me up a bit straighter. "You get a plate number?"

He shook his head and pounded his knee with a closed fist "Big chrome bumpers front and back. There's either no plates or the bumpers are hiding them."

"Phil again," I said. "If there's a plate, he'd find it." *But would we ever find him?* So, what's west of Willow Springs on Archer?"

"A whole lot of nothing. Forest Preserves. Cemeteries. Quarries. Golf courses, millions of places to hide a car."

I stood up. The guy three cells down was now standing with both hands gripping the bars of his cell. "Stupid. Stupid. Stupid," he said again and again. He looked like someone in an old black and white prison movie.

I turned to Terry. "You need a break," I said. "You know the time and the day. The only way you're gonna find him is to go looking."

"I'm not even assigned to this."

"Connect it to the video and you'll get lots of help."

He shook his head. "I can't do that."

"Why not?"

He looked down at his old friend the floor. "Don't we have enough problems already; this video and that video; John Burge and Area Two; that McDonald kid; Homan Square, Minneapolis. It'd just be one more black eye. I'm afraid to even turn on the TV."

"Blue blood," I said.

He looked up. "What's that?"

"Right," I said. They all had it, but nobody knew what it was. "Look, if you're not gonna tie him to the video, then you gotta do it the hard way. Get out there and start asking questions."

163

He shrugged. "I've still got a job, you know."

"Take a leave," I said. "Get Phil's other friends to help. Get out there on Archer Avenue and start knocking on doors. Find people who live on the edge of the woods or the golf course, all those quiet places. Talk to them. Did they hear or see anything odd in the middle of the night. You've got the time and the day. That's huge."

"They could have been going to St. Louis."

I shook my head. St. Louis was 300 miles. "If they were going far, they would have been on the highway."

"He could be dead," he said.

"Then you could at least find his body, so Virginia has something to bury."

"Fuck," he said.

We talked for a few more minutes and then Terry stood up. "Christ, it smells rank in here. How do you take it?"

"I try not to think about it. Thanks for reminding me."

He called to the turnkey and turned back my way. "You want me to get you anything? Food, coffee, cigarettes?"

"You know what I'd really like, a shower and some clean socks."

That got me a real smile. and a headshake. "I'll see what I can do." He didn't look hopeful.

The turnkey came down and unlocked the door. "Any chance you get him a shower?" Terry asked.

"You gotta be kidding." He locked the cell door and followed Terry out of the lockup.

Two hours later, I was still dirty as can be. I was heading into another wagon when the turnkey brushed past and stuffed something into my jacket pocket. "Socks," he whispered.

THIRTY-FIVE

Ten hours or a week or two days later, I woke to the smell of coffee, and sat up to find Sergeant Sheehan, my old childhood friend towering over me.

"Thought you might like some real coffee." He handed me an extra-large Dunkin Donuts cup and a paper bag.

I devoured a cream cheese bagel and half a cup of coffee, and then said, "Jim, can you do me a favor?"

He shook his head. "I can't get you out, Nick. Sorry. Not yet anyway. They want to teach you a lesson."

"I'm learning more and more every day," I said. "But that wasn't what I was gonna ask. Can you call downtown for me?" I gave him Lenny's name and saw his eyes widen. "Just tell him they've got me on the merry-go round. You don't have to leave your name or anything."

"The merry-go-round. Is that what they call it now?"

"That's what we used to call it. It was pretty-funny when I was on the other side." We'd usually use it to keep lawyers at bay, not as punishment.

"Big clout like that," he said. "You ought to be out in no time."

"I doubt that."

"Where'd you find him?"

"The academy."

Lenny had been voted least likely to finish his probationary period. He was just too nice to be a cop, too soft, and he had a stutter that was way too easy to imitate, which made him one of the class jokes.

But he stuck with it. He even made sergeant, which kept him off the street much of the time and in the safety

165

of the station house. When his father, a legendary police captain, died, Lenny got up at the funeral mass to say a few words and the stutter was gone. Lenny was as surprised as everyone else.

Without the stutter, he became a rising star in the department. He was now near the very top. If anybody could get me out, he could.

Sheehan smiled. "Old friends are the best, aren't they?"

"I hope he feels the same way."

"Anything else I can do for you?" Sheehan asked after a while.

"I heard a rumor they've got showers in these new stations," I said.

He thought it over for a few seconds then shrugged. "Sure. Why not?"

I followed him out of the cell, down the hallway, out of the lockup, into the locker room, and then to a shower stall. Sheehan reached in and turned on the water. "How hot?"

"Medium," I said.

"Good, that's as hot as it goes," he said as I undressed. "I'll try to find you some clean underwear."

"I've already got socks," I said, and showed him my fresh pair.

"Unbelievable," he said.

THIRTY-SIX

It was a crowded night in one of the modern lockups. One woman was wailing-drunk and kept calling out the names of big shots she knew, cops, politicians, and movie stars. A woman two cells down was wearing a paper suit. "You know if you'd shut up, they'd let you out of here," she called during one of the drunk's few pauses.

"What did you say?" the drunk shouted. She sounded like she wanted a fight.

"You're in for drunk driving, for fuck's sake. Just shut up and they'll let you go."

"Really?"

"Trust me," the woman in the paper suit said.

When I woke an hour or two later, the place was quiet, and they were both gone.

One night in the depths of an old stationhouse they stuck a young guy in the cell with me. "Shouldn't you be in juvenile?" I said, and then I took a closer look. It wasn't a guy at all. It was Rita Cunningham, the cop from the 15th District, disguised as one. She was wearing baggy jeans and a leather jacket with extra wide shoulders. Her hair was hidden under a blue watch cap.

She moved over and sat next to me on the bunk. "You don't look so bad," she said.

"Same to you," I said. "How long's it been? Do you know?"

"You came through 15 at least twice," she said in a whisper. "But everybody knows me there. I couldn't risk it. I've got a friend here. She snuck me in the back door."

"Now you just have to worry about getting out," I

said.

She rolled her eyes. "I want to ask you about that photograph," she said.

This would be the photo of the kid from that corner store, the one with the gap in his teeth and the whiskey bottle in his pocket "Ask away," I said.

"It's from that video, right?"

"Uh huh."

"So why were you looking for him?" She put a hand on my knee and then quickly took it back.

"I wanted to know what that shakedown was about. He was the only one left standing. Everybody else is dead."

"Except the clerk," she said, and she looked up. I followed her eyes. A series of dark pipes were suspended from the ceiling, twenty feet above our heads. Thick piles of accumulated dust were waiting to fall.

"Yeah. But I already know his story," I said. "I talked to his uncle. Hell, anybody who saw the tape knows his story. They set him up. The question is why."

"But who cares about the shakedown?" She stood up and came around to face me. "Once you've got that shooting, nothing else matters."

"Let's say I have personal reasons." I wanted to have as much information as possible for my report to Kate Daniels' grave. "So, what are your reasons?"

"Months back a tactical sergeant came to roll call to ask us to be on the lookout for a guy with most of his front teeth missing, and with a star on a tooth right next to the gap."

"Why'd they want him?"

"Funny thing." She spread her arms wide and smiled. "They never said."

"So, you took that photo to the Sergeant, and he

168

wanted to know where you got it."

"*She* wanted to know."

"And?"

"I told her I'd have to talk to my source first." She sat down next to me again. "But you were hiding out somewhere, and other people were looking for you too. She kept pressuring me. And then I saw the video and it was pretty-clear where the still came from."

"You never told her my name?"

She held my eyes for a while and then shook her head. "No. I did not give anyone your name, Nick. And I haven't heard a word from the sergeant since that video surfaced. But now I'm on some kind of department shit-list. I get the worst assignments, the worst partners, all the pigs, the smokers and the stinkers. They had me working a wagon the other day. That's how I found out about you. You were going out while we were coming in."

"So why are they fucking with you?"

"My guess, the video. They think you're the guy who dropped it and because of that photo, I'm connected with you. So, they're punishing both of us."

"Well, I'm sorry," I said.

"Oh, fuck sorry," she said, and she stood up again. "Where's that supposed to get us?"

"Tell me about this Tac Sergeant," I said. "Where'd she get that clout? What's her name?"

"Barbara Yates. I guess she inherited the clout. Her father was a bigwig somewhere on the South Side years ago."

Yeah, my very first boss. "Okay. Anything else?"

"Well, she hangs out at this big convenience store on Chicago Avenue, place called the 365-always open. Her and her crew, sometimes they're in there for hours at a time. And I just have this feeling there's something funny going on."

"They probably give 'em free coffee and donuts."

She shook her head. "I asked about that. Coffee only. Anyway, I used to stop down the street at this little Turkish place. Very good people, and I'm half Armenian, so that's really saying something. They made the most wonderful coffee. It got me through some tough shifts. Anyway, two months back, my Turkish friends are busted for selling alcohol to a minor and the city pulls their liquor license and revokes their business license, and they've got no choice but to close. They can't even sell coffee." She looked up at those dusty pipes again. A spider taking a stroll might start a toxic snowstorm.

"You think it was a set up?" I asked.

"It wasn't a city sting or anything like that," she said. "Somebody called in a fight inside the store. When our guys get there, they don't find any fight, but they find a kid with a half pint in his jacket pocket that he says he got right there. Sound familiar?"

"Does the guy have a star on a tooth, by any chance?"

"No. That's not the description and there's no video." She nudged me with her leg. "They won't make that mistake again."

"Who?"

"My Turkish friends."

"Was your Sergeant Yates involved in the bust?"

She shook her head. "It was her day off. But her crew was the first to respond. They were right around the corner, probably hanging out at the 365 again, so they beat the beat car."

"Nothing unusual about that," I said.

"No. But they're not on the paper at all."

"That's not unusual either. They didn't want to waste

170

their time with the paperwork on a nickel-dime case, and then end up wasting even more time testifying."

"Why are you apologizing for the people torturing you?"

Apparently, she'd never heard about John Burge and his infamous torture crew at the old Area 2. Yeah, the good old days, when they really knew how to get those confessions. Too bad so many of them were from the wrong people. "It's nice that you care," I said. "But I'm waiting for you to tell me something that's really unusual."

"It's just a feeling," she said. "The 365 is a big store in a little store neighborhood, big parking lot, and guess who they've got working security?" She nudged me again and I thought, I could get used to that. "Off-duty cops, 24-hours a day."

"Keep the assholes and the gangbangers away," I said.

"Sure," she said. "But it doesn't make sense. We're so short-staffed, you can work all the overtime you want. Why waste your time for 20 or 25 an hour when you can make four times that much on the job?"

I couldn't stop myself from doing the math, $80 to $100 an hour for working an extra shift. And I was on the outside working for chump change.

As Cunningham kept talking, I remembered another big convenience store a couple miles east on Chicago Avenue. 24-7 Fast Food & Groceries was not too far from Sweet's Mini Mart. It was also a store where off-duty cops provided security. Suddenly I was interested in what Rita was saying. "Well, look, if they're drumming up business for that big store by getting your little store closed, they might be getting other stores closed too. Why stop at one? Go to City Hall; see if you can find a list of all the revoked business and liquor licenses. Funny. Someone sent me one a few weeks back in an official Police Department envelope."

"What's so funny about that?"

"Somebody knew I wanted it before I did." I pointed straight down at CPD concrete. "Somebody on the inside."

"What do I do with the list?"

"Pretend you're a detective. Go through it and see if any other revoked stores are close to that big-one you're talking about. Look for a pattern. And while you're downtown go to Business Affairs. See if you can find out who owns that 365 store."

"Okay, partner," she said and winked.

Before she left, I asked her to call Shelly for me.

"The merry-go-round," she said. "Funny. It doesn't look very amusing."

"That's 'cause I'm on the wrong side of the ride."

THIRTY-SEVEN

The cell door opened. "Come on," the turnkey said. I followed him down the hall and out the back door. I wasn't wearing handcuffs and there was no wagon waiting. The turnkey gave me a slight nudge at the top of the stairs. "Just keep going," he said behind me.

I found myself sleepwalking down a sidewalk. I walked and walked and walked, like a blackout drunk coming back to consciousness; a city side street in the middle of the night; no houses; only a few parked cars at the curb. *Where have all the houses gone?*

The ghetto somewhere, except you weren't supposed to call it that anymore. And weren't ghettos supposed to be crowded? Not this one. Lawndale or Englewood, East Garfield Park. The city was full of neighborhoods like this. No cars. No houses. No people.

Except for one. "You got a smoke?"

And then I was face down on a broken sidewalk, hands patting my pockets. "Man, somebody already got you."

And then back walking. Find a cab. *Man, somebody already got you.*

Pat my own pockets. Nothing. No money for a cab. No phone. No keys. No wallet. My pants are falling down. No belt. No shoelaces. They kept everything.

A street sign says "E. 89th St." the other sign was gone. What a corner. Use it as an advertisement for a nothing city; nothing on any of the four corners; the houses gone to the wrecking ball or to fire. The people have gone to the suburbs, or maybe back south. Black Flight. Get out while the getting is good. No cabs out here anyway. No nothing. Keep going. Must be four in

173

the morning. Even the drunks and the gangbangers are home.

Find a bus to take you downtown. No. You're in no shape for downtown. Find Western Avenue. That's the bus for you.

The street signs still say East which makes it at least three miles to Western. No way I can walk that far. Gotta get out of here before they find me, the police, the gangbangers, before the assholes of the world wake up.

After a while the neighborhood's a little better, more houses, cars, an old guy walking a big black dog.

"Mister, which way is west?" The words don't work. A croak. The dog growls. The man pulls the dog into the mouth of an alley, and they wait for me to pass.

Okay, straighten up and fly right. The numbers are going down. That must be north. Keep talking to yourself. Gotta get home.

87th Street. And there's a bus stop sign. "No Owl Service," it says. That's a hoot. What time is it? Wait there. Cold. They took my coat, too.

I don't know how long I waited and then I stumbled up the stairs onto a westbound bus. The driver has a brown face, gray hair, and dark eyes behind wire rim glasses. I can smell his morning coffee. It's in a travel mug resting on the dashboard. I get a flash of my childhood kitchen.

I put my hand on the fare box, like swearing on a bible. "Got robbed," I say.

"Three choices, pay, get off, or I call the police."

"Police. They're the ones took everything."

"Police robbed you." He looks down at my lace-less boots. "Took your shoelaces, too?" Everyone knows what that means.

But he takes me to Western Avenue. Someday I'll pay

him back. Swear I will. But he won't tell me his name.

"Walk that way. Keep walking 'til you see the turnaround. Make sure you get on the one going north."

Longer walk than I thought. Another bus. Another promise.

"Get back there and sleep it off. I'll wake you when we get there."

16 miles straight north on the longest city street in the world-- or was that just more Chicago bull? --straight as the edge of a yard stick. Straight as Lenny, who never came. No Shelly. No Frank. No John or Andy. Left me there alone. But I'm out now and heading for home, an army of one.

"Okay, buddy, far as you go."

I open my eyes. The bus driver is standing over me. I can see the windows of my own apartment. "Thank you, sir." My fellow riders turn to watch me go out the back door.

Two CTA bus drivers, my only friends.

Down the steps, across the street, and around to the curving sidewalk. Ring my neighbor's doorbell. No answer. She's already left for work.

Back on the narrow sidewalk to the first gangway. I go up the back stairs and then over the banister, drop down to the roof and scramble across to my window. Locked, of course. The roof is black tar, not a rock in sight. Shadowboxing. Pop. Pop. Pop. Not too hard. Pull the shards of glass out, unlatch the window, and then fall into the room. Home sweet home.

Hours later, I turn over in bed. The crinkling of the tape I used to repair my mattress wakes me.

I sit up, still half-dressed in my grungy clothes.

I get the coffee going and then take a long shower, and torture myself with a worn razor. I put on fresh clothes. Pour black coffee. Pour the spoiled milk down the drain.

I look at that pile of rags I'd been wearing for who knows how long. Beyond saving. Beyond repair. Only the boots are worth keeping and they'll need work. Check the pockets before I toss it all in the garbage. On a folded cocktail napkin are a few drunken scrawls from my night at the Third Base Inn. *You are a force of one.* That great insight was underlined twice. Underneath was another line: *Nobody ever got in trouble by keeping their big mouth shut.*

THIRTY-EIGHT

The light on my answering machine flashed, the phone that the telemarketers called. But now there were actual messages.

The first is from Frank Stringfellow. "Nick, something's wrong with your regular phone. No message. No nothing. I just want to give you a heads up. I might need you to go back to Paris and find Al Raven again. Hang tight."

Shelly: "I just heard. Don't worry. I'll get you out."

Al Raven: "I'm coming in at O'Hare, 1:45. United. If you could meet me, I'd appreciate it. Something happened. Yeah, something happened all right. My son died." He could hardly get the words out. "Oh, sweet Jesus, I'm sorry. I thought it might be easier, saying that to an answering machine. *Putain.*"

Shelly: "I just missed you at the 4th District. Son of a bitch, where'd they take you?"

John Casper, my old partner, now retired and living in Arizona: "Nick, what the fuck did you do now? Anyway, I'm making some calls, even though I figure you've probably got it coming. Don't hurt yourself falling off. And then get your ass out here. I'll teach you how to golf."

Stringfellow: "Okay, forget Paris. Raven's back in town. He wants to see you, if you ever get around to answering your phone. Just remember whose client he is. I hope those cops didn't give you too hard a time."

Lenny: "You kno-o-o-o-w who. I got all your stuff. The fuckers sent you out the back door while I'm sitting out front like a fool."

Shelly: "Supposedly you're out. I'll believe it when I

177

see you."

Rita Cunningham: (a whisper) "I got that stuff we were talking about. You were right. It wasn't just one. We gotta meet."

#

Rita Cunningham didn't look anything like a boy this time. She wore a low-cut white blouse under a black blazer, and sexy black jeans over high heel boots. Her black hair was tied in a ponytail. We were in a Mexican restaurant around the corner from my apartment.

"You have any trouble downtown?" I asked. The busboy dropped chips and salsa on the table.

She shook her head. "Never went. I got the corporate name from Business Affairs online." She pushed the chips to the side and slid a single sheet of paper across the table. The name was the address of the store with LLC behind it. "And I got this," she waved several sheets of paper, "from my alderman. He likes me. He thinks a cop moving into the hood is the first sign of gentrification."

"Can we find out who owns this corporation?" I reached for a chip.

"They just give the name of a lawyer, Salvatore Placa. I tried looking him up online and nothing came up at all. That's suspicious right there. I'll go downtown and see if I can find more."

She slid the other sheets across to me. It was a citywide list of all the revoked business licenses for the last two years. "What I did, I got my district map out and I tried to find stores within a few blocks of that 365 store."

She'd drawn a big 365 on the map. Around it seven Rs sat next to Xs. Those were all revoked licenses. They almost made a circle. The open end was the city line. Across the street the village of Oak Park began.

"But how many stores are still open in the same radius?" I asked.

"I'd have to go out and look," she said. "At least a couple. Probably more. But if somebody went out of their way and got them all closed, that would look way too suspicious. We won't get anywhere thinking people are stupid."

A waitress brought our food. Rita had ordered a single fish taco along with rice and beans.

I'd ordered one of the combination plates, a half order of carne asada and a single chili relleno.

"That's probably the worst thing on the entire menu," Rita said. "The steak's okay. But chili relleno? My god."

"What's wrong with it?" It tasted pretty good to me.

"It's deep-fried cheese. In other words, grease wrapped in bread and dropped in more grease."

"Hey, I've been eating baloney sandwiches. Don't I deserve a special dispensation?"

She leaned across the table and looked right in my eyes. "You should probably do that a couple of times a year."

I kicked her under the table, not too hard. "What?"

She ignored the kick and flashed a sly smile. "Ride the merry-go-round. You should see your eyes. I'll bet the whites haven't been this clear in years. You lost weight, too."

"Well, thanks," I said, and took a swallow of beer. I had to make up for lost time.

After the busboy cleared our plates away, I drew my own map on the back of a paper napkin. I put ABS in the middle for the big store out near Sweet's and then began placing my own Rs on the sheet as I went through the revoked list.

"ABS?" Rita said.

"Another big store," I said. "It's on Chicago Avenue too, a couple of blocks from Sweet's. Big parking lot. Off duty cops working security."

"What's the name of the place?"

"What is it? 24-7 Fast Food & Groceries."

"Interesting," she said.

I ended up with nine Rs. They went around in two neat circles. Sweet's was on the outer circle, about three blocks away.

"If they just got half the business from nine stores, how much would that be?" Rita asked.

"Okay, let's assume that whoever owns these stores are the ones behind getting the licenses revoked. How do we prove that? And how do we prove the stores didn't deserve to get revoked anyway?" I held up the list of revoked licenses. "I mean, look at the size of this thing."

Rita reached for my map. She put a line through ABS and wrote "24-7," above it. She drew an arrow heading west and wrote "365," at the end of it. "Kind of go good together, don't they. 24-7, 365."

"How'd I miss that," I said. "So where do we go from here?"

"We'd have to get the reports," Rita said.

"We'd need a lot more than that. And another thing, who's paying the bill?"

"Is that who I think it is?" Rita asked, and I looked up to see Lenny standing just inside the front door. He was wearing a black topcoat, which hid his well-braided uniform, and taking a casual look around. I waved him over. "You know him?"

"He's bringing my stuff," I said.

Lenny didn't sit down. "I can't hang around," he said.

"My driver's double-parked." He dropped a crumpled paper bag on the table.

"Meet Rita," I said. "She's one of the good guys out in 15."

He reached out a hand. "Any friend of Nick," he said.

"It's a real honor, sir," Rita said.

"The most important thing to remember," Lenny said in a whisper, "I was never here." He winked and then turned and walked away.

"He gave a great speech at my graduation," Rita said.

"If you knew how funny that sounds," I said, and tried to imagine a speech by Lenny back in his stuttering days.

I opened the bag. It was almost all there, the wallet, the keys, the dead phone, my belt and shoelaces, even my money, everything but the pocket change and my notebook. *Was there anything special in the notebook?*

Most of it was about Phil missing. Names and phone numbers. I couldn't think of anything else.

"So how do we proceed, partner," Rita asked.

The waitress brought our coffees. "I think we take what we have to the Feds," I said.

"Are you nuts?" It was her turn to kick me. "That's the last thing we want to do."

"They've got the resources." I took a sip of coffee. It came with a touch of cinnamon. "This is way too big for us to handle."

"The FBI will make it bigger." She pointed her pen at me. "And you know it. They'll try to indict the entire department."

"Years ago, we could have gone to one of the newspapers."

"That's almost as bad." She drummed the pen along the rim of her coffee cup.

———

"They don't have the reporters now, anyway. So, what's your suggestion?"

"We do it together. You work on the outside, go down to the liquor board, file freedom of information requests on any arrests, talk to the owners of those stores. I'll work from the inside, trying to find out what I can about Yates and her crew. Who knows what else they might be up to?"

"And then what?"

"When we have it all, we'll tie it in a big bundle and take it downtown. We could even use your friend." She turned her pen towards the door where Lenny had gone.

"Did you see how fast he got out of here?"

"He got you off the merry-go-round, didn't he?"

I shook my head. I wasn't so sure about that. "Maybe they just got tired of listening to me cry," I said. "So, if I get you right, you're going to keep getting a paycheck. What am I supposed to live on?"

"Which reminds me, I've got some shopping to do before my shift starts."

"Well, before you go," I said, and over a second cup of coffee I told her all about Phil Laubett.

She couldn't even say it. She looked at the waves in her coffee. "You think somebody in the department . . ." She was another true-blue cop.

I nodded. "It's the only thing that makes sense."

"That's ridiculous. Why would . . . It's more likely he just walked away."

"His wife doesn't think so. His friends don't think so. He hasn't used his credit card. Didn't pull money from the bank. And the last thing he was working on before he left the store was that video. And nobody's seen him since."

"It's a classic," she said. "Everything looks fine. The

wife thinks life is just grand. The little kids are happy. They love nothing better than playing with their great dad. But the guy is going crazy inside. He wants to be out in the wild hunting lions, not at home tied down with a family."

"Lions?"

"That's word for word from my marriage counselor."

"How'd that work out?"

"Well, now I'm a single mom with two kids and he's married to a different woman. Everybody says she sort of looks like me. She's pregnant. So, pretty soon he's going to have a new family and my kids are going to have a half brother or sister to play with a couple of days a week."

"I'm sorry to hear that," I said, and drained my coffee.

"It's kind of funny, when you think about it. He made it out in the wild for about three months. I'll bet he never got anywhere near a lion. He probably never even went to the zoo."

THIRTY-NINE

I met Al Raven at a place called Milano's in Arlington Heights, a suburb on the far side of O'Hare. I got stuck in traffic and ended up almost a half hour late. Raven was waiting in the darkest corner of the bar, away from a group gathered under a TV watching a hockey game.

"Sorry I'm late," I said, and started to explain.

He cut me off with a raised hand. "You sound like one of my drivers. What are you drinking?"

"Bourbon rocks."

"Anything special?"

"Whatever they've got," I said.

Raven relayed the order, and then turned back to me. "You like rotgut?"

"If it tastes too good, it's harder to stop."

"That's one way of doing it, I guess."

The bartender placed my drink in front of me, along with a small bowl of shelled peanuts. I was about to reach for one when Raven pushed it back to the bartender. "We're having dinner," he said. The bartender took the bowl away.

We sat sipping our drinks. A cheer came from down the bar and a few minutes later the TV went off. "I'm really sorry about your son." I broke the silence.

"Yeah, me too," he said. "But let's talk about something else first. Something easier. Tell me about that video."

"All you gotta do is open a newspaper or turn on the TV." I turned to look down the bar. All the hockey-game watchers were gone.

"I was following online in Paris, believe it or not. You upset the applecart, my friend. Any blowback?"

"Nothing I haven't been able to handle," I said. I was just hoping my merry ride was the end of it.

"Well good work," he said. "We're friends, right?"

"Of course."

"Let's go sit where we can talk."

He dropped a twenty on the bar, said, "Thank you, Andrew," to the bartender, and then we carried our drinks down a hallway, past two busy dining rooms, and into a small room with two large booths. One of them was set for two.

"We've got the place to ourselves," Raven said, and hung his cane on a hook.

A waitress came in and said hello. She placed a basket of bread and a relish tray on the table, filled our water glasses, and then left us alone.

Raven stared into his glass. I twirled my ice with a finger.

"It's my own goddamn fault," he said after a while. "You know I never understood him. Never. Not even when he was a little kid. Never. So why didn't I just leave him be? He was doing fine in New York without any help from me.

"But I talked him into coming back here. You know why? Because I didn't want to sell out and have some schmucks turn my moving company into just another half-assed operation. I wanted it to go on after I was gone, the biggest and best moving company in town. I wanted that to be my memorial. I wouldn't even need a tombstone." He laughed short and sharp, the bark of a wounded dog.

"But that was my life. Not his. That was my big mistake, not seeing that." He grabbed a piece of celery from the relish tray, sprinkled it with salt, and then brushed most of the salt off. I reached for a cherry pepper.

"I made him work on the trucks, summers, a couple of years when he was in high school. He hated it," Raven said. "He could do the work. He just thought it was pointless. He told me once. 'Here's the entire business. You pick up something one place and put it down somewhere else.' He didn't get that it was how you went about doing it. That was the important part.

"Another time he says, 'If this is what you want me to do with my life, I should quit school right now. Why waste time on an education?' And I couldn't argue with him. I never went to college. Hell, I never even got out of high school. So that was it. Next summer he got a job at a bank instead, and he was in finance after that. I never did understand what he did exactly. But he made enough to afford a place on the Upper East Side and send his kids to private schools."

"He picked up money one place," I said. "And put it down somewhere else."

"You're probably right," he said. "And I should have let him keep right on doing it. But instead after years of trying, I talked him into coming back here, and taking over. He left his wife and kids behind. That's something I had nothing to do with. At first, it was supposed to be just until the school year ended, and then it was one thing and then another thing, and they never came."

We spent a few minutes comparing New York with Chicago and then Paris with Chicago. The pros and cons, the weather, New York hot dogs versus Chicago hot dogs; the Italian beef sandwich versus a really-good crepe.

"But here's what I just found out. She was never going to come. They were getting divorced. That's probably why he finally took me up on my offer. But he

186

never mentioned the divorce. He pretended everything was fine and the entire family was on the way. He also pretended he was spending every weekend in New York. And I don't have a clue what he was really doing."

He twirled his swizzle stick for a bit and then took a sip.

"Now I didn't quite level with you in Paris. Every month or so, I used to go to the bank, open our box, and grab a handful of cash. Just enough so I could be a big shot at places like this. One day I go in and the box isn't nearly as full as it used to be and, when I talk to my son, he doesn't know anything about it, which is pretty-funny 'cause only two of us have keys. Now I've been with the same bank for over forty-years, so it didn't take me long to find out Steve's been making regular visits to the box, two, three, sometimes four times a week."

"Steve is your son?"

He looked up. "Didn't I say that?"

"I guess you did."

"Anyway, it really fried me he'd lie to me like that. So next time I stopped by work, I waited until he was out of the office for a minute, and then I grabbed the safety box key from his key ring. And he must have known I took it, but he never said a word. And that fried me a little more and I decided I'd teach him how to have a good time with illicit money, and I emptied the goddamn box and bought a one-way ticket to Paris."

"What was all that about you running away from a nursing home?"

"Well, I'm sort of in assisted living. But it's not the kind you're thinking about. Now they call it independent living. I've got my own place and they let us come and go as we please. I think he just made that up for your boss. He couldn't very well tell Frank he'd been raiding our safety-deposit box."

He picked up another piece of celery, then changed his mind and dropped it back in the bowl. "While all this was going on, you know the one thing I never did? I never asked myself why Steve needed the money."

"Did you ever figure how much was gone?"

"Not that much, really," he said. "Twenty, thirty grand, something like that. And then my great gag; sending back that key to an empty box, but it wasn't completely empty. I'd left a single dollar in there to make it even funnier. And he returned the favor by blowing his brains out while sitting behind my old desk. Some joke, huh?" He finished his drink in one long gulp.

"It probably didn't have anything to do with you or that dollar," I said.

He shook his head. He didn't believe me. I took a few swallows of my drink, and then pushed my empty glass next to his.

"I'd like to ask a favor," he said after a while.

"Name it."

"I'd like to hire you to find out what he was doing while he was supposed to be in New York. What did he need that extra cash for? I want to know about his life, anything at all. Because what I'm finding out is, I didn't know a goddamned thing. And, of course, what I'd really like to know is why he decided to end it. You think you can do that for me?"

FORTY

I was out in River Forest the next morning with the keys to Steve Raven's Lake Street apartment in hand. I was halfway down the hallway, walking on plush blue carpet, when a guy in a gold robe stepped out of an apartment on the left. He walked quickly across the hall, stooped down, and scooped up two newspapers from a door on the right. When he started back with the loot, he saw me coming and didn't know what to do with the papers. Part of his body wanted to get them back on the floor while another part was diving for the safety of the door he'd come out of. The papers were bouncing this way and that like a bad juggling act. Finally, the door won. He danced the papers inside, his robe flowing and his trailing leg high in the air. The door closed behind him with a soft whoosh.

I wanted to applaud but the dancer had left the stage.

I wasn't surprised when I got to Steve Raven's door to find that I was standing in the same spot where those newspapers had started their journey.

It's normally unsettling being in the home of the newly dead, especially when they left planning to return. But that wasn't the case here. I felt like I was walking into a hotel room. Steve Raven had obviously known he wouldn't be coming back.

There were spots on the walls where picture frames had once hung. The refrigerator was empty except for some ice and a few bottles of mineral water. In the bathroom, I found a backup roll of toilet paper and a fresh bar of soap.

The queen size bed was down to a bare mattress. The drawers of both nightstands were empty. I flicked on the clock radio, and it came up on classical music. I checked the alarm setting. 5 a.m.

There was a pair of paint-spotted jeans hanging in the bedroom closet and several T-shirts folded in a dresser drawer. That was it for personal belongings. Within a few minutes, I knew I wouldn't find anything worthwhile. I'd have to do a thorough search anyway. But before I started, I walked across the hall and knocked on the neighbors' door.

The dancer answered still in his robe with the newspapers in hand. "I should probably put these back," he said, and had a hard time meeting my eyes. He was a slender guy with thinning hair, dark, bushy eyebrows, and a nose that ended with a gentle speed bump.

"I wouldn't bother," I said. "You know he's dead, right?"

He nodded. "The police were here last week. Are you . . ."

"I'm an investigator working for Raven Moving and Storage. Do you have a few minutes?"

"Oh, sure." He relaxed. "I'm Larry." He stepped aside and waved me into his apartment.

The difference was striking. There were plenty of pictures on the wall, overflowing bookcases, not-too-fresh flowers, and the smell of burnt toast. An open box overflowing with paperback books was sitting on the floor next to a large stack of newspapers, alongside a comfortable looking armchair.

Larry gestured towards a sofa, and I sat down. "So how well did you know Steve?" I asked.

"Oh just, you know, to say hello. I'd see him in the hallway or out in the parking lot."

"No wild parties?"

"Oh, god no." He laughed and looked very much at home in the armchair. "That's me. But Steve never complained." He pointed down. "That's where the complaints originate."

"How about women?"

"No." He hesitated and then shook his head. "Not really."

"But occasionally." There was something telling in that hesitation.

"Once." I won the bet. "I was going out and she was coming in, and she mistook me for Steve." He smiled. "It was funny. And then Steve opened his door and that was that. *C'est la vie.*"

"A working girl?"

"Wow! Impressive. How'd you figure that out?"

"Trade secret," I said. Larry didn't look anything like Steve. "But only once, huh?"

He nodded. "I don't spend much time thinking about my neighbors' lives. But from what I saw, I would say that Steve was a very serious guy. He went to work. He read the New York Times and the Wall Street Journal, the Tribune and the Economist. He was serious about his job. He went out of his way to tell me that his men were the best damn movers in town and then told me not to take his word for it. I checked the reviews online. They all agreed."

"Did you ever see him outside?"

"I used to see him on the running trail. But then I stopped running. I'm a waiter again. That's enough exercise for anybody. I saw him in the restaurant once. But he wasn't in my station, so we just pretended not to notice each other. You know how that goes."

I got up to take a closer look at one of the framed photographs. It was the old man himself, Mayor Richard J. Daley standing with a boy of about ten in front of a big sign that said, "GOOD FOR CHICAGO. RE-ELECT

RICHARD J. DALEY." The sign never mentioned what office Daley was running for but that was something everyone already knew.

"Is this you?"

"Yeah," he said, and he got up and came to the picture. "I was a paperboy at the time, the Chicago American. I was on my bike and the photographer flagged me down. He wanted a kid for the picture. It was in the Belmont-Lincoln Booster. My mom wrote to the paper, and they sent us the copy. My friends were jealous as hell. He was like a god back then. Remember?"

Sure," I said, and then got back to work. "About Steve, anything else you can think of?"

He shrugged. "He was a nice guy, I guess. He maybe seemed a little lonelier than most. The newspapers usually came at five in the morning. Sometimes I'd just be coming home. But what I figured out, if I stayed up and had a nightcap or two, I could go downstairs and pick all three papers from the recycling bin after he left at seven. And they'd all been read, front to back."

"So now you don't have to go down to the recycling bin," I said.

He smiled. "Yeah, but one of these days the subscriptions are going to end, and I'll be back to reading online. It's not really the same. But who can afford real newspapers anymore?"

"When you saw him at your restaurant, was he with someone?"

"He was alone. That isn't unusual where I work. A lot of our customers just come in for a quick bite on a break. But I got the feeling with Steve it was almost a permanent state."

"Did he say anything about moving out of his apartment?"

192

"I was wondering about that," he said. "He gave me these books." He reached into the cardboard box alongside the chair and pulled out a couple of ancient paperbacks. "He said he didn't want to give them to the Salvation Army. And then later that day, I saw a Salvation Army truck out back. They were there for a while, carting stuff away. I was kind of wondering if he was planning on moving. But I guess he was just planning to do what he did, and he didn't want to leave a bunch of stuff behind."

"Can I borrow those books?"

"The whole box?"

"I'll give you a receipt and I promise to bring 'em back."

"Sure. Don't worry about the receipt. But please bring 'em back. Oh," he started to stand. "Wait, I'm reading one in the bedroom. Let me get it."

"That's okay," I said. "This is plenty." They might give Al Raven some idea about his son.

We talked for a few more minutes, said goodbye, and then I carried the books across the hall and began my search.

An hour later all I'd found was a small sponge, well used, a cap to a jar of tomato sauce, a pair of tweezers a lone sock, and a postcard from Florida from 1992. It was addressed to a woman named Linda Hendrickson at this same address. I also found thirty-seven cents in loose change and, my big find, two $100 chips from the Surf Casino.

I put the chips in my pocket and everything else in the garbage and left with the box of books. On the way out, I knocked on Larry's door. I was about to give up when it finally opened. He had a red robe on this time, and was wiping sleep from his eyes.

"Oh, sorry," I said. "I didn't mean to wake you up."

"It's okay," he said. "It's one of the drawbacks of working nights." He stepped to the side, but I stayed where I was, twiddling my thumbs in the hallway.

"You don't happen to work at a casino, do you?"

He almost jumped. "Now how the hell did you come up with that?"

"You do?"

He nodded. "The Surf."

"And that's where you saw Steve?"

"Uh huh."

"He was a gambler?"

"Like I said, I only saw him that one night. But I assume he was gambling." He lifted an open hand. "I don't know why else you'd come to eat at a casino."

FORTY-ONE

If you want to get thrown out of a casino in a hurry, walk in, start showing a photograph around and asking questions.

In less than five minutes, I was sitting in a windowless security office with uniformed guards on both sides of me. The guy sitting behind the desk looked like a mix between a high-end executive and a very old bulldog. He wore a dark pinstripe suit with a bright blue necktie that seemed to be tied tight enough to cut off circulation. He held my PI license in hand.

"This was issued years ago," he said.

"Right." I shifted in the chair, another in a long line of losers. The chair hadn't been designed for comfort.

"When they told me you were a P.I, I said it must be his first day." This cracked up the two goons. They couldn't keep the smiles off their faces. "Don't you think you should know better by now?"

"Look, he's dead." I felt foolish but I was in an admit-nothing mood. "What's the big deal?"

"Dead or alive, we do not give out information about our customers unless we are ordered to by a court of law after a very lengthy legal battle. We don't have a sign to that effect on the door because everyone else seems to understand."

"Okay," I said. "I'm sorry I bothered you." I held out my hand. "I'll just take my license and run along."

He handed me the license. "You're welcome to come back and play anytime. But please don't try a play like that again."

I left with my tail between my legs. Bulldogs. They'd get you every time.

I called Frank Stringfellow and he said he would put

his "best casino man," on the job.

"Also, I'm wondering if he spent some of those weekends in 'Vegas," I said. "You think you can check that?"

"Not a problem, Nick. But let me ask you a question. What the hell does Raven need you for, if I'm the one doing all the work?"

"We had a good time together in Paris," I said. "I think that's what it is."

"Just don't forget who you're working for," he said.

No. I knew, and I wasn't likely to forget. When I'd gotten myself tossed off the force, Frank had come to the rescue. I'd worked under his P.I. license for two years before I'd managed to get my own.

#

It was another nice day. I walked the two miles down to my office, and spent some time on my computer, looking at maps of the area west of Willow Springs. This was where Phil's car was last seen.

His friend Terry was right. The area was nothing but hiding places.

My phone rang. "Ellis says I can tell you about my uncle now," my squeaky sounding friend said.

"Which uncle is this?"

"The one in your picture," he said. This was the kid with the star and the gap in his teeth. The one Tommy Burroughs and Billy Daniels had used to set up the clerk at Sweet's.

"Everybody's looking for him now," I said. "What can you tell me that I don't already know?"

"I'll ask Ellis," he said, and the line went dead.

I punched in Terry Lopher's number. It was the first time he ever answered one of my calls. "I heard you were out," he said.

"Any luck? Anything new?"

"No. And I just rotated to afternoons. That's gonna make it harder to get anything done."

"Did you get out along Archer Avenue yet?"

"A bunch," he said, and he sounded excited for a moment. "You know what's buried out there? The waste from the Manhattan Project. It's the first nuclear waste dump site in history. You could probably hide 10,000 cars and still have room left over."

"Nothing else interesting?" I swiveled over to my computer and searched the map for a nuclear waste dump.

"There's a junk yard," Terry said. "Remember that movie, they leave the body in the car and turn it into a junk cube?"

"Vaguely."

"Anyway, they don't do the cube thing, the guy tells me. They flatten 'em like pancakes instead. I'm going out tomorrow to watch."

"What time?"

"I figured I'd get out there about ten."

"I'll meet you," I said. "Where's this junkyard?"

He told me, and then I zeroed in on my map. Pretty soon we'd never have to leave our chairs.

FORTY-TWO

I called Rita Cunningham and invited her to come along. "After the junkyard, we can canvas the neighborhood a bit."

"Why not?" she said. "I never manage to get to sleep in the morning anyway."

The next day, I parked on the side street behind the 15th District station. It was just after eight o'clock when Rita walked down the block towards me. She was in street clothes, a light leather jacket, jeans, and running shoes. But there was no bounce to her step. A night patrolling the West Side could make you drag your feet.

But then a bit of sunlight peaked through the clouds and caught her in stride. A smile creased her face. She brushed some hair away from her eyes, playfully stepped over the cracks on the sidewalk, and slid into my rent-a-dent, a Toyota which wasn't too battered. "What happened to that fancy SUV?" she said as I made a U-turn. "I would have bet you were a buy-American guy."

"I know there's an insult in there somewhere," I said.

A minute later we were following the curves of Jackson Boulevard through Columbus Park. "Even in the winter this is great," I said. The exquisite landscape always got to me. On our left was a 9-hole golf course, on our right a bridle path left over from the good old days, back in the early years of the last century, when you could rent a horse and go galloping along.

"Yeah, it's nice," she said. "Do you golf?"

"Oh, once or twice when I was a kid. How 'bout you?"

"I keep thinking it's for rich old men. But I never see many of those out here."

On the way southwest, I told Rita just about everything I knew about Phil Laubett. "He even helped me find you," I said. "He enhanced the red-light video when you were chasing that clown in the wig. That's how I got your beat number."

"And who's this guy we're meeting?"

"Terry Lopher," I said. "He grew up with Phil. Now he's on the job in Roger's Park."

"You're sure we trust can him?"

"Pretty sure," I said. "He wants to find Phil. He feels a little guilty." I told her my theory about Phil asking Terry to find out about Burroughs and Daniels, and eventually the information about Phil and his video store somehow getting to the wrong person.

"Well, you're right about one thing. Cops do love to talk," she said. "But I still don't quite believe someone would . . ."

"You're true-blue, alright."

"Yeah, maybe," she said. "But everybody defines that their own way. That's the problem."

We stopped for breakfast at a diner in LaGrange. I ordered an All-American breakfast, eggs, bacon, hash browns and toast. Rita, who'd been working all night, ordered half a grapefruit with a side of wheat toast.

She took a long look at my overflowing plate and decided not to comment. I watched her re-cut the grapefruit segments and returned the favor.

"And why the junk yard?" Rita asked over her coffee mug. "What's there?"

"Probably nothing." I told her about the sightings of Phil's car heading west on Archer Avenue.

"That's it," she asked, and she stole a few ice cubes from her water glass and dropped them in her coffee. "That's all you've got?"

I shrugged. "You gotta take what you find and work with it," I said. "That's something you're going to have to learn if you want to be a dick someday."

"What gives you the idea I want to be a detective?" She twirled the ice with one finger.

"Hell, you're talking to me. You showed that picture around. I can see it in your eyes."

She smiled. "I already took the test, but the list is about three miles long. There's a sergeant's test coming up. I'm thinking of taking it."

"You should wait," I said. "Otherwise, you're stuck." In Chicago, detective was the grade between patrolman and sergeant. If you became a sergeant without first being a detective, you'd probably spend your entire career in the patrol division. You'd never wear plain clothes.

FORTY-THREE

Mel's Scrap & Automobile Recycling was on a wedge of land between Archer Avenue and the Sanitary and Ship Canal. "I better park this thing out here," I said, and joined a couple of cars parked in a gravel strip along the fence line. "In case Mel gets the wrong idea."

Inside the yard, Terry Lopher stood with a tough looking old guy who wore grungy overalls. They were watching junk cars being turned into metal pancakes on a portable crushing machine mounted on the back of a huge flatbed trailer.

Terry introduced us. "This is Mel," he said. "He's been here since 1976."

"Meet Rita," I said.

While Rita and Terry warily circled each other, Mel gave me a handshake that might have crushed a subcompact. His white hair shot out the sides of his Make America Great Again hat.

"I've seen a lot of cars come and go but not that many Subarus," he said. "By god, I wish somebody'd drop a banged-up Forester. I'd squeeze $10,000 out of that baby."

"So, you would have remembered?" I said.

"Damn-straight, I would," Mel said. "You might want to talk to old Jack over there." He pointed towards the man operating the crushing machine, who looked quite a bit younger than Mel. "He goes from one yard to the next, all day long. But I already asked. He don't remember seeing none neither."

I walked over to the crushing machine. Rita and Terry stayed put. Terry looked very interested in his fellow cop. Rita seemed a bit wary.

Jack was playing some kind of game on his phone while waiting for the forklift operator to drop another car on top of the two he'd already crushed. He slipped the phone into his pocket and shook his head. He hadn't seen any Subaru Foresters in the past few weeks.

"You go to a lot of junkyards," I said.

"That I do," he said, and I could hear the forklift approaching behind me.

"You know any out this way that work the edge a bit?"

That got me a grunt. "Now a couple years back I would have had to lie to you. But with these new laws they got, even the biggest crooks are so busy stripping every damn part off these cars, hell, they ain't got time to steal."

"What new laws?"

"Laws that say you can't always use that cheap aftermarket shit. Sometimes you got no choice but to use the genuine part. That means you either got to buy it direct from Ford or Chevy for a thousand or so, or you come to old Mel here and give him a couple of hundred for one that's used. Mel built himself a brand-new house and got himself a fancy Mercedes Benz. It ain't junk no more. Recycling. It's heaven-sent. Hell, it's damn near gold."

"He bought a German car and he's wearing that hat?"

"Know what's even funnier?" The forklift operator dropped the car in the crushing machine. It sounded like a head-on crash. I had to wait for the sound to subside to hear the punch line. "His father got shot down over Dusseldorf in '44."

FORTY-FOUR

Terry draped a detailed area map over the hood of his pickup truck and we stood outside the junkyard coming up with a plan. Terry would go west towards Lemont, the old quarry town. Rita and I would go south and east.

"Maybe Rita should ride with me," Terry said.

"Why?" I asked. Could it have something to do with the fact that he couldn't take his eyes off her?

"Well, we're both on the job. You know, so . . ." He flashed a hopeful smile and looked to Rita.

Rita looked back without a hint of a smile, and then turned and waved a finger from me to her. "But we're partners, right?"

"Yep," I said. "I want to show her a bit about canvassing."

"Oh, well," Terry said. "Maybe next time."

"Maybe." Rita barely looked back. She wasn't making any promises.

"What's this?" I pointed to the map. Terry had put X's where he'd stopped and asked questions. One of the X's was circled.

"An old house, just in on a gravel road. I've been by twice. Nobody answers. But there's always a car out front. You guys will be close. Maybe swing by and try again."

We agreed to meet again for a late lunch. Rita and I drove around knocking on stranger's doors. It was a weekday, and many of those strangers had jobs.

"So how was it, being a detective?" Rita asked, as we waited on a front porch at a large house that backed up to a golf course.

"Best job I ever had," I said.

"You really don't think I should take the sergeant's

test?"

"You'll end up riding around by yourself telling guys to put their hats on and not to swear at the people. That's ninety percent of the job."

Rita leaned over the banister to get a better look in one of the windows. "Looks like nobody's home."

"You're divorced, right?" she said when we were back in the car.

"Uh huh," I said. But it had been so long now, I liked to tell myself I'd almost forgotten the entire marriage.

"Sucks, right?"

I lifted a hand from the steering wheel. "At least we didn't have kids." How many times had I said that in the past ten years?

Our next stop was at a house alongside a cemetery. Once again, nobody was home.

"You still hate her?" Rita asked a few minutes later, back in the car.

"I never did." I could feel my stomach rumbling. Maybe I'd try a grapefruit for breakfast some morning.

"So why?"

I shrugged. "Who knows?" Not me, that was certain.

I turned on to Archer Avenue. This was the road where Phil's car was last spotted.

"You lost everything," Rita said.

"Oh, I don't know," I said. "I like to think I still have my sense of humor."

"You miss it?"

This was a question that every cop eventually asked. I always pretended I had no idea what they meant. "What?"

"The job."

I shook my head. "Not anymore," I said, and I goosed the gas. We were in the middle of the Forest Preserves.

"But I miss this, having someone to talk to. It sure beats wandering around alone." This was my usual condition.

"Well, thanks," Rita said, and then, "Wait. Make a U-turn."

I followed directions. "Now what?"

"Slow down," she said. "Turn right." I turned onto a narrow gravel lane, heading into the woods. "Stop. Is that the house Terry was talking about?"

We both got out. It was a small wooden cabin that had probably been built the century before last. Three steps led up to a sturdy looking, one-chair porch.

Before we got there an old man came around the side of the house, pulling a garbage cart. He was a little guy, a bit pudgy, with a round face, dark hair and white eyebrows. He looked a bit like the man in the moon. "You can't park there," he croaked. "Pull it up ahead. You'll see the spot."

I got back in the car and found the pull off.

When I got back to the house, the old guy was looking at Rita's badge.

"Chicago, huh? Came all this way, huh? Must be something important."

Rita introduced us. I was her boss, she said. The old man was Bob Marsh.

Rita asked the questions this time. But we ended up with the same result. Marsh didn't remember anything special about the night in question.

"Where's this road go?" I asked.

"Nowhere. Just goes down a bit." He waved a hand back and forth. "But you gotta come out the same way."

"What's down there?"

"Swimming holes and old quarries. You should take a ride all the way to the end. Used to be sort of a lover's lane. Not anymore." He smiled and the man in the moon likeness disappeared. "Don't know what happened to all those old lovers."

"If somebody went down in the middle of the night, you'd probably hear them," Rita said.

"Oh, I sure would," Marsh said, "and I . . ." He stopped suddenly, and then turned away as his face darkened. "That's if-fin they ever did."

A few minutes later, we said goodbye and started down the gravel road. The leaves were gone from the trees, but the woods were still thick.

"Did you catch that?" Rita asked.

"He almost slipped up and told us something," I said.

"Slow down," Rita said after I'd picked up speed. She was looking out her open window. "I want to enjoy being out in the wilds. I get so sick of buildings. Don't you?

"Nothing like the wide-open spaces," I said.

"Oh, right," Rita said. There was nothing wide-open about this landscape.

Dead trees rotted where they fell. If there wasn't room to fall, they just leaned on their neighbors. There were patches of snow the sun would never find. I thought I saw some movement off to the left but by the time I looked it was gone. "I'll bet there're plenty of deer back here," I said. But the only wildlife I saw was a single black squirrel.

A little further on a sign on a chain link fence off to the right said KEEP OUT.   NO SWIMMING. NO FISHING. PRIVATE PROPERTY. Thick vines covered the fence and the gate from top to bottom. A rusty padlock dangled from a chain. But even if you got through the lock, you'd still have to spend quite a bit of time cutting vines. The gate hadn't been opened in years.

"I'd like to come back when those vines flower," Rita

---

said, and we continued deeper into the woods.

We came to another trail of gravel that went off to the left. I turned and we followed it for a few hundred yards and came to a small clearing where a large pile of rotting railroad ties served as a roadblock. You'd have a hell of a time getting a car over those. Ten feet beyond was a lake of murky water.

"This is silly," Rita said as we came to a stop.

"What?" I threw open the door and got out. We were far away from all the city noise. I could hear some early birds singing. Huge sagging spider webs hung between trees. "I wouldn't want to meet those spiders," I said and pointed.

"Probably caterpillars," Rita said.

"Really," I said. "So, what's silly?"

"The entire idea." Rita came around the car. "First that someone grabbed your friend. Second that they hid his car out here, and third that we might find it."

"Never gonna find it if you don't look," I said. This was rule-number-one. If you didn't get out of bed in the morning, nothing would happen that day.

I kicked a beer can into a shallow fire pit and picked up a charred piece of wood and pretended to examine it.

"What?" Rita said.

"Good place to roast marshmallows." I looked up. The water was dull and motionless, covered by a thin layer of scum.

"It's pretty desolate," she said. "I think I'd rather have my picnics a little closer to civilization."

We got back in the car and went back out to the main gravel road and started down again. A minute later, a bicyclist flew by about twenty feet in front of the car, going from left to right.

"Where'd he come from?" I asked and flicked on the

headlights. A new-looking sign said, 'Bike Crossing.' We crossed a trail wide enough for a couple of bikes abreast, and then continued on to the clearing at the end. This was the defunct lover's lane, according to the old man who lived up the road.

There was another cyclone fence and another bunch of signs forbidding this and that, and the other thing-- but they forgot to mention private eyes or pretty cops. Another bunch of railroad ties blocked a padlocked gate.

We parked, got out, and walked up the ties, which were laid out like shallow steps. Beyond the gate was another large pool of murky water. More ties served as a deck. This was the perfect place to sunbathe after taking a swim. But first you'd have to wash off the pond scum.

"I guess that's a quarry," Rita said.

"Think so," I said. "Lemont limestone. The rock that built Chicago."

"Look!" Rita whispered. "Eagles."

I looked up to see several large birds circling high overhead.

"Really? What are they doing here?"

"Looking for something to eat, more than likely."

"Speaking of which," I said, and my phone rang.

"My uncle can tell you who's in charge, Ellis says." It was the squeaky-voiced kid again. "He'll give you her name."

Her name? "In charge of what," I said.

"In charge of them B.B. boys," he said.

Could that have been a stutter? "Would you say that again?"

"The B.B. boys. That's what my uncle calls them, Ellis says."

"Can I talk to Ellis?"

"No. He says my uncle gonna call you. But before he

does, we got to talk about the reward."

"Okay. What do you want? Assuming your uncle gives me something good."

"Something for my mother."

"Okay. What?"

"A new home."

"Say that again." I looked up. Rita was standing next to me waving a foot-long twig. A couple of autumn leaves were still attached.

The kid on the phone said the same words again. "That's what she needs. Someplace away from these streets."

"I don't know," I said. "I'd like to help but that's a pretty tall order."

"You're the man. You're white. Ellis says you can do anything."

I looked at Rita and shook my head. "I wish that were true, kid," I said. "I really do. Come up with something else, okay?"

"My uncle, he gonna call," he said, and he was gone.

"Oh, goddamn," I said.

"What?" Rita said.

"You wouldn't believe it if I told you," I said, and started back for the car. "Hey, you ever heard of the B.B. boys? Something like that?"

"Yeah, when I first got to 15, I used to think they were talking about breaking and entering, B and E. Then I kept hearing it and realized it was B. B. or maybe B.B's. But I never figured out what it meant. I haven't heard it lately. Was this from that call?" Her twig was brushing her chin.

I leaned against the car. "This kid keeps bugging me. He says his uncle's the one with that star on his tooth. And he can tell me who's in charge of the B.B. boys. He'll give me *her* name."

"Oh, now that's interesting," she said, eyebrows raised.

"The only problem is, he wants a big reward." I stuck my phone back in my pocket.

"How much?"

"He doesn't want money. He wants me to get his mother out of that fucked up neighborhood."

"See," Rita said, as a single leaf floated to the ground behind her. "That's why I hate the job half the time. The poor kid."

"Oh, Rita," I said. "You can't let your heart get broken over every little thing. You'll never get anywhere."

Her eyes flashed. "It's not a little thing to him," she said, and she swung her twig at me. "He's trying to help his mother."

"Yeah, sure. Sorry." He was trying to help his mother but eventually he'd break her heart. I kept the thought to myself, but she must have heard it anyway.

"You know, I'm never going to be like you." She opened the passenger door of the car, then changed her mind and slammed it shut. "I might end up being a cop for 40 years but I'm never going to end up like you." She turned her back on me.

"What'd I do?" I waved my arms around, the last innocent man.

"You didn't do anything," she said. "That's just it."

"Oh, goddamn." This had been going on my entire life, one woman after another, and I could never figure out what they were talking about. I lifted my foot and took aim at the nearest bush. The bush didn't talk back, of course. Not for the first time, I wished I still smoked.

I spotted a beer can and gave it one kick and then another. I ended up on a narrow path, which curved along following the fence. I hadn't gone far when the fence stopped. A 10-foot section was missing. I kicked the can into the water and watched it float away.

The edge of the quarry was ragged. The limestone started a few feet down, the water a foot below that. I found a rock and tossed it in. I was still waiting to hear it land when Rita appeared next to me. "Be pretty easy to push a car in right here," she said.

"Yeah," I agreed. "But nothing went in this way recently. All we've got is a foot path."

"I'm not so sure," she said and climbed up on a fallen tree. "What do you think that is?"

I joined her for a look. It was another narrow path, and it followed that same curving line as the first. They were about four feet apart. From this vantage point it was easy to see the pushed down prairie grass. A car had been over the path sometime recently.

"No way to tell if it ever came back out," I said. "Could just be a couple of lovers."

"Sure," Rita agreed.

"They could have backed in. That's the way I'd do it. Then you've got the entire clearing right in front of you."

"And then when you hear the hook hand scraping your roof . . ." Rita said.

"Now I'll never get to sleep tonight," I said.

We walked back towards the Toyota. The sun had come out but was having a hard time breaking through the tangle of trees. A couple of streaks had found a broken beer bottle and was making it sparkle.

We got back in the car. Nobody said a word until we were almost back to the main road. "Stop," Rita said.

I stopped. She laid her twig on the dashboard and opened her door. "I'm going to ask Mr. Marsh if I can use his bathroom," she said.

211

"Can't you wait until we get to the restaurant?"

"I could," she said, and she closed the door and walked around and up the steps to the porch, and then disappeared inside the cottage.

I waited, and waited a bit more, and then went out and pissed on the side of a tree. After a while she was back. I started the car and pulled away.

"We're gonna be late for lunch," I said once we were heading southwest on Archer. "You get anything?"

"No. But he's hiding something for sure." She picked her twig off the dashboard and gave it a sniff.

"He's probably got a patch of marijuana somewhere in the woods," I said.

"Could be," she said. "I might come back and talk to him alone."

"Don't you dare," I said.

"You're kidding right?"

"About what?"

"You're too much, Nick." She lowered her window, stuck her head out, and started talking to the forest.

FORTY-FIVE

Terry looked conspicuous sitting all-alone in a booth in the Troubled Water Bar & Grill in downtown Lemont. "They were just about to evict me." He toasted us with a nearly empty beer.

I slid in next to him. Rita got the far side of the booth all to herself. "Sorry," she said. "It was my fault."

"I got nothing and more nothing," Terry said. "How about you guys?"

"That house you wanted us to check out," Rita said. "Turns out it's an old one-room schoolhouse."

"Really?" Terry said. He didn't sound very impressed.

"Yeah. I had a very nice conversation with the owner. He told us there was an old lover's lane down at the end of the road. You know what else we found down there."

He nodded. "A couple of fenced off quarries."

"Except one of them isn't really fenced off," Rita said.

"Really?" Terry said. Now he was interested.

"And we found tire tracks," she said.

Terry looked at me.

"Not really tracks," I said. "But there's a path and it sure looks like a car has been across it sometime this winter."

"I've got a friend who's a diver," Terry said. "He's on the list for the Marine Unit." These were the cops who patrolled the rivers and the lakes. "I could talk him into checking out the quarry if it's not too deep."

"If we're going to let every cop in town know what we're up to," I said. "We might as well call a press conference right now."

"No press," Terry said, using his empty beer for a

microphone.

"I agree." Rita agreed.

"Let's not be so impatient," I said. "Maybe we will use your friend. But what do you say we come back out tomorrow. Maybe we can find a couple of other places to search."

"I'm okay with that," Rita said, and looked towards Terry.

Terry shook his head. "Tomorrow's bad for me," he said.

"And there's another factor, too," I said to Terry. "You ever hear of the B.B. boys?"

Terry shook his head. "Who's that?"

"I don't know," I said. "But there's something funny going on out on the West Side. These little Ma and Pa corner stores keep losing their licenses. We think there might be some kinky cops involved."

My phone buzzed. I pointed to Rita and, as she started to talk, I slipped out of the booth and walked outside. I'd missed a call from Stringfellow.

"All right, Nick," Stringfellow said when he answered. "You're on the money again. The boy liked to gamble, an hour or two just about every night, blackjack, hundred-dollar table. Good player. Knew the odds. Won some, lost some. Tipped generously. Always polite. Went to Vegas every other weekend. It's gonna take a while to get that end checked out completely."

I looked around at the old western-style buildings. Wooden facades hid the peaked roofs. Before Lemont was a quarry town, it was a canal town. The Illinois-Michigan Canal was the last link of the waterway from the East Coast to New Orleans. And this was one of the boomtowns that helped build it.

"No personal angle," I asked.

"Not from the casino end. Maybe we'll find something in 'Vegas."

"Why don't you hold off on that end for a while." I'd left my jacket inside and was now regretting it. "Let me talk to Raven, tell him what we've got so far."

"We just got off the phone."

Suddenly I didn't need the jacket. "You called him?"

"Yeah, I figured I better give him a heads up. He is my client after all, and I wanted him to know who did the actual work here. Nothing personal, Nick, but if I don't toot my own horn, who will?"

"Gee, is it okay if I call him?"

That got me a forced laugh. "He wants you to call A.S.A.P."

"O.K.A.Y.," I said.

When I got back inside the food had arrived, but nobody was eating. Rita was looking down at an extra-large salad. Terry was staring at a club sandwich. I picked up my hamburger and was ready to dig in. Nobody else moved. I put the hamburger back down.

"So, they could sell more candy bars," Terry said after a while. "You really think that's what this is all about? That's what happened to Phil?"

"It had something to do with that tape and that shooting," I said. "And, yeah, I believe the shooting was about selling more candy bars. Well, probably mostly liquor, tobacco, and lottery tickets."

"That'll make Ginny and the girls feel better, I'm sure." Terry stabbed his sandwich with a toothpick.

"You know, we can just forget the whole thing," I said.

"Fuck that," Terry said.

"One way or the other, you're not going to make any friends on the force," I said.

"You think I give a shit," he said. "I didn't join up to cover for a gang of dirty cops. I hope they're the ones get buried."

I looked from one to the other. "Means we're all on the same page, right?"

Rita nodded. She watched Terry. Her eyes were gleaming. He nodded back.

"Fuck 'em," he said, his jaw set.

FORTY-SIX

When I called Al Raven, he invited me to stop by for a drink. He gave me detailed directions and told me to tell the guard at the gatehouse I was expected.

"The gatehouse?" I said after the call ended. What kind of assisted living was this?

Blue Skies Village looked nothing like a nursing home. Al Raven's bungalow was several blocks beyond the guard shack, on a quiet curving drive lined with ample one-story houses, attached garages, and wide, well-tended lawns. A golf course was out the back door. Beyond the course stood two five-story buildings.

Raven was waiting out front. He waved me into the driveway. "Thanks for coming, Nick," he said. I followed him into the house.

I whistled when I saw the living room. It was as big as my entire apartment. There was plenty of dark leather and well-polished wood. A stained-glass chandelier added just enough color. "And I was feeling sorry for you," I said.

"Pretty posh, huh?" Raven said. He moved behind a four-stool bar, which was set into a corner. "What'll you have?"

"Bourbon, if you've got it." I picked a high-back armchair.

"Makers, okay?" He placed two rocks glasses on the bar. They chimed when they touched.

"Sounds good," I said.

"I'll be sure to pick up some rotgut next time I shop."

"This'll do just fine," I said, as he placed the drink in my hand.

"I guess it's not that surprising," Raven said. "He liked money. So that's how he spent his time." He sat in a matching chair across from me.

"He also read a lot," I said. "Three-four newspapers every morning. Magazines. Books. He gave his across the hall neighbor a box of books. I've got them out in the trunk if you want to see them."

"You took the books back?"

"I borrowed them. I thought you'd be interested."

"Okay, thanks. But let's finish these first. And I want to talk a bit more about the gambling."

"Okay." I took a sip of the drink. It had come out of the right bottle.

"It doesn't sound like much of a life to me," Raven said, and he raised his glass to his lips.

"Maybe he enjoyed it," I said.

"You gamble?" He set his glass down on a side table in a circle of light cast by the chandelier. It looked like a whiskey advertisement in some fancy magazine.

"Years ago, I was in a steady poker game with a bunch of detectives. Other than that, no."

"But you're with your friends." He picked up his glass, took a sniff, then set it down without drinking. "He's sitting around in a casino with strangers. I don't get it."

"If we weren't all different, Al, there'd be long lines everywhere we went."

He picked up his glass again. This time he took a taste. "You know, I've been wondering about Steve since he was a baby. He always seemed to miss what was going on right in front of him. He lived in his head. It always seemed like a lonely place to me."

My phone rang. I looked at the screen, a blocked number.

"Go ahead answer," Al said. He held up his almost full drink. "I've got to catch up with you."

"Hello," I said into the phone.

"You been talking to my nephew," a very low voice said.

"I've been talking to your nephew?" I looked at Raven and shrugged.

"Showing my picture."

"I've been showing your picture?" And then I understood. "Okay. What you got for me?" I stood and walked over to the corner bar.

"You going to take care of my little man?" Silver Star asked.

"I'll do what I can," I said.

"No. No. That ain't even close."

"Do I look like a housing service?" Raven came up behind, dropped my drink on the bar, then went back to his seat. "And how do I know you really got something solid?"

"You want to know what the game was in that store?"

"It was a shakedown. I can see that on the video." I lifted my glass and took a sniff.

"It's bigger than that, man. Didn't you see that movie? Follow the money."

"Ain't much green in a corner store."

"B. B.'s boys," he said. "You know about them? You know who's in charge?"

"Not yet." I faced Raven, lifted my glass and took a drink. He did the same.

"You think about doing my nephew right, you'll know everything."

"Even if I could find him new digs," I said. "I gotta take your word, you're the star of that video."

"I can show you that," Silver Star said. "You keep thinking about that reward and I call you back." The line went dead.

"Oh, well," I said, and I put the phone away.

"That sounded interesting," Raven said. I dropped back into my chair.

"Supposedly it's the guy from the video, the one with the star on his tooth."

"You know you were sounding like a black guy there for a minute."

"Sorry. I had a partner who used to do that," I said. "Drove me nuts."

"It wasn't a very good imitation." He shook his head.

"Everyone's a critic," I said, and lifted my glass.

"So what'd he want?"

"He says he wants to tell me what was really going on at that store. And maybe he knows something worthwhile. But, if you remember that video, they sent him out the door pretty-damn fast."

"With the bottle," Raven said. "That was the first sign that something funny was going on."

"His nephew's been calling me for weeks. And he wants me to get his mother out of that fucked up neighborhood. I promised him a reward if his uncle came through. But finding them a new home, that's a little out of my reach."

"Can I touch up that drink?" Raven asked as he stood.

"Sure," I said. "But go light. It's a long way home."

After a bit, we walked outside. Raven pointed towards the two large buildings on the far side of the golf course. Lights were on here and there. They might have been hotels, or even hospitals. "They try to force me into one of those, I'm going to call you and your job will be to get me back to France. Maybe I'll try to buy my way into *Pere Lachaise.*"

I opened the trunk of my car and then the flaps of the carton.

Raven began picking through the books. "What the hell is this?" he said a minute later. He had couple of paperbacks in hand. "These are my books, my old books. How the hell. . . He must have gotten into my storage locker." He was pulling books out of the box and setting them alongside.

"You're losing me, Al."

"When I moved here, I put a bunch of stuff in storage. It's one of the advantages of owning a moving company, you don't have to throw your old junk out, you just put it into storage for free." He pulled another book from the box. "Some of these books are damn near 50 years old. I used to buy 'em in truck stops when I first started out. But how the hell did Steve end up with 'em?"

I reached in and grabbed a couple of books. "The Deceivers," by John D. McDonald and "One Tear for My Grave" by Mike Roscoe. Both had vivid, pulpy covers.

Raven hung his cane on the lip of the open trunk. He put the books he'd taken out back into the box and then picked it up.

"Al, let me get it," I said.

"The day I can't carry a box of books," he said. I grabbed his cane, closed the trunk, and followed Raven and the carton into the house.

He set the box on the coffee table. "This is very strange," he said. "But it'll be fun going through these again."

"Just remember, I promised to bring them back to his neighbor."

FORTY-SEVEN

Rita called at six in the morning. "I'm going to have to cancel," she said. We were supposed to head out to Archer Avenue in a few hours to search for more hiding spaces.

"Oh, well," I said. "Maybe we can get Terry back tomorrow."

"What do you think of him?" she said.

"He's pretty good. You know he didn't really want to get involved at all. But he was willing to follow the evidence."

"I sort of like his eyes," she said.

I couldn't stop a quick laugh. "Can't say I've noticed," I said, and rolled over and went back to sleep.

Several hours later, the phone rang again. "Remember that old man on that gravel road," Rita said.

Of course. I remembered asking her not to go alone. "Bob Marsh," I said.

"I know I went against your orders here, sir." She was talking fast now. "But I went out and talked to him. He said two cars went down the road that night, about one-thirty in the morning."

"What night?"

"The night your friend Phil disappeared. "

"Keep going." I sat up in bed.

"He said it's been happening as long as he can remember. Two cars go down the road in the middle of the night, and then a half hour or an hour later, one car comes back."

"He told you that?" I headed for the shower.

"Yeah. He said the headlights usually wake him up and he can't get to sleep until the car comes back. It's like living under a drunk and waiting for the other shoe to fall."

"When did the car come back that night?"

"He said it was a pickup truck this time, a pickup truck with a big chrome bumper on the front. It came back at two-fifteen. Alone."

"He have any idea what might have happened to the other car?"

"He said some of those quarries are more than 100 feet deep and full of murky water."

"And in all these years, he never thought to call the police?"

"He says he doesn't have any love for insurance companies."

"That's what he thinks they're doing?"

"Yeah, he says some cars are worth a lot more in the book than they are on the street."

"You feel like going swimming tomorrow?"

"You know I sort of do."

"Maybe you should call Terry and see if he can get his diving friend to come along."

"He keeps calling me," she said. "All I have to do is wait."

"Well, that's easy." I was fiddling with the shower and just about had the temperature set when one of my neighbors flushed their toilet.

"You really like him, right?"

"Sure," I said. "He seems like a good guy." Especially now that he was answering my calls.

"I'm sort of taken with him," she said.

"Really?" Lucky devil, I thought.

"I might ask him to marry me."

"Doesn't it usually work the other way around?"

"You know it's not the 50s, Nick. A girl can ask. Of course, I could wait for him to pop the question. But what if he doesn't do it?" The line went dead.

I put the phone down and slipped under the water.

FORTY-EIGHT

Al Raven and I met in that same restaurant in Arlington Heights and sat in that same booth in that semi-private room. "I had a crew spend half the morning digging through my storage containers," he said.

"And?" I tasted my first drink of the day, always the best.

"Steve got there first," he said. "It's funny. When he started reading, I was always trying to get him to try some of my books. But, as far as I knew, he never did. I don't know why he suddenly got interested in them. Maybe he was finally trying to understand his old man."

"Strange." I picked a cherry pepper from the relish tray.

"You probably couldn't even find most of those now, cheap paperback mysteries most of 'em. But they opened my eyes to a bigger world, if you know what I mean."

"Sure." I remembered the first time I read Nelson Algren and realized he'd gotten the city I lived in down on paper. My neighborhood looked nothing like the one Algren described but, somehow, I knew they were linked.

"I mean, there's some Hemingway in there and Jack London, some other big names. But mostly it's guys you probably never heard of. You could buy a book for a quarter or fifty cents back then. I was on the road for two and a half years. I'd be in some strange town where I didn't know a soul. I was always trying to save money, so I'd sleep in the truck even though there wasn't a sleeper. The books are what got me through. And they gave me the idea I could control my own destiny if I really tried. I didn't have to be a loser just 'cause my father was. And I didn't have to drive somebody else's truck either."

He paused to pick through the relish tray and finally settled on a carrot stick.

"Now Steve, he liked science fiction when he was a kid. And then later he read a lot of history, the Roman Empire and dynasties in the Far East, stuff that didn't interest me in the least. Now I'm thinking maybe I should have looked at some of those books. Maybe that would have made a difference. Maybe I would have understood him a little better. There weren't any other books in that apartment?"

I shook my head. "He cleaned it out," I said.

"He didn't want to be a bother to anyone," Raven said. "Let me ask you this, you think that next door neighbor would be willing to sell me my books back?"

"I'm sure he would."

"Price is no object. I'd really like to have them."

"I don't think we'll have to go too high," I said, and then I remembered the $100 casino chips in my pocket. "You know these would probably do it." I flipped them on the table like a real high roller. "I found them in Steve's apartment."

"The Surf? Is that the place you got thrown out of?"

That moved me back in my chair. "Where'd you hear that?"

He smiled. "Frank Stringfellow."

"The son of a bitch," I said. "He told you that?"

"He's afraid you're going to try to poach my business."

"He keeps telling me not to forget I work for him."

"I'm selling out as soon as I can," Raven said. "There won't be any business to steal."

"You're really gonna do it?"

"It's either that or go back to work full time."

"That's easy. Sell."

"Right." He took a sip of his drink. "And I'm going to have more money than I know what to do with. I always thought it would end up with Steve. I've got my grandkids, of course. We're not very close but blood is blood." He picked up one of the casino chips and spun it with a finger. "So anyway, I've been thinking, we work with several relocation firms. They're kind of a one-stop operation for people who are moving, usually long distance. They'll find you a mover and, since we're the best, that's me. They'll buy your old house for you, so you don't have to go through all the hassle of selling it, and help you find a new one in the right neighborhood. They'll help your spouse find a job in the new town, schools for the kids. You get the idea."

"Sure."

"So, I could probably get you a house."

"Well, thanks," I said. "But I'm pretty happy in my little cave." I looked into his eyes and tried to telegraph my thoughts: Did you ever think about cash instead?

"Not for you, Nick." He put an end to my dreaming. "For the kid who wants to get his mother out of that neighborhood."

"You're gonna buy her a house?" I drained my glass.

"Sure," Raven said, as if he were talking about the next round. "Why not?"

I could have given him several reasons. The look in his eyes told me not to bother.

He held up his glass. "One more to cinch the deal?"

———

FORTY-NINE

On the way back into the city, Terry called to tell me his diver couldn't make it tomorrow. We'd have to wait one more day to see what we might find at the bottom of that Lemont quarry.

A half hour later, I was standing outside Rent-a-Dent looking at the enticing glow coming from the Third Base Inn across the street.

"Not tonight," the angel on my right shoulder said. *"Walk home. You need the exercise."*

"Just have one," the angel on my left shoulder whispered.

The phone rang before I could make my pick.

"No more slo-mo," Silver Star said. "We rollin' tonight or we ain't rollin'."

"Tell me where," I said, and turned back towards Rent-a-Dent.

"You taking care of my little man?"

"It's in the works," I said. "You giving me something good?"

"Good?" he said. "You're getting more than good, you getting dynamite."

"Where?"

"You come down Ohio Street," he said. "It's right in the middle between Chicago Avenue and Franklin. "

I felt that little shiver I'd come to trust. "No side streets," I said. "Not after the sun goes down."

"Okay, good to be careful. How about Franklin, just past Homan? Give you plenty of room to escape."

"And then?"

"We ride around, and I show you a bunch of empty corners. What's your ride?"

"Call me back in five minutes and I'll let you know."

228

I walked back into Rent-a-Dent as Caitlin was dousing the lights.

"You know Nick, you're not our weirdest customer," she said, "But you're pretty damn close." She tossed me a set of keys. "Take the Ford Focus out front. We just got it. You can put in the first new dent. We'll do the paperwork tomorrow." The lights went out.

#

At my office, I opened a file cabinet and then a thick folder that said "Misc. Insurance." I pulled out a 5-shot Smith and Wesson .38, checked the load, and then turned to leave. Both angels spoke at once. I went back to the file and got the small ankle holster with the 2-shot derringer inside.

I took the boulevard route out. These were a series of wide, tree lined streets, where the rich had lived a century ago, before they'd escaped to the suburbs. Now most of the boulevards were in marginal neighborhoods. None more marginal than Franklin, which besides losing the rich, the middle class, and most of the working poor, had also lost most of its trees.

I slowed as I passed Homan. A guy with his hand up to his mouth started my way. He lowered the hand, and I noticed the dark gap next to a silver star. The hand went back up and then came down, and now a set of gleaming white teeth filled that hole. Even the star was gone.

I stopped, reached out and unlocked the passenger door, and he slid into the front seat. He'd lost weight since he'd appeared in that video.

"Nice teeth," I said.

"Make a U-turn," Silver Star said, and the scent of breath mints filled the air. "Left on Kedzie."

"Used to be a little store, right here," he said as we waited for the light at Kedzie to change. "Burned to the ground one night." It was now an empty lot. A few blocks up, he pointed to the wreck that used to be Sweet's Mini Mart. "You know about this one," he said as we passed. As we continued our tour, he pointed out several more sites where corner stores had once stood.

We were on Chicago Avenue, silently passing the People's Food Store, that tiny store in a trailer. "They missed this one," I said.

"Oh, hell that ain't no store," he said. "No potato chips, no dip. That woman's crazy. Now I'm gonna show you where all those people who used to shop at all these empty places shop now. But we gotta go by quick . . ."

"'Cause there's always a cop in front at the 24-7."

"You're pretty good at your job, huh?"

"So who owns it," I said. "That's what I need."

"B.B.'s boys," he said, and he drummed the dashboard, two beats.

"Who's that?" I asked.

"B stands for Barbara."

"Barbara Yates," I guessed. This was the Tactical Sergeant in the 15th District that had been looking for the man sitting right besides me.

The 24-7 was doing business. The parking lot was crowded but the only one hanging out front was a single patrol officer. He had his back to us, watching the action inside the store.

"You real good," Silver Star said. "But that Yates. That's her new name. See that comes from her new husband. You gonna tell me the old name now?" He turned both hands like a teacher prompting a class.

"Whalen," I said. She was John Whalen's daughter.

"That don't make any sense." A single beat on the

dashboard. "It got to begin with a B." He pointed for me to make a right turn.

I followed his direction. "Sense or not, that's the name she was born with."

"How's Barbara Burroughs sound?" Two beats.

"You're telling me she was married to Tommy?"

"Uh uhh." He shook his head. "His big brother Ray. He's dead too."

"Well, well, well," I said. "And you're telling me Barbara Yates owns that store we just passed?"

"Her and the last brother. And they got other stores too."

"And they sent you into Sweet's with that bottle."

"Sweet's, and other places."

"And you're willing to testify?"

"Won't need no testifying. I show you something that put her away forever. Just keep going straight. I tell you where to turn."

We were on Sacramento Boulevard. I continued along past the old Kraft Food site--I wondered if this the birthplace of a billion boxes of macaroni and cheese--and under a viaduct.

"Make a U-turn and come back in that lane on the right." He drew a backward U in the air.

I made the U-turn into a high-clearance truck lane. "Where're we going?" I asked as we went back under the viaduct. A narrow street went off to the right. Straight ahead, the lane merged back into the main boulevard.

"Turn right," he said.

I slowed to look at the street, really a dark lane that climbed a hill and disappeared. A sign read: UNION PACIFIC RAILROAD COMPANY. I hit the brakes and felt that familiar tingle. "What's up there?"

"It's where the trucks go. It's what I got to show you."

I pulled my .38 out and set it on my lap.

"That's cool," he said. "Better safe than sorry." He reached into his own jacket.

"Hold it!" I put a hand on the gun but I'd never been very good left handed.

"Just getting something to drink," he said.

"Slowly. Slowly."

He pulled out a half pint of Vodka. "Now you got me sweating," he said, and pulled a handkerchief from the same pocket.

Lights came up behind. High beams flashed.

I started into the turn. Out of the corner of my eye, I saw the bottle tilt upwards. But it didn't go to his mouth. Before I could process that, he reached out and stuck the very wet handkerchief in my face.

I swung the gun his way, pulled my head away from the handkerchief, and pushed down on the gas. Those high beams flashed again, and then all the lights went out.

FIFTY

"What we waiting for?" I heard a familiar voice say in a thick fog. I'd obviously had too much to drink.

"Just sit tight," came the answer.

"I'm sick of sittin'."

"Hey, you want to be back there with him?"

"I'm just saying."

"Don't!"

Snap. The radio went on, heavy metal music.

"Oh, man," I heard Silver Star say under his breath. He was the one who was sick of sitting. Back where? I wondered.

I opened my eyes. I was on my back looking up at the dome light of a car. I was wedged between the front and back seat of a small car. My hands were bound together. My face burned. A sweet chemical smell lingered in my nostrils. I was shivering cold, trying to remember a day long ago.

I was with my uncle, one of those sub-zero days in the heart of winter. The hood of his old Packard was open in the garage. He carried the battery in from the house, wrapped in a grungy blanket, set it in place, and then handed me an aerosol can. He pointed towards the carburetor. "When I give the signal, you spray right there. Hold it for one, two, three, and by that time you'll hear this old engine rumbling. You know, Nicky my boy, we never had to do this with horses back in the old days."

The odor stayed on my gloves for days. Ether, that's what was in the can. That's what I was smelling now. I suddenly remember Silver Star and his wet handkerchief. *Did I get a shot off? Where was my gun?*

It had to be gone, probably with the tough guy up front. *Was this my Rent-a-Dent?* I tried to move my legs.

They were tied too. I couldn't move them apart, but I managed to rub them together. The ankle holster was still there, the derringer tucked inside. Two shots. Tough guy first and then Silver Star if he wouldn't listen to reason. But how would I get my hands free?

"Okay, hang tight." The driver's door opened. "How do you like your coffee?"

"Cream and sugar," Silver Star said. "Lots of both." The door closed.

Silver Star twirled the radio dial and got nowhere. What was he looking for? Something else horrible, I was sure.

Where the hell were we? I tilted my head back and saw a gas station sign against the night sky. I tilted it the other way. "Huck Finn Donuts." Some of the best donuts in town, right there on Archer Avenue. I had a pretty good idea how this ride was supposed to end.

Turn the fucking radio off! I want to talk to you.

And a miracle happened. He read my mind. The radio went off.

"They're going to kill you, too," I shouted. My voice came out in a hoarse whisper. I felt slightly drunk.

"What?"

"You heard me. They could have got me anytime, at home, at the office, at the saloon. They knew where to find me. I wasn't the one hiding. You were. You think they used you to get me. It's the other way around. They used me as the bait to get you. Bring us Acropolis and all is forgiven. And you believed them."

"Shut up!" His hand flashed above me as he banged the back of the driver's seat.

Nearby, a car pulled in with a loud rumble. "I hear another car," I said. "But I don't think it's a car. I think it's a pickup truck with a big chrome bumper on the front. You know what that bumper's for?" As I said it, I realized the truth. "It's to push this car with both of us inside straight into a quarry full of water." I wondered if we'd have much company down below---or would it just be my old pal Phil?

"Look, I'm trying to go straight, man. But I gotta get these fuckers off my back. And they wanted you."

"You're a fool if you believe them," I said. "And you're gonna be a dead fool if you don't listen..."

He banged the seat again. "Shut up! Here he comes."

"When he asks you to drive, ask yourself . . ."

The door opened. "Coffee and donuts. Got a half dozen assorted. But don't make yourself sick."

"Don't want no donuts!"

"What the hell are you mad about?"

"Donuts for pussies and cops."

"Careful," the driver said and put the car in gear. So, the tough guy's a cop. But it's not Craig or Swanson. It's not Barbara Burroughs or Yates, whatever her name is. I wondered if Silver Star's story was true at all. "Well, if you change your mind . . ." And the bag came sailing and landed on the seat behind me. "Did he wake up?"

"No."

"Maybe he needs some coffee," he said, and some hot coffee landed on my head. I groaned and tried not to move. "You might have overdone it with that shit."

"The man was trying to shoot my ass."

"You better pray he doesn't die," The cop said.

"Shit, he gonna die anyways, right?"

Tough guy didn't answer. He kept me in suspense about my own future. "So that's how you figure it, huh?" he finally said. And I could almost hear him wondering what else Silver Star might have figured out.

FIFTY-ONE

Was this my last case, I wondered as we headed southwest on Archer with bright lights following us all the way. I knew it was the pickup truck, the one with the shiny chrome bumper. But who was behind the wheel? Was it Barbara Yates? Would she do her own dirty work or was she still following her father's advice, keeping her hands clean.

This wouldn't be a very successful conclusion to my checkered career, I decided. But at least I knew the truth now. I could whisper it directly to Kate Daniels, if I ever found her in the great beyond. Billy was helping Tommy who was helping his ex-sister-in-law Barbara shut down corner stores so they could make more money from the much bigger stores they owned. Is that clear, Kate? It was all about nickels and dimes, thousands and thousands of them, and that weight landed on Billy. He wasn't having an affair, and he didn't want a divorce. He was trying to break up with the police department. But that's very hard to do, especially if you're thinking of turning in your own partner. It's usually not done. In fact, it's almost unheard of.

Would the kids finish the case for me? Rita and Terry, would they see it through? Could they pull it off without the help of the Feds or the newspapers or somebody big downtown? Would they be willing to throw the dirty laundry on the street where the entire city could see it? Or would they turn away and stay true-blue?

Would they find me in this car down at the bottom of the quarry?

Al Raven. He was going to miss me. I'd done okay with a case that shouldn't have needed a private eye at all. A family book club about 40 years ago might have made a world of difference. Would Al think I'd just walked away? No. He knew me better than that. Plus, I hadn't submitted a report or my final bill. We regret that we must charge our friends, but we find that our enemies do very little business with us.

Rita. Rita and Terry probably. I'd seen the look in his eyes outside that junkyard. If Rita was serious, she probably wouldn't have too hard a time convincing Terry to go along, and now I was going to miss the wedding. Too bad. There was nothing as wild and crazy as a good old-fashioned two-cop wedding. But please make sure all the cops check their guns at the door and, as an extra security measure, frisk the dancers before they go out on the floor.

And then we left the lights of the city behind. The bright lights of the pickup stayed in place behind us. It wouldn't be long now.

If it wasn't Barbara Yates in that pickup truck, maybe it was Swanson and Craig. No. It was hard to believe that homicide dicks would be involved in anything like this. The cream of the crop. When your day ends, ours begins. *Please pick three assignments in order of preference.* I picked Area 4 Homicide, Area 6 Homicide, and Area 1 Homicide. I'd been so proud those first couple of years. Swanson and Craig. They didn't look proud. They looked old and tired. They looked like they'd given up.

Cut the number of dicks and increase the caseload. How did that work out? Now you've got a 17 percent clearance rate. Congratulations Mayor. They said it couldn't be done but you did it. In 83 percent of Chicago murders no one was even charged, much less convicted. The 17 percent, those were the guys found with the gun still in their hand and the victim at their feet. Who says you can't get away with murder? That must be some other city they were talking about.

And where were the watch commanders and the chief of detectives? There couldn't be doing much if Swanson and Craig could waste days following me around.

I'd been wiggling my hands all the while. They were bound at the wrist and around my waist. I'd gotten the binding a bit looser. But what was it? Rope burned. Handcuffs dug into the skin. Duct tape caught your arm hairs. That's what I was feeling. That's what was holding me in place. Everybody's favorite tape, good for everything but air conditioning and heating ducts, its original purpose.

I twisted my body a bit and got my hands under the back seat. I found a latch of some kind. I got my fingers locked around it and managed to pull myself a half-inch closer. I found no sharp edges. What would happen if I unlatched it? Would the seat spring up? No. My body was tight against it. Okay, I gave it a try. The seat moved just a bit. The bag of donuts rustled and that quick the radio went back on. Was Silver Star trying to muffle my movement? A sharp edge was revealed. Could I get my wrist to it? I'd have to lift the seat to make enough room and that meant getting my big, overweight body, out of the way. And even if I managed that without alerting the guy behind the wheel, whoever was in that pickup truck would probably see me moving in their bright lights.

That concealed derringer wasn't going to do me any good if I couldn't get to it.

The turn signal came on, and we turned off the smooth asphalt of Archer Avenue onto that rough gravel surface. The two sets of lights would shine into the old one-room schoolhouse, starting a clock with a very fast second hand, and Bob Marsh, the old man who looked a bit like the man in the moon, would sit up in bed and wait for the big truck to come back all alone.

FIFTY-TWO

"Man, this is like Mars or something," Silver Star said as we moved slowly down the gravel road. He sounded a bit shaky.

"You should see it during the day. It's almost as bad."

"Where's it go?"

"Just down a ways. Oh, that's funny. You'll see."

They had to stop before the end. Tough guy had to get out, and they had to do something about Silver Star. They couldn't leave him conscious and untied or he might just swim away.

Unless I was the only intended victim?

We kept moving, going deeper and deeper into the woods, and now I had to take the chance. We were getting closer and closer to that watery grave. I unhooked the latch, twisted my body, and let the seat rise enough to get my hands underneath, holding it in check with my head.

Lights flashed behind us. They had seen me moving? The car stopped. "Hold on," tough guy said. "Let me see what she wants." A door opened and closed. We couldn't be too far from that played out limestone quarry.

She.

"When he comes back," I whispered, "he's gonna ask you to get behind the wheel and that . . ." I cut the tape with the sharp edge, talking all the time, reached down, lifted my pants leg, and grabbed hold of that tiny gun.

A "Shhh," came from Silver Star and I froze in place. A moment later the door opened again. My legs were still tied together but I had two shots, and my hands were free.

But tough guy didn't get back behind the wheel. He

239

stayed outside, where he could look down at me if he wanted. "Hey, slide over here, L. You're gonna drive."

"Me? I can't drive."

"Shit. The first time I arrested you was in a stolen car. You drove it right into a fire hydrant."

"See what I mean?" He sounded very shaky. Maybe he was beginning to believe me. "And I ain't got no license."

"Get the fuck over here." Tough guy growled.

"I'm coming. I'm coming."

"I'm gonna walk ahead with a flashlight. Follow me but stay the fuck off my heels. You got it?"

The door slammed shut.

"Don't get too close to him," I said, as we started up. "There's a bike path right before the end of this road. That's how we're getting out of here."

"A bike path. You crazy?"

"It's too narrow for that pickup." That was my hope, anyway. "Where is he walking, right or left?"

"He's kind of in the middle, waving the light around. Maybe more to the left."

"When you see the bike path turn left." That would give him less of an angle if he decided to shoot. I held my own gun with two hands. I'd had bigger squirt guns when I was a kid.

"We're gonna drive a car on a bike path?"

"There's a little sign off to the right, just before it, picture of a bike. Tell me when you see it."

"I'm thinking maybe I'll just keep straight." His confidence was coming back.

And maybe I'll shoot you in the head. But where would that get me?

"Don't be stupid," I said. "They're going to kill you. And remember your nephew. You got to get his mama a new house."

"Oh, come on, man. You don't really think I believe that shit."

"It's all set. She's gonna get to pick where she wants to go. Now tell me when you see that sign."

"There it is!" he said a moment later.

"Okay, turn easy and as soon as you straighten out hit it."

The car continued straight at the same steady pace. *TURN!*

I thought he'd changed his mind. But then he turned a bit too fast. The rear end slipped on the gravel, fishtailed, and then straightened out. "Now step on it," I shouted, and the car took off.

"Man, ain't no fucking room," Silver Star shouted as I unhooked the latch again.

I pushed the seat up and forced my body into a sitting position and then reached down and ripped the tape that was holding my legs. We were scraping trees and being beaten by bushes, bouncing along. Shots rang out behind us.

"They behind us."

I closed the seat and then looked back as I pulled myself up to the seat. The headlights were a hundred yards behind us and were falling further back. The pickup truck was way too wide for the lane.

"A bridge!" Silver Star shouted.

I turned. A narrow bridge went over a creek. It was twice as long as it was wide. Cement pillars on either side at the front would stop the pickup truck dead.

"Never make it," Silver Star shouted.

"Hit it fast," I shouted back. "Don't worry about the car. Faster! Faster!"

Silver Star floored the gas pedal. Sparks flew on both

241

sides. Metal rattled. And then we were across. No way was that big, fat, ugly, pickup truck getting across that little bridge.

"Where's this path go?" Silver Star said. He'd calmed down a bit.

"It's gotta go somewhere." I leaned over the front seat and peered ahead. There was no end in sight.

"You tell me to follow the bike path and you don't know where it's goin'?"

A few minutes later, we came out above a parking lot around a picnic grove. We were in the Forest Preserves, somewhere south of Archer Avenue.

"Turn your lights off," I said. "And pull over there." I pointed off to the right, towards a small clearing that sat behind a cluster of thick bushes.

The lights went off.

"Keep your foot off the brake. We don't want any lights."

"Why you the one giving orders?"

I held up the derringer and braced it against the passenger head rest. "And I'm sitting behind you," I said.

"Man, you full of surprises," he said. "What are we waiting for?"

"See, if they come up that street out there. They know this area better than we do. They might be waiting for us to come out. Hey, you have a phone?"

"I got one, but it needs a charge. How about I put my Superman cape on, and fly us away," he said "Lights!"

The lights were in the woods, bouncing along the same way we had come.

"They must have gone around, probably right through the creek," I said. "They're not going to see us. Watch. They'll go right past." That was my prayer.

"Bicycles!" Silver Star shouted.

"Wow!" Four bikes came shooting out of the woods, their lights bouncing up and down. Four riders in a pack, helmets and fancy spandex. They were peddling as if their lives depended on it. Maybe they'd heard the shots. When I turned to follow their path down along the edge of the parking lot, I saw the pickup pulling into the parking lot without lights.

"Look!" Silver Star saw it too.

"They thought the bikes were us," I said.

"Here they come."

The pickup truck waited until the bikes passed, then jumped a curb and started back on the bike path. A single headlight came on. The big bumper had failed to protect the other light.

"Don't breathe," I said as they approached.

"Man, you an old lady," Silver Star whispered. "Would you shut the fuck up?"

The pickup passed no more than 100 feet in front of us, beyond that wall of thick vegetation. The surviving headlight shone on the chrome bumper. The truck was extra-long, with a king size cab and an extra seat in back. I couldn't see who was inside.

"Wait a minute," I said as the truck disappeared into the woods. "Can you get it going without hitting the brakes?"

"Like this?" he said, and the car began to roll.

We went through the parking lot and came out to a street. The pickup must have come from the left. "Turn right," I said. "And turn your lights back on. We don't want to get pulled over out here."

"You sure about that?"

"You ready to start trusting cops again?"

"Where are we?"

243

"Damned if I know. Let's just keep going till we find a cross street. Hey, is my phone up there by any chance? Check the glove box."

He leaned over and opened the box. "Nice dream," he said.

A few minutes later we found 123rd Street. We turned left but were still in the woods. After a bit, civilization appeared, gas stations and shopping centers. "See if you can spot a pay phone," I said.

Who would I call? Rita and Terry's numbers were in my phone. How could I get in touch with them? I knew a few numbers by heart. Shelly's. Stringfellow's. Lenny's. He was probably my best choice. Lenny, who had called in the favor I owed him and was probably now regretting it. Did that mean he now owed me a favor? Lenny, who had never called back after I'd dropped that tape in his lap. But he'd gotten me off the merry-go-round. Did that make us even?

We couldn't find a phone. The entire world got cell phones in case of emergency and now if you lost your phone, or somebody blew up all the cell towers, there were no pay phones to help when that imaginary emergency actually arrived.

"Let me get up front," I said at one point. Silver Star pulled over but then I couldn't open either door. The trees and the bridge had hammered them shut.

"Oh, fuck it," I decided and sat back. "Nice to be chauffeured for a change."

"Just so you know, I ain't got no license, man."

I patted my back pocket. My wallet was gone. "Me either," I said.

We came to an entrance ramp to the Tri-State tollway. This was the bypass around Chicago. The city I was now afraid to enter. We took the ramp heading north and a few miles later pulled into a service area, an oasis.

Silver Star managed to kick his door open. I almost got stuck climbing out the window. "Wish I had my camera," Silver Star said. "I'd make you a star."

FIFTY-THREE

I patted my pockets. My phone and wallet were gone but I still had my keys and some of my money, a twenty, a five, and two singles. How had they missed that?

The keys were worthless. I couldn't go home or to my office. That's where they'd be waiting. If the B.B.s had wanted me dead before, they'd want me even deader now. They knew I had Silver Star, and what he knew might send them all away. My derringer wasn't much in the way of protection, two shots against the entire police department.

"Come on," I said to Silver Star. "I'll buy you a cup of coffee." We walked inside and down the hall past a row of pay phones to the McDonald's. "What's your name, anyway?" I asked as we waited in line.

He winked. "Ellis."

"So, you're not the uncle," I said. "You're what?"

"That's my little brother you been talking to." He dribbled an imaginary basketball and bumped the guy in front of us. "Sorry," Ellis said. The guy looked around, and then quickly turned back front. He was next in line.

"He sounds like a nice kid," I said.

"He is." He put his hands together like a priest praying and looked to the ceiling. "I got to save him from them streets."

"What happened to you?"

"Man, you don't know what it was like when I came up."

"Probably not," I said. I pointed at his chest. "You testify against Barbara Yates and her boys, your little brother's gonna get his house. Keep that in mind."

"Shit, wait years for a trial. He gonna want his reward way before that."

"Okay," I said. "But you gotta give me everything.

The whole truth and nothing but the truth."

"That wasn't the deal."

"It's the deal now," I said. "And then you're going to have to give it to the police, too."

"The police?" He rolled his eyes. "Who you think that was, goin' kill you?"

"The FBI then," I said.

"Oh, fuck them. That's a TV show."

"You can start by telling me. I'll write it down and you can read it back and sign it, then you won't have to talk to anyone."

"Ain't signing nothing."

That was okay, I decided. I didn't have a notebook or a pen, they were somewhere with my .38, my wallet, my phone, and the rest of my money. "Just tell me what you know." I said, and then gave up. "How do you want your coffee?"

What was in that notebook? All I could remember was my inventory of Steve Raven's apartment. And then I was patting my pockets again. My two poker chips were gone. I'd been rubbing them together like good luck charms. They hadn't worked very well. On the other hand, maybe they had. I wasn't at the bottom of that quarry.

I paid for the coffees and got a couple of dollars in change. We found a table at a window overlooking the highway, just across from that row of pay phones.

"Man, everybody in a hurry," Ellis said. "You ever notice that?"

I looked down. It was mainly big trucks speeding by, probably trying to get around town before everyone woke up. Two pickups shot by out in the fast lane, one behind the other. Neither had a chrome bumper.

"So, what you want to know?" Ellis said.

247

"For starters, who was in that pickup?"

"B and B," he said.

"They got real names?"

"Barbara and Corny Burroughs."

"The last brother?"

"That's the one."

We took a break while he poured four packets of sugar into his coffee cup.

"So Corny. Is he a cop, too?" I asked, as he stirred the mix.

"He tried but he couldn't pass the psychological. So, he's a Cook County Sheriff."

"And he's a partner in those stores?"

"Far as I know." He took a long drink of coffee.

"And who was that riding up front with you?"

He showed me a face full of disgust and shook his head. "Frank James."

"Another relative?"

"Don't know."

"But he's a cop?"

"Oh, yeah." He pointed a forefinger my way, then brought the thumb down and fired away. "He's proud of that."

An air horn sounded nearby. I looked down as two huge trucks passed side by side. "You said there were three stores?"

"Three for sure. Could be more."

"Where?"

He pointed straight down. "The one you know on Chicago, another one on Chicago--the 365, out west near the bus turnaround, and one way south on Racine. I was only there once so I can't say where exactly."

"You worked for 'em?"

"I did favors for them." He held up one finger. "I sold

248

to them." Another finger. "Most of the times I was there I was dropping off a load." He clunked the tabletop.

"What kind of favors?"

"You seen my movie, right?"

"What'd you say you were dropping off?"

"Cigarettes or whisky. Usually both. That's what they liked."

"Where'd you get the stuff?"

"Sometimes I stole it myself. Sometimes I bought it off some other thief. Didn't make no difference to B.B.s. "

"You're putting me on." This sounded a bit like the old Summerdale Scandal, where the cops had acted as lookouts for burglars, way back in 1960.

"About what?" he said.

"Stolen cigarettes and booze." It wasn't just hard to believe, Silver Star/Ellis seemed a little too forthcoming.

"That's what they wanted and that's what I got 'em," he said. "No Indiana shit either. Everything had to have Chicago tax stamps."

We sat there sipping coffee, watching the traffic pass.

"You ever use a U-Haul truck?" I asked.

"Nice thing about rentals." He gave me a big smile. "People careless with those keys."

After a bit, the sky brightened. Dawn was coming. It was time to make my phone call.

For some reason, the call I really wanted to make was to Al Raven, my new best friend. But, once again, I didn't know the number. I'd have to wait for Raven Moving and Storage to open. But what could Al do, besides give me a suburban hideout. What would he say if I brought Ellis along? What would the guard at the gatehouse think?

Rita would be getting off work at seven. That's who I wanted to talk to, I decided.

"You got a safe place to go?" I asked.

Ellis reached into his pocket and came out with a phone. "If I could find somewhere to charge this thing."

"How about protective custody? Would that interest you?"

"Sounds like jail."

"The difference is, you can leave whenever you want and the food's better. But if you're really tied to that double homicide in Austin, then all bets are off."

He put a hand up like he was swearing on a bible. "I didn't do no double homicide. Not in Austin. Not anywhere. No singles. No triples." The hand came down and he pointed a finger at me. "You a fool if you believe that shit."

"And you'd have to testify."

"Against who?"

"The ones who just tried to kill you," I said. "Remember?"

"I'm still not sure that was the game," he said. "I keep thinking I should have just gone straight."

"That's what you should have done about ten years ago."

He made a pillow with his hands. "I could be sleeping right now."

"In the bottom of a limestone pit," I got up. "I'm gonna make a call."

I dropped two quarters in the phone, dialed Lenny's number, and then a recorded voice asked for even more money. Lenny answered on the second ring. He sounded wide-awake, and not very happy to hear from me. "What now?"

"Is that any way to greet an old friend?" I turned my back on the phone. Ellis was staring into his coffee.

"Sorry," Lenny said. "It's just every time your name

comes up lately, it seems to be bad news."

"Here's some more," I said. "Barbara Yates tried to kill me a while ago."

"Oh, boy," he said, and he took a long break. "But, you know, if you're looking for a motive, she was married to Tommy Burroughs' brother for a while. Maybe she didn't like that video that someone dropped. What happened?"

"I don't have much in the way of evidence. That's what I'm working on now. I just wanted to give you a heads-up." I told him about the Burroughs' family stores, and all the stores they'd run out of business.

"Can you prove any of that?" he asked.

"You should be able to track ownership of those stores," I said. "I've got an accomplice that might be willing to testify." I looked back at our table. Ellis was staring into his dead phone. "He sold them stolen cigarettes and booze at three different stores. He also helped set up some of the stores that lost their licenses. I thought you might want to offer him protective custody."

"I'd sort of like to stay in the background on this, if you don't mind. I can tell you who to call."

"Can you do me one small favor?"

"I'm listening," he said.

"I need the phone number for Officer Rita Cunningham. She's in 15. I'm pretty sure she's working right now."

"That's the officer I met, right?"

"Yeah. I lost her number when they took my phone. I guess they figured I wouldn't need it down at the bottom of the quarry they were gonna push me into." I looked up. Ellis was gone.

"Okay. That should be easy enough. You want me to

call you back?"

"I'm at a pay phone. I'm not sure it takes incoming calls."

"Just hang tight," he said. "I'll use the other phone."

I waited and waited, and pumped more change into the phone, and waited some more. An older couple came down the hall and sat at our old table. Ellis was nowhere in sight. I checked my pockets. None of them held car keys.

"Nick, you still there?"

"I'm here," I said, and if Ellis took the car I might be stuck there.

"She's waiting for your call," he said, and gave me the number.

"Say it again slow," I said. "They took my pen, too."

I memorized the number and then called.

"Nick, are you okay?" Rita said.

"I'm fine." I just needed another cup of coffee. "How are you?"

"Who was that who called me?"

"Remember the guy at that Mexican restaurant?"

"That was him?" she said in a whisper.

"Yeah, but he really doesn't want to get involved. Look, Barbara Yates and her buddies tried to push me into that quarry a while ago."

"What?"

"You heard me." I turned, leaned into the phone. "Remember that bike path. That's what saved me. I want you to call Terry and see if he can get his diver out today. Promise him anything. It's an emergency. And if he's got some diving friends, tell him to bring them along."

"Why the big rush?"

"We've got to find some real evidence before they

find me again. And I've got a witness, too, and they know it. Remember that picture I showed you."

"Oh my god, you've got him?"

"Uh huh," I said with more confidence than I felt.

"I'll call Terry and call you right back."

"I'll call you," I said, just as the recorded message kicked in demanding more money. "Gotta go."

"Remember we're on..." she said and my time expired.

FIFTY-FOUR

Ellis was nowhere to be seen. I checked the McDonald's and the washroom, and then walked outside. The car was right where we'd left it. It looked like it had spent a year in a war zone and ended up on the losing side. Ellis was stretched out on the front seat.

I tapped on the roof. "You taking a nap?"

"Charging my phone," he said.

"Where'd you find the charger?"

He sat up. "You know some people don't even lock their doors."

"I thought you were going straight?"

"That don't mean I can live without a phone." He opened the door and got out. "And you can forget about protective custody. Ain't me."

"You got any money?"

"What I need money for?"

"For me. I need a phone." How could I get by without one? "I'll pay you back."

He pulled out a healthy-looking roll, found a fifty, and handed it over. "Thirty-five bucks at Walgreens. That's all you need."

"Thanks. Now we need a Walgreens. Who's driving?"

"You," he said, and he climbed into the back seat.

By the time I walked around and got behind the wheel, he was snoring softly.

I cranked the starter and then changed my mind and turned the key back the other way.

FIFTY-FIVE

Ellis shook me awake from the back seat. "I thought we were going to Walgreens," he said.

"What time is it," I said as I sat up. It was full daylight.

He held up his phone. 10:13. We'd been asleep for almost three hours. "Can I use that thing?" I asked.

He handed me the phone. "You gotta block it," he said.

I did and then I dialed Rita's number and got out of the car. "It's Nick," I said when she answered.

"You okay?"

"I'm fine. Where are you?"

"We just got to the quarry. Terry's friend Chris is setting up his diving equipment. Are you going to join us?"

"As soon as I can." I had to do something with Ellis and with the car. I knew the BB's would be looking for both.

"Remember the old man at the one-room schoolhouse?" Rita said. "He was out front when we came by. He said a car and a big pickup truck went in last night. He can't say for sure, but it looked like the same truck from the other week."

"Okay," I said.

"There was a commotion. Shots fired. And then the pickup came out all alone, driving way too fast. Mr. Marsh called 911 and reported the shots. And then the pickup truck came back and went down the lane again. It was there for about ten or fifteen minutes. It was just leaving when the police arrived."

"County cops or Lemont?"

"County. They talked to the guys in the pickup for a

few minutes, not long, and let 'em go."

"That's huge, Rita. Good work."

County cops wouldn't have much reason to protect their Chicago cousins. And then I remembered what Ellis had told me. One of the Burroughs brothers was on the County Police force. He'd been unable to pass the psychological test for the CPD.

"That old man," Rita said. "I think he likes me."

"Really?"

"He told me that right before the cops pulled up, he saw somebody drop a bag out the window of that pickup."

"Did he tell the cops?"

"He didn't want to bother them. One of the cops is a Sergeant named McCarthy. A couple of years back, he gave the old man a ticket for an untended fire."

"An untended fire?"

"That's what he said. So, I've got this bag. What's the password on your phone?"

"My last name, what else?"

"Oh, look at that, it just lit up on me. You've got several missed calls."

"Really?"

"You didn't happen to lose a 5-shot Smith and Wesson?"

"You know what? I'm going to make you a full partner."

"Do you mind if I look through your wallet?"

"And next time I'm buying you two fish tacos." I pounded the roof of the car. Was I more excited about getting my phone back or the gun?

FIFTY-SIX

Ellis and I walked back inside for a junk food breakfast. He made a few whispered phone calls and then said, "You know Buona Beef on Roosevelt Road?"

"In Berwyn?"

He nodded. "You take me there."

"And then what?"

"Then you on your own."

"How do I get in touch with you?"

"Call this phone."

I borrowed a pencil from a girl behind the counter and wrote the number on a napkin.

"Same deal," I said to Ellis. "You give me the B.B.'s, we get your brother his house."

"You just call me when you're ready." He gave me a fist bump. You couldn't get a better promise than that.

I borrowed his phone one more time to call Rent-a-Dent, then we got back in the car and headed to Berwyn. This was a western suburb that had once been predominately Czech. Lately the yuppies had been moving in, the new Bohemians. No one would think to look for Ellis there.

"There's your Walgreens," Ellis said, as we cruised down Roosevelt Road, twenty minutes later.

"Don't worry," I said. "Somebody found my phone."

"That's cool."

"So, you've got friends out here," I said as we turned into the parking lot at Buona's.

"You worry about your own friends," he said and pointed. "Now go all the way around to the back."

I followed directions. "Now what?"

"Go get yourself a dog. When you come back, I'll be gone."

I opened the door, and then leaned back in. "Be careful," I said.

"Ain't you forgetting something?"

"What's that?"

He held out his hand. "My fifty dollars."

I dug it out and handed it over, and then went inside for a cup of coffee.

When I came out Ellis was gone. I pulled the car around to the front of the lot. Twenty minutes later, Caitlin from rent-a-dent pulled in behind the wheel of a grey minivan.

I got out to meet her. She stuck her head out the window. "Wait right there," she called.

She opened the door but didn't get out. She stood on the running board with her phone in hand. "Okay, now smile," she said, and she took a picture of the car and me. She then got out and walked around, snapping pictures here and there.

Both side view mirrors were missing, as were three out of four door handles. The paint was almost completely gone on the right side. What was left had been scratched by that bridge and by a thousand bushes and trees.

"Are these bullet holes?" Caitlin asked.

I walked back. The two holes were within an inch of each other on the trunk lid. "That's pretty good shooting," I said. That would have been the tough guy who had poured coffee on me. Frank James. "The insurance will fix it, right?"

"Fix it? Are you nuts? This is going to be one of our most popular cars, especially with the movie people. They're always looking for bad guy cars."

"A Ford Focus?"

"Now it's a Rent-a-Dent special. We'll just grind off

the sharp edges, make sure the doors open and the lights work. I do have one question. Are the police looking for it?"

"Well, they might be, but they don't want the car, they want me."

"No hit and runs, anything like that?" She twisted her face and looked into my eyes.

I shook my head. "But I should sign the paperwork so it's all on the up and up."

"Don't worry." She gave me a smile. "I already forged your signature."

"You're the best," I said, and then I borrowed her phone and called Rita.

"Anything?"

"Yeah," she said. "There're all sorts of cars down there. Chris says at least ten."

"Okay," I said. "That's a beginning."

"One of them is Phil's."

"Oh, dammit." My stomach sank to my knees.

"We wanted evidence," she said.

"Right," I said, evidence of my incompetence. "Anybody inside?"

"It looks like it. Chris took a picture. It's not very clear but it's clear enough."

"Okay. Now we have a decision to make. Downtown or the FBI?"

"That's no decision at all. Downtown. We'll go together. Where should I meet you?"

"How about Terry?"

"He's going up to see Virginia."

"Maybe you should go with him."

"I don't even know her," she said. "It'll be better if it's just him. Plus, they're going to want real evidence. I'll bring you Phil's license plate."

"Okay. Meet me at 31st and Michigan. I'll be in a grey minivan."

"Ten-four."

I handed Caitlin back her phone. We exchanged keys. She got behind the wheel of the Ford, waved, and drove away.

I stood there for a moment, remembering two little girls running down the stairs.

FIFTY-SEVEN

Lenny was doing paperwork. The license plate from Phil's car sat on his desk. I was relaxing in a side chair, waiting for Ellis to call me back. Rita was at the window looking down to 35th Street.

It was another one of those Chicago-style success stories. At one time the neighborhood had been filled with thousands of poor people living in high-rise housing. The projects, which were pretty-much controlled by various street-gangs, were long gone. The poor had been dispersed to some very nice black middle-class neighborhoods. The gangs had followed along and now those neighborhoods were nowhere near as nice, and no longer very middle-class.

After a while Terry joined the club. I introduced him to Lenny. They shook hands and Lenny went back to his paperwork. If he worked hard enough maybe we'd all go away.

"Ginny said she's known almost from the beginning," Terry said. "He wouldn't just walk away. We all knew that."

My phone rang. "Talk fast," Ellis said.

"Things are happening," I said. "It's time to come in."

"Come in where?"

"35th and Michigan."

"You think I'm going to walk in that door alone."

"You got a lawyer?"

"I can find one," he said. "Where do we go?"

I gave him Lenny's name.

Lenny spoke up. "Tell him he can talk to the superintendent himself if he gets here before four." Lenny had already made a trip to the head office.

I repeated his words into the phone.

"That fat fuck," Ellis said. "Why would I want to talk to him?"

FIFTY-EIGHT

My phone rang as I was heading to the quarry the next morning. The Stevenson Expressway was choked with traffic.

"Ellis says you were going to call me." My squeaky sounding friend said.

"Yeah, sorry. I've got to make a call first. Give me ten minutes. How's that sound?"

"Ellis says to tell you to hurry."

"As fast as I can," I said. "Hey, what's your name, anyway?"

"Ellis didn't say," he said, and he was gone.

I punched in Al Raven's number. We talked for a while and then I said, "About that house. We're still on, right?"

"I've got a list of about 20 available places sitting right in front of me."

"Good. Maybe we can pick up the family later in the week and try to find them a place." I took the curving ramp for the Kingery Highway exit and headed south.

"Sure," Raven said. "You know, I've got friends think I've lost my mind. One of 'em might have a point. He says if everyone decent leaves those neighborhoods that will just make them that much worse."

"Oh, fuck him," I said. "You ought to load all his stuff on one of your trucks and move him to the West Side. And then ask him how he feels."

"I'll make him the offer, Nick. Thanks. That should shut him up."

"Anybody who could figure a way out has been gone for years," I said. "The rest are trapped. You're going to spring one family."

"When you put it like that, it doesn't sound like

much, does it?"

A few minutes later, I turned left on Archer Avenue.

There was a five-squad-car roadblock at the head of that gravel lane, three Chicago cars and two from Cook County. I gave them Lenny's name. They called in and then waved me through.

Birds were out. I spotted some buds on bushes and trees. It looked like an early spring. I slowed down when I saw the sign for the bike path. I could hear Dinah Washington singing about the difference a day could make.

I pulled off to the side near the end of the lane. A dozen or more squad cars from the city and the county, several detective cars, a morgue van, and three tow trucks, blocked the way. Two divers stood on a boat anchored in the middle of the quarry. A big guy in a CPD baseball cap manned a winch. A county crew was busy setting up portable lights.

A multitude of cops stood in a wide circle in the middle of the clearing, the old Lover's Lane. Lenny detached himself from the crowd and waved me over to a flat bed tow truck. A mud-covered convertible sports car sat on the bed leaking cloudy water. In patches, here and there, a gleaming red finish shone through.

"Recognize it?" Lenny said. "Red Mercedes Roadster."

"Oh, yeah. Who was that again?"

"Marge Dooley," he said, and he gave me a wink. "Ring a bell?"

"The missing heiress," I said.

She'd disappeared about ten years back, the day after she'd supposedly told her husband that she wanted a divorce. The husband, Vincent Dooley, told police his wife had never mentioned a divorce to him. She'd gone out for a ride and had never come back. He was a lawyer, Shelly's biggest competitor. He defended half the cops in town. Shelly got those who couldn't afford him.

"So, where's Marge?"

"We think that's her in the trunk, kind of hard to tell after all these years. We're sending the car and everything to the Medical Examiner. See if they can figure it out."

"You caught a break," I said. "This should take the heat off."

The newspapers and TV would be screaming about Marge Dooley, the missing heiress. Phil Laubett, the missing video storeowner, would get a bit of space towards the end of the story. He would never be tied to the video of Tommy Burroughs shooting that clerk.

"Not much of a break. You were right about who the county cops stopped coming out of here the other night.

"Barbara Yates and Corny Burroughs," I said.

He nodded. "And one other."

"Cop named Frank James," I said. "Fucker poured coffee on my head."

"Real name is Thomas Clancy. He's got a thing about appropriating other people's names. He was on the Yates team in 15. We took 'em both off the street last night."

Lenny looked across the clearing, where Rita and Terry were standing side by side talking to a pair of detectives. Three mud-covered cars were behind them. The one in the center was a Subaru wagon. "I think your friends are going to get meritorious promotions out of this," Lenny said.

"Rita's already on the detective list."

"They both are," he said. "And they both deserve it. Official word is they did it all on their own. That's right, isn't it?"

"Sure is." I nodded. "Is Phil Laubett in that Subaru?"

He shrugged. "Him or somebody else. They'll figure it out at the morgue."

"So how about charging Yates and her pals with murder."

"That's up to Cook County not us," he said. "And they're going to want more evidence than just the word of a gangbanger."

"Don't I count?" I pointed at myself.

"Oh, that's right, and a private eye. That's a few steps above, right?"

"You know, I think I liked you better when you stuttered." I turned and walked across the clearing.

I couldn't bring myself to look inside the Subaru. I wanted to remember Phil as he'd been, a guy with a big beard and a smile, munching on a donut, happy that his very own Sam Spade had shown up again.

Rita and Terry stood side by side, about as close as they could get without touching.

"Do me a favor," I said to Terry, and I turned my back on Phil's car. "Let me know about the funeral. Or should I just stay home?"

"It wasn't your fault," Terry said. "It wasn't mine either. Ginny knows that."

"But . . ."

"Yeah." Terry nodded. "But . . ."

"Oh, knock it off, you guys," Rita said. "You want to feel sorry for someone, think about Ginny and her two little girls."

FIFTY-NINE

The newspapers played it as predicted. Marge Dooley's picture was on every front page. Phil Laubett was buried deep again. This time in the second to last paragraph.

"A Chicago Police Department investigation that began with an anonymous tip," the Sun-Times reported, "ended more than a hundred feet down in rural Lemont with the recovery of 7 unidentified bodies and 23 missing cars from a water-filled limestone quarry."

The body found in the oldest car, a 1959 Ford Fairlane, was presumed to be that of Michael O'Brien, the registered owner of the vehicle. He had gone missing in 1960, a few days before he was scheduled to testify as a prosecution witness in a murder-for-hire trial.

Two bodies were found inside an old Volkswagen Beetle. The car had gone missing in 1987 along with a couple of local teenagers. This one didn't float.

A Tribune reporter and a photographer were let into the clearing not long after I left. A few days later, they ran a full-color two-page spread of the 23 mud and slime-covered cars that had come up from the depths. Most had been reported stolen years before. Many were found with the steering wheel tied in place and bricks on the gas pedal. The owners had collected the insurance money, and they wouldn't be giving it back. The statute of limitations for insurance fraud in Illinois was only three years.

Rita and Terry stood in the background in one of the photos, both in street clothes. In the newspaper they were identified as detectives. They'd been working cold cases, according to the Sun-Times, when they'd received a tip about Marge Dooley and her car's whereabouts.

SIXTY

"You didn't even get a mention," Al Raven said a few days later, as we headed west from my office in his huge Cadillac SUV. I was behind the wheel.

"I've got enough trouble already," I said.

"And those crooked cops go free, is that how it's going to work?"

"They're trying to throw Yates and Clancy off the force. I don't really know what's going to happen."

"It seems to me . . ." He was busy looking out the window. "Fullerton Avenue's around here someplace, right?"

I pointed to my left.

"Do you mind?" Raven asked.

I turned left, took the new suspension bridge over the river, and went west again on Fullerton. "I grew up right around here," Raven said when we got past Western Avenue. "Until I was six years old, that is. Then we moved to Schiller Park."

It would have been a middle-class neighborhood way back then. The Puerto Ricans had come along a few decades later, followed by the Mexicans. Now the Uber-craft-beer generation was taking over.

"I don't remember which street," Raven said. "My brother used to know. When he got his first car, we used to go all over. Sometimes we'd drive by the old place." He kept looking down the side streets as we passed. "It was one of those courtyard buildings. Yellow brick. We were in a basement apartment at first, pipes all over the ceiling. And then my old man got a raise or something and we moved up to the first floor. That was a big day in the family. I remember that."

At Sacramento, I turned and followed the boulevard through Humboldt Park to Chicago Avenue, and then went west again. "There it is," I said a few blocks later, and pointed to the 24-7 convenience store. It had been formally linked to the Burroughs family and the B.B. boys. For once there wasn't a uniformed cop outside. The store was shut tight. A big REVOKED sign was pasted on the front door. A couple of kids bounced a ball against a wall. "How about that for poetic justice?"

"So now where are these people supposed to shop?" Raven said.

"You're a bleeding heart, Al, you know that?" I patted his shoulder.

"Too bad it took me all these years, huh?" He reached out and tapped my leg.

The neighborhood wasn't bad looking, not at ten in the morning with all the gangbangers sleeping. There were several empty lots on the street we wanted. Most of the buildings looked pretty good. If you squinted a bit, you might believe you were in Lakeview or Lincoln Park.

We stopped in the middle of the block where a woman and a young boy waited on the porch of a two-flat. "Something funny's going on," I said when I recognized the woman.

"What's wrong?" Raven said, as they started down the steps towards us.

"I talked to her a few weeks back," I said. "She's got a little grocery store in a trailer. No junk food. No alcohol or tobacco. Oh, I'll bet I know what it is." She was looking for a different kind of home. I'd seen the artist's rendering on that grocery-store wall. "Al, I think we've been conned."

"I've been conned by some of the best," Raven said.

"But she looks okay to me. Let's hear what she has to say." He opened his door.

I got out and came around to meet them.

Raven stuck out his hand. "Hi, I'm Al," he said.

"Regina," the woman said as they shook hands. "And this is my son, Owen."

"And you already know my friend, Nick, I hear," Raven said as he shook Owen's hand.

Regina gave me a big smile, as if we were long lost friends. "Hello again," she said, and held my eyes for a long moment. Was that a plea I was reading in them? Her son gave me a shy smile. He had a hard time meeting my eyes. He wasn't quite as sly as he'd sounded on the phone.

"Hello, Regina. Hello, Owen," I said.

"Now I've got a list of houses we were planning to show you," Al said. "But Nick seems to think you might have other ideas."

"If we could just drive up to Chicago Avenue, I could show you," Regina said.

We all climbed in for the one-block ride. Regina directed me into an alley and then into the lot with the trailer sitting in the middle. I pulled alongside and we all got out and walked up the steps and into the People's Food Store.

Another familiar face was busy behind the counter.

"This is my son Ellis," Regina said.

Ellis looked up and smiled. He was wearing his new teeth and a striped apron. He gave me a wink, and then went back to packing a shopping bag.

"Now let me show you what I have in mind," she said, and she led Raven to the artist's rendering.

Raven had plenty of questions and Regina was prepared with answers. Above the grocery store a

270

neighborhood center would include a gym, child daycare, a computer center and classrooms. "If you don't know how to use a computer, we'll teach you. We'll do job training. We'll hold seminars on the criminal justice system. We'll offer cooking classes. One of the reasons people eat so much junk food out here is they never learned to cook properly."

After about fifteen minutes Raven said, "And where do I fit in?"

"Well, Mr. Acropolis promised my sons that he would buy us a house if they helped him with his investigation," Regina said. "And I believe they have more than fulfilled that obligation."

"Nick?" Raven turned his cane my way.

"I promised them a home out of this neighborhood, not necessarily a house," I said, "not a grocery store right in the middle of it."

"This is the home I need," Regina said and pointed at the display. "I already have a house in Berwyn. But this is where I grew up, right down the street where you picked us up. And this is the neighborhood I want to help. Running away never solved anything. My heart is still here. And this neighborhood desperately needs a real grocery store. Do you know what a food desert is?"

Raven did not and Regina began to explain. There was a rush of sorts. A series of customers came and went as Regina went on and on. Owen went behind the counter and began bagging groceries. Ellis ran the register.

Right next to the register was the store's answer to junk food. HEALTHY ALTERNATIVES a big sign read. There were sweet potato chips, dark chocolate, popcorn, trail mix, and various nuts. "No Salt," "No Sugar," "Baked is Better," various packages proclaimed. None mentioned the word taste.

Regina ran out of steam as the last customer went out the door. "So how can I help you?" Raven asked.

"Well, if you took the money you were planning to spend on a house and donated it to our certified non-profit, we would use it to build a house right here in the city, a house for this entire neighborhood, a neighborhood in need."

She was sounding like a preacher again. I was waiting for her to tell Raven that his donation would be returned one-hundred-fold.

"So, if I've got you right," Raven said, and he suddenly looked like a serious businessman, "the idea is to fund the neighborhood services with the profits from the grocery store."

"Correct."

"You're confidant that you can turn a profit with the store?" He pointed at the display.

"Very confidant."

"How much do you know about the grocery business?"

"I worked my way up from cashier to store manager at Dominick's. I would probably still be there if Safeway hadn't come in and destroyed what was a wonderful and successful chain. I also managed an Aldi for several years."

Raven smiled. "Well, it sounds like you know what you're doing," Raven said. "That's good. But I'm uneasy just turning over money without limitations, no matter how good the cause." Her tapped his cane and walked in a tight circle, looking around the store. "Now this is just a thought," he said a minute or two later. "What if I paid to build the store."

"That would be very generous," Regina said.

"But I would want to retain ownership or control of the building for, oh, I don't know, say five years, something like that. Long enough to make sure that everything was progressing."

"We would probably be agreeable to that," Regina said. "I would have to talk to my board, of course."

"And I would want to have a seat, no probably two seats on that board. I'd want to bring in someone with construction experience, preferably in the grocery industry. How would that sound?"

"It sounds like that old master-slave trick," Ellis said behind us.

Regina pivoted and pointed a steady finger. "If those shelves are not stocked in the next two minutes, you are going to find out who the master is around here. Do you understand?"

Ellis was quick. By the time Regina finished talking, he was busy stocking.

SIXTY-ONE

I was flipping through my road atlas one summer day when Jack Banks called. This was an investigator who usually worked for Shelly. "How're tricks?" he asked.

"Just planning a little road trip," I said, and closed the atlas.

"I'm jealous. Where to?"

"North Dakota." This was where Kate Daniels was buried in the small town of Spring Valley. It was beginning to look like a trip that would never happen. I just couldn't get going.

"Now I'm not jealous," Banks said. "Shouldn't you wait until the middle of winter? That's when it gets exciting up there. Make sure to wear your long johns."

"You call to give me a hard time?" I put my feet up on the edge of the desk. Banks didn't appear to be in any hurry.

"Truth is, I'm looking for a bit of help," he said.

"What flavor?"

"Shelly is getting buried with work. You heard about Dooley, right?" Vincent Dooley, Shelly's biggest competitor, had been indicted and charged with murdering his wife Marge, the missing heiress. "Well, Vince is so busy working on his own case," Banks said, "that he's not taking any new cases and Shelly's getting everything. Thought you might like to pitch in."

"Shelly knows I don't do police work," I said, and put my feet back on the floor.

"All she really needs is contact info for your video guy. She says he's the best, by the way."

My video guy. That stopped me. The last I'd seen of Phil was a closed coffin at Cooney's on Irving Park Road. It was a pretty big turnout. All of Phil's old friends were there, along with a bunch of kids from the store; kids who had worked for him after school; kids he'd helped with videos and recordings though the years, many of them no longer kids. Phil's parents were sitting side by side with a small knot of friends. Virginia came from a big family. They were crowded around her, keeping her steady. The two little girls were wearing identical dresses. I wasn't sure if they really understood what was in that closed gray box in the front of the room. Rita and Terry were there, too, the only cops in the room.

"You still there, Nick?" Banks asked after a while.

"I'm here," I said, and I opened the atlas.

"Look, what's the big deal? The guy would probably like the work, don't you think?"

"Yeah," I said, and pushed the button to end the call. "I think he would."

I let my finger trace the route to Spring Valley: northwest to Madison and Minneapolis, west to Fargo, due north to Grand Forks, and that was as far as the interstates would take me. Now I'd be on U.S. 2 going west. It was one small town after another, and then north almost to the border with Manitoba, to a tiny dot on the map. I got the office bottle out and grabbed the pad I'd been scribbling on for months.

I know I'm responsible for what happened Kate and I'm sorry. I really did want to help. I'd just forgotten how to do it. And I was blinded a bit. Because the truth is, I fell for you the minute you took your hat off in that elevator. When you showed up back at my office an hour later, I thought it was just the beginning.

Pretty funny, huh?

Billy was thinking of turning Tommy in. That's my best guess. If he had wanted to protect Tommy, all he had to do was destroy that tape. A flick of a cigarette lighter would have done the trick.

I don't know what he was doing on those nights he stayed out late but wasn't drinking. Maybe he was just driving around, from one street to the next, from one highway to the other, circling the city, trying to talk himself into it. Because it just isn't done, turning your partner in. And driving around with no particular place to go is sometimes the best way to really think about what's on your mind. I think it was just him and that tape, night after night, Kate. And then, when he still couldn't make up his mind, he decided to see his brother.

He couldn't talk to you because he knew what you'd say. If he decided he couldn't turn Tommy Burroughs in, he'd forever be a coward in your eyes.

Who was I kidding? I put the pen down. I'd spent less than an hour with Kate Daniels and now I was an expert on her true feelings. Maybe she would have wanted to protect Tommy even more than Billy had. What did I really know?

I knew that cops protect other cops for the same reason that doctors protect other doctors and priests cover for other priests.

Why did good priests protect or cover for their pedophile brothers? Why did bad surgeons continue to operate when everybody at the hospital knew to keep their own friends and relatives away from that surgeon's operating room? Why did good cops cover for bad cops, even for guys they didn't particularly like?

"That's just the way it is because that's the way it's always been," was not something I could comfortably say to anyone's grave, even from 1000 miles away.

The funny thing, I'd been waiting for someone like you to come along, Kate, someone with an actual case. No, it wasn't a homicide--until I made it one--but it wasn't a personal injury or a worker's compensation case either. You wanted answers to a few simple questions. And I should have found them without getting you killed in the process.

I never talked to Billy's brother or any of his non-cop friends. I never asked around in the neighborhood. It's funny the stuff you pick up at a gas station or the hardware store, talking to the neighbors. I did want to help you, Kate. Honest, I did. But I'd grown lazy through the years. I'd become a telephone detective, and that's what I did. I picked up the phone without really thinking.

Maybe while watching the tape in that Iowa motel Billy realized that, if it ever got out, his career as a cop was over. That might have been enough to bring on a heart attack in a family so prone to them.

The tape did get out Kate, and you were responsible for that. You knew something funny was going on, and everything followed from that. A convenience store clerk named Sharma got out of a prison, a place he never should have been. A woman named Regina Thompson is about to get her dream grocery store and neighborhood center, in a place that desperately needs both. A couple of young cops met and fell in love. I got an invitation to their wedding just the other day.

Everybody knows what happened at Sweet's Mini Mart now, but they don't know why. Nickels and dimes Kate, that's what it was all about. But we're keeping that part a secret, Rita and Terry, Lenny and me. The department's had too much bad publicity. I'm pretty sure your late husband would agree. We're conveniently forgetting a bit of the truth, one of those lies of omission. But I thought you should know.

You probably met Barbara Yates somewhere in your travels with Tommy. They were in-laws at one time, and they went into the corner-store trade, and they became outlaws. They used their police powers to run a bunch of their competitors out of business.

All their stores are closed now, making those neighborhoods

even bigger food deserts, and Yates and some of her pals are in the process of being tossed off the police force. She's been indicted on a variety of charges and odds are she'll end up in prison. But not for Phil's murder. Nobody was being charged with that. Those videos showing that extra-large pickup truck following Phil's car down Archer Avenue has been ruled inconclusive.

Inconclusive, meaning we don't want to know. And what was one more unsolved murder in a city where that was the rule not the exception?

SIXTY-TWO

I didn't bother with any looking-for-work phone calls but, as autumn approached, my phone started ringing again. Unlike cops, lawyers tend to forgive and forget.

On days when I happened to have a car, I'd try to swing by and have a cup of coffee with Al Raven. He'd sold his moving company to a big mover out of Texas and was now at the construction site five days a week, conferring with the contractors and Regina, keeping his eyes on the future home of the People's Supermarket. He still carried his cane but usually used it as a pointer. "I'm having the time of my life," he told me one day as we watched one group of workers set refrigerated cases while another crew ran copper lines. "But if we ever get this place up and running, I'm going back to Paris. You want to come along?"

"Just say the word."

#

One afternoon I was paging through the morning Sun-Times and there was that startling photograph. The baby was in mid-air. The mother was leaning out the window with the flames right behind her. On the edge of the frame were the outstretched arms of the cop as he waited to make the catch. "See openings this weekend," the photo caption said.

I followed directions. "A Career Cut Short. Kate Daniels' Photographs. Opening reception Friday, 7:00 to 11:00 p.m."

I hadn't been to an art opening in many years but the gallery was in Bucktown so I figured I couldn't go wrong with a sports coat and blue jeans. If anything, I'd probably be overdressed.

When I got there, the fire photograph was front and center. Next to it were several pictures of the aftermath. In one series, several firemen in the bucket of a snorkel unit rescued the woman from the burning window. In another photo an overweight cop was sitting on his ass in the middle of the sidewalk. He still had the baby in his arms. The weight must have knocked him to the ground. He was holding the kid up to his partner, like the winning touchdown in a last second victory.

Many of the frames held other news photographs, fires and accidents, crime scenes, shots of politicians and celebrities. Kate had the ability to find the people in the stories and put them front and center in her photographs.

But, left to her own, she seemed to like lonely people and places; empty churches, saloons, and courtrooms, solitary women and men; a kid with emotionless eyes looking out a grimy picture window; a skinny dog scrounging for food in a quiet, early-morning alley; the hallway outside my office.

That one stopped me. She must have shot it before she knocked on my door. It was the view from the far end of the hall, looking past my office to the elevators and the travel agent in the front suite. The hallway was empty. The light spilling from various offices cast soft shadows on the black and gray marble floor. As the light rose towards the ceiling the color faded into a pure white. Instead of an office-building hallway, it might have been the road to heaven.

As I continued looking, I noticed that there were no signs of winter. The floor was as smooth as glass; no slushy footprints or bits of road salt carried in by winter boots.

"Nick Acropolis." A woman laughed behind me. "What in the name of god are you doing here?"

"Paula?" I said as I turned. I'd know that laugh anywhere.

"Who else," she said, and the smile was as bright as the last time I'd seen it five years before. "You told me we'd meet again, remember?"

I didn't remember saying that, but I'd certainly had such hopes. In my head she was the girl who got away. "And here we are," I said. "As promised." We shared a quick embrace, and I inhaled that familiar scent.

"So, what the hell are you doing here?" Paula asked. "Did you know Kate?"

"I met her once," I said. "I saw the notice in the paper and wasn't doing anything. How about you?"

"We were neighbors for a while," she said. "Remember my back porch? Kate and I used to sit out there drinking wine and telling stories."

I remembered the porch. It was a third-floor rear, with a view of the North Shore commuter line. Every so often a train would shoot past with suburbanites heading in or out of the city.

We walked along looking at the various pictures. "How's married life?" I asked after a while.

Paula had gone back and forth between me and her future husband. He kept asking her to marry him and I was happy just the way things were. Paula could never decide which future she wanted, and one day I decided to try a bit of reverse psychology. "Why don't you just marry him and get it over with." A week later she sent me a note letting me know that they'd tied the knot and wished me luck. She had obviously missed the reverse part of the psychology.

"Don't laugh when I tell you," Paula said. "Promise?"

"Sure," I said, and waited for her to tell me how great marriage was. I knew it had to work for some people.

"We didn't make it a full year," she said.

"I'm sorry to hear that," I said, and then I gave it a beat. "You should have called."

She smiled. "I'm not so sure about that," she said and then she was looking into my eyes. "But I'm standing here now, Nick."

The last five years of nothing-special romance vanished as if it had never happened. "What do you say we get the hell out of here?"

She shook her head and gestured across the room. "The only other guy in a sports coat," she said.

His coat would never fit me. He looked like an ex-football player, a big tight end or a fast linebacker. He was holding eyeglasses in hand as he peered closely at a photograph. "The latest flame?"

She nodded. "A couple of months but we've already figured out it's not going anywhere."

"Well, how about I call you in a couple of days?"

"That sounds perfect. Wednesday or Thursday. We'll figure something out."

"I'll bet we will," I said.

"You know what happened to Kate, right?"

I nodded. "Yeah. I heard."

"She didn't deserve it. She really didn't. She was such a cool girl and she loved it here, all the action, the cops and robbers, and that's what ended up killing her. She had great stories from her job, and I told her some of mine and a couple of yours too. Those were right up her alley, of course. But we'd get in fights sometimes. I'd be down on the city, dreaming of getting the hell out, and she'd tell me I was so lucky growing up here. She was from some small town in North Dakota. She said I didn't know how good I had it."

A few minutes later, we hugged and said goodbye, and then I went back to look at that photograph of the hallway outside my office.

Maybe Kate had used darkroom magic to make all the signs of winter disappear. Maybe she'd come by later that night after the cleaning crew had been through. Maybe she didn't really get off on the wrong floor. Maybe she'd been walking by my door for weeks without ever knocking.

"Maybe this, maybe that," she'd said at my office that day.

Maybe she'd never stopped at all.

ACKNOWLEDGMENTS

Sometimes a village is not enough. This one took an entire city.

I'd like to thank Pat Arden, Scott Baker, Michele Barale, Maudemarie Clark, Caitlin Devitt, Ryan Gantes, Steve Grossman, Paula Kamen, Kathleen Kimmel, Francis Leroux, Sydney Lewis, Michael Ramsey, Robin Rauch, Rose Spinelli, and several others who wish to remain anonymous.

I never would have got off page one without your help.